FALLING *for* ALASKA

AN ALASKA DREAM ROMANCE

Shannon L. Brown

Sienna Bay Press

D1153642

Sienna Bay Press

PO Box 158582

Nashville, Tennessee 37215

www.shannonlbrown.com

Book Layout ©2015 BookDesignTemplates.com

Publisher's Note: This is a work of fiction. Names, characters, places, and incidents are a product of the author's imagination. Locales and public names are sometimes used for atmospheric purposes. Any resemblance to actual people, living or dead, or to businesses, companies, events, institutions, or locales is completely coincidental.

Falling for Alaska/Shannon L. Brown. —1st ed.

ISBN: 978-0-9898438-4-3

Library of Congress Control Number: 2015918278

FALLING
for
ALASKA

To my husband, Larry,
Thank you for giving me a chance to make my dreams
come true, for helping solve plot problems, for
proofreading romances and mysteries for kids when
you'd rather be researching ancient Greece or Rome.
But most of all, thank you for loving me.

Chapter One

"Bench or bookshelf? Which do you want to be?" Jemma Harris walked around the beat-up old dresser sitting in the garage next to the house her great-aunt had recently left her in Palmer, Alaska. She removed the drawers and stepped back. Nodding once, she said, "Bench." Jigsaw in hand, Jemma began the transformation.

Out of the corner of her eye, she saw Mr. Gorgeous from across the street open his front door. He wore his usual neatly pressed chinos and dress shirt, his dark, wavy hair adding the only element slightly out of control. Refocusing on the blade in her hand, Jemma cut off the dresser's top, then started a curve on the right side.

Something poked her shoulder. When she reached out to brush it away, her hand met with warm skin. Jumping backward, Jemma stood with the jigsaw in front of her like a weapon.

"What are you doing?" Mr. Gorgeous shouted over the sound of the saw.

1

Gorgeous but none too bright. She pushed the off switch and removed her protective glasses. "I'm sawing wood."

"No." He sighed with obvious frustration. "What are you doing making so much noise?"

"Um, creating a bench?" She pointed at the half-altered dresser. Seeing it in her mind in a fresh yellow with white trim and a matching padded seat, she knew it would be beautiful. "A parent will happily buy it for their daughter's room— at least I hope so."

Her neighbor's mouth dropped open. "This is a business? The noise I've put up with for weeks isn't temporary?"

"Yes. No. Yes, I'm planning to open a store."

"So you won't continue making noise here and being a general nuisance?"

Now he had her hackles up. "A nuisance?"

His hand swept over the area. "Noise. Grime. Chaos."

Focus on patience. He was her neighbor, so they needed to get along. Forcing a calm note to her voice, she said, "I'm Jemma Harris. It may appear chaotic to you, Mr. . . . ?"

"Nathaniel Montgomery."

"But I can assure you everything is under control."

With a little too much eagerness, he asked, "Will you be gone soon?"

As soon as I can make this pay, she thought, wondering how someone so attractive on the outside could be the opposite on the inside.

Ready to ask him to leave, Jemma saw a truck come around the bend of the road and pull into her driveway, saving her from herself. Wondering who could be visiting when she'd lived in Palmer all of three weeks and hardly knew a soul, she noticed the load in the back. Travis, the man she'd met at the community yard sale and hired to deliver goods for her, was here, and his truck was filled to the brim with what she knew were great things. When she ventured a glance at her neighbor, his expression said otherwise.

Travis stepped out of his truck. "My sister had a few things left from her yard sale. I added the ones I thought you might want." He pointed at the back of his truck toward several items she hadn't bought.

Jemma climbed onto the side to see better. "Thank you, Travis. The bench and stool are great." She pushed a music stand aside. "And that lamp. What's in the box up there?" She pointed past the dresser, headboard, and coffee table she'd bought to right behind the cab of the truck.

"Some old tablecloths. Maybe some old fabric too. My mother doesn't even remember who gave them to her. She had the box stored in a closet, and no one at the sale wanted it, so she told me to throw it away. I thought I'd see if you wanted any of it."

How had she missed that at the sale? Jemma swallowed and tried for a nonchalant appearance so he wouldn't know how much she loved old linens and up the amount he wanted. As she scrambled into the back of the truck and over furniture, she realized she might have spoiled her attempt. When she reached the box, she folded back the flaps—and discovered a treasure trove of tablecloths from the 1940s and 1950s. "I can take these off your hands." She gulped. "At the right price."

"Just take them. Mom will be happy someone wants them."

She added extra to the amount she paid for the other goods. Jemma knew she'd gotten a good deal and from the expression on Travis's face, it looked like he thought he'd gotten a good deal too. That was how she always hoped to do business.

By the time Travis drove off, Nathaniel was standing with his mouth hanging open. "But that's junk! You paid for junk!"

"No, I paid for things I can revamp into products I can sell. This isn't junk." She picked up the lamp that had a shredded shade over a black-and-gold base from another, perhaps less appealing, era. "Well"—she shrugged—"some of it might be junk *now*, but everything will be beautiful when I'm done with it."

Nathaniel leaned over her pile of goods and nudged the stool with his foot. "I know I wouldn't want any of it. This just solidifies what I said earlier. I've put up with the noise for two weeks, and now we have truckloads of junk dropping by. This business," he said in the same tone she'd use to describe smelly garbage, "must be against the law."

"Mr. Montgomery—"

"Nathaniel."

They definitely were not on a first-name basis. "Mr. Montgomery, my business complies with all laws and codes. In short, it's legal."

His cell phone rang as Jemma inhaled, ready to impale him with her words. Speaking into the phone, he crossed the street to his house. About halfway, he gave a halfhearted wave in her general direction.

That was that, Jemma thought. It was probably best that he'd left because she didn't like the way she had been about to act. Nathaniel Montgomery seemed to bring out the worst in her.

Her sister Holly's silver compact came into sight about the

same time he reached his front steps. Jemma's nieces waved out the window, bringing sunshine that helped clear out the Nathaniel Montgomery storm.

"Hi, Aunt Jemma!" Abbie shouted out the window.

"Me too!" Ivy added.

When the car stopped, Jemma pulled open a door and helped unbuckle the four-year-old twins from their car seats. As they climbed out, their mother directed them to the old swing set in the backyard, the same one she and Jemma had used as children when their family visited Great-aunt Grace.

"I noticed Mr. Gorgeous going into his house," Holly said. "Did you get to meet him? Is he as swoon-worthy up close as he is from a distance?"

"Yes. And n-o."

Holly's brow furrowed. "What's yes?"

"I met Mr. High and Mighty."

Her sister winced.

"And I've brought chaos into this neighborhood."

"Great-aunt Grace sold him land to build his house, and the other thirty acres to a builder for the subdivision around the corner—but on the other side of the woods. You and he *are* 'the neighborhood.'"

"And I've apparently ruined it with my sawing, junk deliveries, and general sense of chaos."

"I think I'm speechless, and I didn't know that could happen." Holly glanced at her watch. "I'd like to hear more, but I have to get to my job interview. If I don't find something soon, I'm going to have to get a job in another field. Wish me the best, and thanks for watching the kids."

"You're a great teacher, and you'll land a job soon, Holly. You graduated less than a month ago, so *don't* worry. And you know I'm always happy to watch the girls. I didn't get to spend much time with them before I moved here, but I can make up for that now." Just then, the furniture in her driveway caught Jemma's eye. "Hey, Holly. If you have a minute to spare, give me a hand getting this dresser into the garage."

Her sister grabbed one end, Jemma the other; then they hoisted the dresser off the ground and shuffled it into the open garage, setting it on the sawdust-covered, concrete floor.

Looking up, Holly reached over and pushed on one of the garage's loose wall boards. "This building is a little rickety."

"It's solid. It's just old." Jemma brushed off her shirt front.

"Speaking of old, you seem to really be getting into your new vintage fashion look." Holly raised one eyebrow.

"I'm thrilled to be able to wear whatever I want, to not adhere to the company's business conservative dress code. Suit. Closed-toe shoes. Stockings." Jemma shuddered. Glancing down at the hippie-ish peasant top she'd tucked into 1970s-era high-waisted jeans, Jemma asked, "Do you think it's too much?"

"It's . . . unique." Then, shaking her head, Holly said, "I'm off."

Jemma followed her sister back outside, then stood with Abbie and Ivy at her side as Holly climbed back into her little car and drove away. When she asked her nieces, "Would you like to sew later?" they gave an enthusiastic reply of "Yes!" Laughing, she picked up the box of linens and set them inside the front door.

When she came out, the girls were chasing each other around the garage. Jemma spoke above their happy-at-play sounds, "Stay in sight of the garage's back door, and I'll work for a little longer." She heard squealing as she went back in and settled into her work.

Glancing up every couple of minutes, she kept an eye on her nieces while she finished sawing the arms of the bench. Finishing this piece of furniture kept her complying with her plan. She would make this business a success.

Before Jemma began sanding, she stepped out the door and found the girls swinging. Happy to find them having fun, she went back into the garage. Back at work, she gave an initial sanding to the arms and back edge of her bench, then switched to a finer grit to give the whole piece a once-over. After brushing on a coat of white paint—she'd re-coat it later today and add the trim—she checked her watch and knew she'd better sew with the girls, or it would be too late.

"Girls!" She waved them over. "Ready to make something fun?"

When they stepped into the entry and Abbie saw the box of fabric, she shrieked with glee. Jemma knelt beside her and went through the box with the little girl, who cared as much about it as she did, while Ivy happily played with Stitches, the cat Jemma babysat for her other sister, Bree.

Jemma hoped she'd have a little girl just like one of her nieces. Someday when she wasn't so busy with life. Of course, she'd first want a man who loved her for who she was, not someone like Mr. Montgomery, who wanted every-one to conform to *his* rules.

Nathaniel set his phone on his desk and stared down at his neighbor's property from his office window. When he'd bought land across the street from a sweet old lady with a house as old as she was, surrounded by a white picket fence, he figured this would be a quiet place to live, a change from the condo he'd owned in downtown Anchorage. The old lady was gone, Jemma Harris had inherited, and she might be cute at first glance, with her long, blonde hair, big blue eyes and slender figure, but she was chaos through and through.

He should probably try to get along with her, and he *would* try to be neighborly. Her apparent love of garage sale finds even made her clothing chaotic, the different eras clashing loudly. Pushing off from the window, he chuckled to himself. As a marketing consultant, he'd learned a little bit about a lot of things, including fashion and football. He'd admit to the second but never the first.

A shriek pierced the air. He started to run for the stairs, but when a second shriek sounded, he realized the sound came from a child at play. Back at the window, he saw two identical little girls running around the front lawn of his neighbor's house. Great: sawing, hammering, and screaming. What more could one ask for during his workday?

Reaching for his phone, he scrolled down, found the number of his lawyer, and called. After a brief but odd delay, during which he heard the secretary pushing buttons on the phone, she came back and said she would try again. Moments later his lawyer came on the phone. Nathaniel asked, "Pete, do you have a minute?" The other man answered that he did, so Nathaniel outlined the situation with his neighbor.

When Pete said, "I'll check into it," Nathaniel asked, "That's it? No, 'I'll get an injunction' or some other legal-sounding answer?"

"I'll give you a shout when I know more later today. I'd ask if you'd like to shoot some hoops later, but I have a brief to finish and will probably be here late."

Nathaniel would have bowed out of it anyway. He'd given in after a string of requests last year and played basketball with some of the guys he did business with in town. Now they all assumed he'd want to do it again. He hadn't had anyone close enough to be a friend since middle school and didn't see that changing anytime soon. "Thanks. If anyone can help, I know you can."

When he'd hung up, he put on one of Mozart's flute concertos and felt the soothing music calm him. Good thing, because when he checked his e-mail, Nathaniel discovered a mess he had to sort out for a client. He loved his work. He truly did. It had a rhythm and a sense of order that suited him. He was good enough at what he did that the fires he had to extinguish were minimal.

With the mess sorted out, he spent more than an hour on Paris Expressions' branding and marketing. So far, he'd taken them from being called "Today's Fashions," a women's clothing store with a lackluster name and sales to match, to a business with respectable sales. He put his phone on speaker and punched in the store's number. The owner answered on the second ring.

"Evelyn, I want to confirm our meeting today."

"Are you kidding? I wouldn't miss a meeting with my marketing expert unless I were in the hospital. Even then I'd ask to move the meeting there."

Nathaniel could picture the energetic, fiftysomething woman doing exactly that. He grinned. "My guess is that business is up."

Evelyn sighed. "I was so close to losing this dream. Just giving us a new name and sign has made a huge difference."

Jemma's business dream popped into his mind, but he

pushed it away. There was no way he'd get involved in her used furniture and assorted junk mishmash. He didn't work for free anyway, and he doubted she could pay him.

"Evelyn, today we'll talk about taking it to the next level."

"Hurry." She laughed. "I ordered some of your favorite cookies."

"You do know the way to a man's heart."

"Shh. Don't tell my husband." She was still laughing when Nathaniel hung up.

He dialed his lawyer next.

Pete answered. "You *are* in a hurry. No matter. I'm happy to say I have your answer."

"Please give me news I want to hear."

"That I can't do. It's legal. Her business in the garage is totally legal."

Nathaniel growled.

Pete hesitated, then said, "I could send her a letter. Nicely say that my client asks if she could operate her business in a quiet manner."

"Thank you! That might help. She may even think a letter from a lawyer means she's in the wrong."

"You know"—Pete cleared his throat—"I'd be disbarred if I gave the wrong impression."

"Sure. I know."

"And it might be a couple of weeks." Pete lowered his voice and added, "My secretary is new and hasn't quite gotten the hang of things."

"No problem." Nathaniel started to end the call, then added, "Thank you."

With business out of the way, and his noisy neighbor out of sight, but it never seemed out of hearing range—the sound of a saw slicing through something screeched into his office—he leaned back in his chair and closed his eyes to mentally shift gears.

After a few minutes, he moved back in front of his computer and brought up his current volunteer project, the marketing plan he'd begun for an orphanage in Central America. They needed to reach out to donors. He enjoyed using his skills to make things like that happen. Helping with children's charities gave him a break from his normal clients, and always brought a smile to his face.

After almost an hour spent on the project, Nathaniel had a concept he liked and e-mailed it to them for approval. He checked his in-box one last time, and after finding nothing he had to handle immediately, stood and stretched his arms overhead, thinking about the afternoon in front of him. When he finished his meeting at Paris Expressions in Anchorage, he'd head toward home, stop at the post office, and wrap up the day with a business dinner in Wasilla. At least he hoped it was just dinner with Alexis. She'd hinted at more, but he kept bringing it back to the graphic design work she did for him. He'd learned in the corporate world not to mix business and pleasure, and even if he'd wanted a long-term relationship—which he didn't—Alexis's bold sexiness didn't say *Take-me-home-to-meet-mom*.

He leaned more toward girl-next-door types. But *not* the irritating neighbor he'd been saddled with. Rubbing a hand over his face, he sighed. If he was honest with himself, and he tried to be, he'd admit he didn't want anyone to get that close.

A grinding noise pulled him over to the window. What else could happen today? An ancient, rusty van sat in the middle of the road, blocking his driveway. The grinding noise apparently came from its engine. Jemma Harris stepped out of the driver's door with a more appealing outfit this time, a timeless pair of shorts and a T-shirt. She slid open the van's side door and reached inside, and the two little girls he'd seen earlier stepped out.

When she started to walk away, he raced down the stairs and out the door. "Hey, you can't leave this here!"

She turned around. "I'm not." Her expression clearly told him she thought him a complete idiot. "I'm calling for a tow truck to take it into the shop."

Looking upward for patience, he shook his head in frustration. He'd never make his meeting if he had to wait for that to happen. When she opened the gate and started up the steps to her house, he said. "If you'd like, I'll check under the hood. I can do basic fixes." Actually, he could probably replace the engine, but she didn't need that much information.

Her face brightened, and he felt like he'd been smacked with a sunbeam. The lady's smile packed a punch. "Please do!"

He reached inside the van's open door and popped the hood. Then he checked out the vehicle's engine. It didn't take him long to determine what the problem might be. By the time he'd gone to his garage and returned with the tools he'd need, the two girls were sitting on one of Jemma's concrete steps with drinks in their hands, and she was halfway back to the van. When she got closer, he noticed her T-shirt had a touristy Alaskan giant mosquito on the front.

Jemma leaned over the side of the engine while Nathaniel worked. His hands moved quickly and with purpose. While he seemed like he'd be more at home in a *GQ* modeling session, this guy knew his way around an engine. "I'm lost beyond putting in gas," she said. "Where did you learn to do this?"

"My high school's auto shop teacher took me under his wing, basically treating me like his own son. I spent more time with him than at home."

Interesting. She wanted to ask why, but before she could, he changed subjects.

"Didn't I see you with a red sedan a couple of days ago?"

"It's still there, behind the garage. Even after driving it up the Alaska Highway, it's in good shape." She made sure she had the oil changed on schedule, every service recommendation met.

Nathaniel stared at her. "Why did you buy this thing, then?"

Rudeness seemed to be one of Nathaniel's gifts. Standing tall, Jemma adopted her formal, I'm-in-charge voice, the one she'd perfected during years as a corporate executive assistant. "I needed something to haul furniture for my business. The man who sold it to me said it would be good for that."

He rolled his eyes. "Ms. Harris, you were learning the alphabet the last time this rolling scrap metal was anything close to 'good.'"

"Oh." Jemma felt her lip tremble. This man knew which buttons to push.

Nathaniel blinked, and she thought he knew he'd gone too far. He pointed at the driver's seat. "Give the engine a try." Jemma climbed in and turned the key.

When it started up, she got out, leaving the engine running and came back around to him. He'd saved her both money and time today. "Thank you very much! I'm grateful to your teacher."

She was about to say more when he slammed the hood shut. "There you go. That will hold it—for now. But the clock is ticking on this rust bucket."

She forced a smile even though he'd been a jerk to her. Again. But he was kind underneath, because he could have just helped push the van to the side of his driveway and been on his way. "Thank you very much for fixing my van." To be neighborly, she added, "I'm taking the girls for ice cream, then dropping them at home. Can we get you a cup of ice cream to go?"

He shuffled his feet and wouldn't look directly at her. Yep, he felt guilty. He cleared his throat. "No thanks. I'm going to enjoy the quiet."

As he walked away, she muttered, "Mr. Grouch." *Just when you thought there was kindness in him, pow.*

Nathaniel didn't like hearing her words, but knew he deserved them. And what he'd said wasn't really the truth. He needed to leave in two minutes to make his meeting, so he had about 120 seconds of quiet to enjoy.

His afternoon went well—until dinner.

As he drove home afterward, Nathaniel put on some Bach and slid into the music. Alexis's ideas for the evening *had* extended beyond the offerings on the menu. He'd gotten out of there as cleanly and as quickly as he could. No one could do her job better, but he probably needed to move on and find someone else to work with. Personal relationships had never worked for him, and, he figured, they never would.

When he reached his driveway, he wondered about that

awful van his neighbor had bought. Her outside lights showed it parked on the rise behind the garage, so she'd made it out and back. That surprised him, considering the condition of the engine.

As he recalled her muttered words as he walked away earlier in the day, he knew he didn't have to worry about *her* wanting more than he was willing to give.

Chapter Two

Holding both hands around a cup of tea for warmth, Jemma watched the oranges and pinks of the sunrise from her front porch. She was loving May in Alaska. Compared to Atlanta, Georgia, it was on the cool side, but the brisk mornings cheered her heart.

The view toward Nathaniel's house, the woods beside her own house, and the mountains in the distance couldn't be more opposite those of her downtown Atlanta condo surrounded by a hundred other condos. She could barely make out the sound of traffic on the two-lane highway that passed not far from here. No car doors slamming, no emergency sirens telling their tragic tale, just birds waking up and singing.

This would be a great day, the day she'd been working toward for years. Today she was officially a businesswoman.

Jemma went through to her kitchen, refilled her mug—this time adding a cinnamon stick to flavor the tea—and popped a bagel into the toaster. Yesterday the promise of ice cream had kept her nieces under tight control in the grocery and craft stores so she'd been able to buy some much-needed supplies to feed body and soul. She slathered cream cheese on the hot bread and topped it with what might be considered by many to be an excess of strawberry jam.

As she walked through the house, munching, she surveyed the sewing projects that would add to her inventory. Late last night, she'd spread out the tablecloths she'd bought from Travis and paired them with fabric she already had. Ideas for a dozen projects that excited her resulted—pillows, seat cushions, table runners, aprons, and assorted other pieces that would sell well and decorate her booth at Friday Fling, Palmer's local food and craft fair, and other events as they waited for their new home with a buyer.

Her heart raced as she thought of the risks she'd taken. No one outside of her family understood why she'd walked away from her high-paying corporate job. Jemma had a dream that wouldn't be pushed aside any longer. Neither would her nice boss's twentysomething grandson, who must have five hands since she'd push one to the side and another would touch her somewhere else. She'd saved money earned working long hours to make her dream of owning a business come true. Even without the handsy grandson, she'd have taken the leap into business soon anyway, just probably not this year.

After putting her plate and mug in the dishwasher, she went out to the garage, unlocked the padlock, and pulled open the old-fashioned doors that let in light beyond the single bulb that hung from the ceiling.

Jemma pulled off dust cloths and admired her work. A decoratively painted nightstand, two formerly dilapidated dressers, one now the bench she'd made yesterday and another a media center, a side table made into an upholstered stool, and a framed nature-scened scarf turned art sat before her. With these and her completed fabric projects—five pillows, the seat cover for the bench, and several tote bags— she had a respectable booth ready for the Friday Fling market today. Small like the town it was in, the market had a loyal following and was a good place to test her wings.

The van protested when she turned the key in the ignition, sending her blood pressure sky-high. She had to be on the road by eight to arrive by eight thirty. She took a deep breath, said a silent prayer, and turned the key again. When it started, she gave a cheer. If she drove out of here in the next half hour, she'd arrive on schedule and pretty up her booth by opening time. After backing the van up to the garage, she got busy loading everything inside.

Jemma grinned as she slammed the van's back door shut. For years she'd dreamed of having her own business and making her own way. When she'd discovered what she could do with the castoffs of others, and that she actually seemed to have a gift for making old things new and wonderful, she knew she'd found the rest of her dream. Today it became a reality.

Sitting in the driver's seat, she offered up one more prayer and turned the key. A grinding noise like yesterday's was the engine's only reply. "Please, God," she murmured, and tried again. The grinding noise escalated. She had paid for a booth for the season and needed to be there. It fit in her plan. Her plan would get her where she wanted and needed to be.

Nathaniel woke to a loud noise. Jemma Harris was at it again, and—he glanced at the time on his nightstand—earlier than ever before. He'd worked into the night and wanted to sleep in this morning. Nathaniel pulled his pillow onto his head and squeezed it over his ears. The noise penetrated the down fluff. After tossing it aside, he got up and stomped over to the window.

This wasn't sawing. This was that hunk of junk van of hers, and she had it parked in front of the garage. At least it wasn't blocking his driveway this time. He heard her try the engine again, only to have it produce the grinding noise. He was about to go back to bed when she stepped out of the van and leaned against it, wiping her cheeks. Women cried over the simplest things. When she sat down on the ground beside the van and buried her face in her hands, he gave up, got dressed, and headed over there.

Nathaniel found Jemma unloading furniture from the back of the van and trying to cram it into the sedan she'd moved beside it. She'd managed to fit a couple of pieces, but it was obvious that her car wouldn't work for whatever she'd planned with the van. Tears streamed down her face as she tried to squeeze a large stool next to a bench in the backseat.

"Ms. Harris?"

She swiped at her eyes before looking up. "Yes?" She blinked, obviously fighting more tears.

"I heard the van grinding. Let me look at it and see if I can fix it."

"Oh, thank you!" She reached out like she was going to hug him, then obviously thought better of it. "I have to be on the road in ten minutes." She pointed at her car. "And I can't fit . . ."

He went around to the front of the van and popped the hood. "I made a slight adjustment on something yesterday, but it only held for a while." It didn't take him long to see that any further attempt was futile, so he slammed the hood back down. "This isn't going anywhere."

"What?" She sank back to the ground, eyes closed, and leaned against the van's wheel. "What will it take to fix it?"

Nathaniel shook his head, but he realized she couldn't see him. "It would take quite a bit of money, and I'm not sure it would be worth it in the end. You'd be better off with a newer van."

She quietly said, "No. I can't do that."

"Well, that's all I can do."

"Thank you." This time she spoke in almost a whisper.

He started to turn and leave, but stopped. What could make this so important? "Where were you going?"

"I have a booth at Palmer's Friday Fling." She leaned her head back against the van, then sat forward, her hair now powdered with rust. "This is—*was*—my first try at selling what I've made. Other than to friends and family."

"There will be another event where you'll be able to sell your"—he pointed at her furniture—"unique products."

She stood. "Thank you for your help, Mr. Montgomery."

He hated it when she said his name that way.

Then his mouth disconnected from his brain and said, "I can drive you there." He blinked. *Where did that come from?*

A smile started small, then stretched across her face. "Thank you! You're the answer to my prayers. We have just enough time if you pull your SUV over here now."

Every step Nathaniel took to his house left him more puzzled. He guessed this was like helping a lost child. He couldn't let her wander loose, could he? The metaphor worked to a point. A child wasn't the same as a pretty woman with a sunshine smile.

Once he'd moved his SUV into Jemma's driveway, they transferred all of her inventory into it and headed out. He felt comfortably dressed for any occasion in navy chinos and a navy-and-red plaid shirt; she wore jeans and yet another peasant top, this time in teal, paired with white sneakers painted with yellow and orange daisies. The same they were not.

Trying for conversation, he asked, "What will you do with whatever you don't sell?"

Jemma smiled. "I plan to sell everything. I've carefully chosen pieces for this first market I believe will sell quickly."

He thought over the items he'd shifted into his vehicle. Junk was junk, painted white or given a fancy design. He cleared his throat. "I don't think people will want this." He pointed with his thumb to the back area and watched her smile dim.

"Yes, they will. I believe people will like my style."

"Okay." He didn't say anything else for a few minutes, but couldn't hold his tongue. Helping people with businesses, branding them, promoting them, this was his livelihood, and he was very good at it. New was good. Or a high-quality antique. Something of value. He didn't understand his neighbor's attempted business at all.

When they were almost there, he said, "Your business can't succeed. I hate to see anyone put this much effort into something with no promise of return. I think—"

She cut him off. "It shouldn't come as a surprise to you, Mr. Montgomery, that what you think makes little difference to me."

She didn't say another word as they parked, and then he helped her unload her goods and tote them over to her outdoor booth. Once done, she glared at him and said, "I appreciate your help, Mr. Montgomery. I'll find my own way home."

He reeled back. "You're in for a long walk."

With a smile that didn't reach her eyes, she said, "I know. But I'd rather walk than ride back with you. Good-bye." She turned and started organizing her area.

Nathaniel glanced around and was relieved no one appeared to have overheard. She seemed determined. "Here. If you need a ride." He set his business card on a yellow-and-white bench and walked away. When he looked back over his shoulder, he saw her tearing the card into tiny pieces. She started to throw it into the air, then stopped herself. She was probably against pollution too.

Jemma watched Nathaniel Montgomery climb into his vehicle. A barrage of emotions ranging from gratefulness to annoyance to downright anger assailed her. Just as anger fought to win out, potential customers stopped at her booth and happiness took over. When one of the first bought several items, she let out a huge sigh. This could work. Jemma found she enjoyed the give-and-take of bartering.

She felt like a local when tourists stopped at her booth and asked about the area. Jemma laughed and told them she didn't know any more than they did. Jemma also enjoyed watching Alaskan men walk by. Young or old, they often had a rugged, outdoorsy sense about them. Nothing like her former corporate world. Or her neighbor. These men oozed confidence and what she'd come to think of as natural sex appeal.

Exhilarated by the end of the event, she made a combination deal for two of the last three items, only breaking even on one of them, but she'd been left with just a stool to haul home . . . somehow. In the midst of doing a happy dance, she noticed out of the corner of her eye that the man sitting at the booth across from her was watching her and grinning. Embarrassed, she took down her sign.

"Good day?" he asked.

"The best." When she stared at her now empty space, her problem came home to rest. She was near downtown Palmer. She lived just a ten or fifteen-minute drive away, but that distance would take a long time to walk, and she had to carry the stool, and her table and chair. Her van sat derelict in her driveway, and she'd dismissed her driver. Holly would normally come if she called, but she'd left the girls with a friend so she could go to yet one more job interview, this time in Anchorage.

Jemma felt the tiny pieces of Nathaniel Montgomery's business card that pride had put in her pocket, a bridge that was well and truly burned.

The man across the way spoke again, "Everything okay?"

She shrugged. "Do you know if there are any buses here?"

The small bus line's schedule ran mostly earlier in the day, he told her, but he offered to drive her home.

When Jemma arrived home at six o'clock, she was tired and grimy from her day. She had just put away the things she'd hauled home, then settled on her front porch's rocking chair, when Holly pulled into her driveway. Jemma got up from her rocker and went over to help get the girls out of their car seats. They raced across the yard as soon as their feet hit the ground.

Holly asked, "How'd Friday Fling go?"

"Great! I made a good profit, so I'm on track with my plan and meeting my goals."

"You and your plan and goals. See what planning does?" She pointed at the girls.

"They're a wonderful shift off of a plan."

Holly watched her twins run around. "They are. I love them more than I would have ever imagined possible." Blinking, she turned back to Jemma. "Thank you for taking them tonight for a few hours. I need to focus on getting more job applications filled out."

"I'm glad to help. I may be the oldest, but if you get a teaching job this fall, you'll beat me to having a career in your field."

"Now that Bree is Briana Harris, MD, she's officially ahead of both of us. Me, I'm thrilled to have finally finished one degree." Holly turned toward the garage. "What's missing? Tell me what sold." Before Jemma could answer, Holly gave a quick glance toward the house across the street. "Any more sightings of Mr. Gorgeous But Not-So-Nice?"

"He helped me with the van yesterday." She left out the details about today.

"Oh?" The word oozed speculation. "Is that a blush I see?"

"It's hot out here."

"Right. May in Alaska is baking you after spending years in Atlanta."

"Don't get any ideas. He fixed the van, then just when he seemed to be getting nicer, made a jerky comment." She shuffled her feet and said quietly, "And he drove me and my goods to the market this morning."

"He what?" Holly whirled around to face Nathaniel's house. "Is there a romance brewing here?"'

24

Jemma felt her blood boiling as she remembered her morning. "About as far from it as possible." She described in detail what had happened.

"So he just dropped you off?"

Jemma nodded. "I'd had enough of him by the time I got there."

"And how did you get home?"

She gulped. This might well be the dumbest thing she'd ever done. "That's the dicey part. I let someone I met there, another booth holder, drive me home."

"Jemma!"

"I know. I wasn't sure what else to do. Anyway, the tow truck should be here soon for the van. Which probably can't be fixed. Next time I need to haul a lot, I'm renting a truck." She jerked her thumb across the street. "He isn't what you're picturing."

"Oh, well. I can fantasize, can't I? The handsome neighbor steps onto his front porch and calls my name, inviting me into his house and his life. The four of us live happily ever after."

Jemma made sure the girls weren't around, then leaned forward and whispered anyway, "I thought you'd sworn off men after Daniel."

"I've been so busy with college I haven't had time to consider the opposite sex. But now that I'm done, I'm wondering about my future, career and otherwise." Holly watched her girls climb onto an old stump in the front yard. "I'm lonely. Not every man hates children as much as Daniel did." Tipping her head to one side, she added, "Right?"

"Oh, Holly. There are men who adore children." Jemma hugged her sister and the girls ran in to make it a group hug.

Releasing Holly from the hug, Jemma said to her, "Wait here for a sec before you go," then to the girls, "Abbie and Ivy, I have a treat for you. Let me show you and your mom." Jemma raced up the steps and into her house, returning moments later with her surprise.

"Wings!" Abbie cried.

"Not just any wings. These are fairy wings," Jemma assured her as she strapped the purple-and-green-patterned wings she'd made onto each girl. "Look what else I have."

"Tutus! Oh, Aunt Jemma, you're the best." Ivy hugged her and pulled on her matching tutu, with Abbie not far behind. Both girls raced around the yard, flapping their arms and leaping in the air.

"Where did you get your freewheeling sense of creativity?" Holly asked, amazed. "Bree and I missed out on that gift completely."

"I'm not sure. If I didn't look like Mom and Dad, I'd wonder if I was adopted. Of course, Great-aunt Grace knitted, crocheted, sewed, and dabbled in a dozen other crafts, all beautifully. I guess the genes are out there." Jemma gave her another hug. "Don't worry about a man. I know there's a great one waiting for you, someone who will love you *and* your kids."

Holly replied, "We'll talk when I come back later. I know you'll have the girls in bed asleep so I'll just have to walk them out to the car in their sleepy state." She climbed into her car and drove off, blowing kisses at her girls, who waved at her.

Later that evening, Holly stepped onto the porch after checking on her girls. "Abbie and Ivy are sound asleep."

"Here." Jemma handed her sister a mug of hot chocolate with marshmallows on top.

Holly sat on a chaise lounge beside Jemma's wooden rocking chair and took a sip out of the cup. "You may not be able to cook, but you make a great cup of cocoa. You do know we won't be able to sit out here at night in the middle of the summer. Too many mosquitoes."

"I'm thinking of taking a page from the South and turning this into a screened porch."

"That would be great! There aren't very many front porches around here. It's a good thing someone added this one at some point." Holly stared at Jemma over the rim of her mug. "Now, tell me how you're feeling about Alaska. You seem . . . not quite right."

"I don't know, Holly. I really thought I'd be happy living here. It was fun when we were kids."

Holly took a sip of her drink, giving her sister one of her special, penetrating stares, but not saying a word.

"What?"

"You liked it here before."

"I know. I liked Palmer and I loved the history of this house. Great-aunt Grace was always so proud of living in one of the earliest houses in the area. This isn't one of the historic Colony houses from the 1930s when the government resettled farmers from the Midwest to Palmer, but it's from right after that."

"You're the only one in the family who loves old houses and all things antique as much as she did. Bree or I might have sold it."

"She knew I would keep it."

"And pass it on to your kids." Holly held up a hand. "Don't

worry. I'm not turning into Mom. I mean whenever you get married and have children."

"Thank you. Anyway, when I was here before, I was a visitor, a tourist, so I didn't have time to really know Palmer. Not that it's Palmer's fault I'm having problems."

Jemma ticked off her complaints on her fingers. "One: no flea markets. Two: my friends—other than you, of course— were left behind in Atlanta, and I haven't had success making new friends. Three: I have an annoying neighbor."

Holly set her hot chocolate on the porch floor and moved the bar on the back of her chair to lower it. "That's better." She settled into the chair. "Just be glad Great-aunt Grace found out about a wonderful scholarship I could use here and gave me her little rental house in town so I could keep school costs down. Otherwise you'd be all alone in the great state of Alaska."

Jemma sighed. "I don't know if I would have even moved up here if you didn't live nearby. I'm so glad to have you and the girls close."

"As to your problems, you seem to have found ways around the flea market situation."

Jemma shrugged. "To a point. I've found smaller events, but nothing has truly taken the place of a sale that lasts the whole weekend and that hundreds if not thousands of people visit." She sipped her drink.

"But you've made progress. For friends, you have to get out and meet people—unless you put a sign out on the main road with an arrow pointing over here that says, 'Lonely woman wants to meet strangers.'"

Jemma choked on her hot chocolate. Leaning forward, she thumped her chest. "Don't do that to me!" After wheezing in a deep breath, she sat back. "Your suggestion might not bring in the type of people I'm looking for. But point taken."

"You aren't missing a special man back in Atlanta?"

"On a fishing expedition?" Jemma grinned. "As I've told you, there wasn't a man I felt especially close to. James went to business events with me for a couple of years since we both worked at the company, but it wasn't anything more than friendship." She tucked the rest of the story away, keeping it private even from Holly. She had gotten closer to James than she'd meant to. Business handshakes had become kisses, and she'd started to expect a proposal. Instead, he'd propositioned her on his last night in Atlanta before moving to Dubai for a job transfer. After saying no to his offer of a one-night stand, she'd decided to keep business associates at a distance from then on.

"So, wise one, fix number three," Jemma said.

Holly leaned forward. "That one's a mystery to me. "He's handsome and successful," she said, pointing at the neighbor's dark house. "You're pretty and friendly."

Jemma stared up at the porch ceiling. "Um, maybe not as friendly as I could be."

Her sister asked, "When?"

"Well, I tore up his business card when he dropped me off."

"That wasn't nice. He'd just loaded your stuff and driven you to Friday Fling. And probably helped unload it."

Jemma shifted uncomfortably in her chair. Her sister was right.

"But just tearing up a business card doesn't seem too ugly."

Jemma cleared her throat. "I, uh, tore it into teeny tiny pieces. Shredded it, really."

"Okaaay. Anything else?"

"I called him a grouch, under my breath, and he might have heard it."

"I'm surprised here. You worked for almost a decade in a profession where you kept your cool. Always. What has you so riled up that you're being downright rude to your neighbor, a man who once fixed your van and today helped you get to your first sale?"

"From the very moment we met, he's been nasty about my business. Today he tried to tell me I would fail." Jemma waffled between anger and tears. Anger won. Standing, she said, "No. I've been right all along. I don't get along with my neighbor." Then she stormed into her house. When she was about to let the wooden screen door slam behind her to add an exclamation point to her feelings, Jemma caught it, remembering her sleeping nieces. As she walked toward the kitchen, she heard Holly mutter something she probably didn't want to hear.

Chapter Three

A weight landing on Jemma's chest woke her up. "No, Stitches!" She turned to see the time. "Six o'clock! You couldn't wait a little longer for breakfast?" Flinging her arms to her side, she stared up at the ceiling. She'd hoped to find an event to sell her goods at today, but nothing had appeared. Apparently Alaskans had better things to do this Saturday than shop.

Holly's words last night kept rattling around in her mind. She couldn't rely on her sister as her only friend. Holly had a life here with friends she'd made in college and otherwise. Besides, her sister had to find and interview for jobs, something that had almost turned into a full-time job.

Today was the day Jemma would do something to end her loneliness. She rolled over and sat on the edge of her bed. First in school and then in work, potential friends had surrounded her. It had been easy to find someone she might like to get to know better. How did you meet people when you worked from home?

Technology must offer a solution. Jemma reached for her phone and searched for Palmer activities. A hike caught her eye. The web page said participants could drive to the trailhead together, hike, and return in one day. Perfect. She'd have people around her but not have to spend too much time with any one person. She could get a sense of them and see if a potential friend lurked in their midst. Maybe she'd get to know Alaska better. And even like it. They were meeting in front of the Palmer Visitor Center at eight o'clock.

Jemma got up and headed for the shower, then afterward dressed and pulled her hair back into a ponytail before heading downstairs to the kitchen. After tucking a snack into the small backpack she'd used for a short hike on a company retreat, she fed Stitches and left.

A sense of excitement filled her as she drove to the meeting site. When Jemma reached the parking lot, she pulled into a space. As she got out of her car, she counted seven people milling around. A woman with a clipboard stood off to the side so Jemma approached her.

The woman smiled at Jemma. "I'm Melinda." Addressing the whole group, she said, "We've had a great turnout today, so we'll need two vehicles. I'm taking my minivan—and yes, you can thank me for cleaning out all signs of children under ten, which isn't a simple task." The woman's easy grin made Jemma suspect she had a potential friend in front of her. "Anyone else want to drive?"

Jemma was about to volunteer when a man spoke.

"I'd be happy to."

Oh, no. She gulped. *It couldn't be.* She slowly turned his direction. And yet it was. His jaw dropped when he saw her. Jemma gave a little wave, what she hoped appeared friendly to everyone around her. No need for people to get in the middle of whatever they had going on. She wasn't even sure.

Melinda glanced from one of them to the other. "You two know each other?"

Nathaniel spoke first. "We're neighbors."

"Well, then you can drive together."

"No!" Jemma held up her hand. Melinda jumped at her outburst, so Jemma forced a calm note to her voice. "I moved to Alaska about a month ago, and I'd love to meet new people. I'm feeling isolated in my house with just one neighbor."

"I understand. You can ride with me." Melinda divided everyone up. Then Jemma put her backpack in the open back of the minivan and climbed in the front passenger seat. As the others took their seats, Melinda leaned inside and asked, "Anyone need a potty break before we get going?"

Laughter followed a moment of stunned silence.

Melinda turned bright red. "Perhaps I should have worded that differently."

Jemma waved away her concerns. "How old are your kids?"

"Six and four. Let me phrase my question this way: we have a two-and-a-half-hour drive in front of us. Would anyone like to use the facilities?"

Jemma gasped. "Two and a half hours?"

Melinda said, "You must not have read the whole description of the hike."

"No. I just saw that it was a day hike. I assumed it would be around here."

"You want out?"

"No. I'm on board. Show me your Alaska."

After everyone assured Melinda they didn't need a potty break, Melinda took her seat behind the wheel.

A man from the row behind Jemma spoke as Melinda negotiated her way out of the parking lot and onto the highway. "I'm Matt."

"Jemma."

The others introduced themselves.

Matt said, "Gull Rock Trail runs next to Turnagain Arm. We'll wind through trees and catch glimpses of the water. It has some beautiful views."

"It sounds great. I just assumed we'd be going locally."

They drove to Anchorage and followed the highway south from there. Almost immediately, the road sat next to salt water, a narrow bay with mountains rising high on the other side. "I've never been here before," Jemma said, noticing a touch of awe in her voice. "This is gorgeous! I visited Alaska when I was a kid, but I guess I didn't pay attention."

Matt answered. "You need to explore. This isn't too far from the Mat-Su Valley. And if you're still happy at the end of the hike, you'll have to join us again. We go out every month."

Melinda pointed at a sign they passed that said, "McHugh Creek." "There's a pretty waterfall up that road. I'd like to stop and show you some of the sights along the way today, but we don't have time for them on this trip. You need to come back here sometime soon." Not too much further, Melinda pointed up the Girdwood road. "Ditto on this place. Our best ski resort, Alyeska, is up there. Maybe a group of us could come here to ski sometime this winter."

Jemma glanced up the road as they passed it and around at the scenery. "I can't believe how pretty this is."

"Wait until we're on the trail," Matt said. Everything changes when you're in the middle of the outdoors in Alaska."

Melinda laughed. "Spoken like a true outdoorsman. Not that I disagree with you. My husband, on the other hand, would rather dance naked on hot coals than spend a day in the woods. Which works out well for me today since he's able to watch the kids—and gladly."

They eventually left the main highway for another road. When Jemma saw a sign for a place called "Hope," she felt that emotion fill her. She'd found a nice group of people. Maybe Alaska could grow on her. She had a free house and could find ways to grow her business. She felt like there was a chance this place could become home.

Melinda parked near the trailhead and Nathaniel pulled in beside her. Then everyone got out and grabbed their packs.

As they started down the trail, they entered the woods, now fresh with new leaves. Jemma decided to spend time talking to everyone here, to see who she might like to get to know better. Asking no one in particular, she said, "I honestly didn't read the fine print here, or I would have known we weren't hiking near Palmer. How long is this trail?"

Matt answered, "About five miles."

"That shouldn't take long."

"Each way."

"Oh." Jemma pictured herself as a desk jockey in an office. Could she do this?

Someone else chimed in. Cathy?

"Don't let him scare you. It's level, and families come here." She poked Matt with her elbow.

Melinda said, "Brother and sister."

35

Jemma grinned. "I can relate to that. Only I have two sisters."

Everyone chimed in with their family stats. Everyone except Nathaniel.

Matt asked, "What about you, Nate?"

Nathaniel wore what seemed to be a pasted-on smile. "I'm an only. And"—he smiled wider—"I know it uses more syllables, but I prefer Nathaniel."

As everyone laughed, he stepped to the side of the trail where the trees parted. "Nice view."

The group crowded around him to take a look.

As they moved away and continued down the trail, Jemma lingered. She could see across Turnagain Arm to mountains on the other side.

Nathaniel surprised her by speaking. "Beautiful, isn't it?"

"Yes, it is. No one could ever question Alaska's beauty."

He turned back toward the trail and Jemma followed. "But?"

She wondered if she should open up to him. He didn't seem like the warm-and-fuzzy type. "I'm a long way from my friends and the life I knew."

He frowned. "That woman with children visits."

"'That woman' is my sister."

"Ah, so those are your nieces."

"Twin nieces. Do you have family in Alaska?"

After a long pause, he answered. "I'm a very private person, Miss Harris."

Jemma waited for the rest of his thought, but only heard laughter from their group up ahead. Nathaniel hurried to catch up with the others and she followed behind him. Just when she thought she might be able to like her neighbor . . .

Trailing behind the rest of the group, she wondered about Nathaniel. Why was he here when he didn't seem to want to talk to anyone? She watched him interact with people. He would smile and laugh, then almost catch himself and close back up. The whole thing was odd, and she'd never have anything to do with someone so hard to read. She sighed. If he wasn't her neighbor . . .

Matt had stopped and was staring at something beside the trail. He waved everyone over. "Let's make a tighter group."

"Because?" Jemma asked.

"Bear scat." He pointed at what must be bear poop.

Adrenaline rushed through Jemma as she prepared for a sprint back to the car. Eight other people continued down the trail. "Aren't we going back?"

Melinda replied. "We're carrying heavy-duty bear spray—in case we see not just a smaller black bear, but a brown bear."

"But—" Jemma sputtered.

Melinda walked back to her and steered her toward the group. "If you stay away from places that might have bears in Alaska, you have to stay indoors." She shrugged. "Even then they sometimes find their way inside."

Jemma felt the blood rush out of her head. *Breathe.*

"Don't worry," Nathaniel offered. "I've hiked dozens of trails since I moved here, and I've only seen one bear. And he was more interested in going the other direction."

Now she thought she must be hallucinating. Could a lack of oxygen cause that? Nathaniel had just been nice. She took a deep, slow breath so she didn't hyperventilate.

When they hadn't seen a bear in the next ten minutes, she started to calm down.

The group walked across a wooden walkway over a wet area, then through different kinds of trees, some with leaves and some pine, often stepping over their roots. What looked to be an old road paralleled the trail, so she asked about it.

A man whose name she couldn't remember answered. "It's an old wagon trail that went beyond Gull Rock."

Jemma found herself once again hiking beside Nathaniel. When he helped her over a fallen tree, she knew the oxygen had yet to return to her brain. He'd been nice to her before, but every time he did, he'd do a 180 and become a jerk again. She'd wait and see.

At least he fit the setting here. He might usually be Mr. Gorgeous in his perfectly pressed dress shirts and chinos, but if the women she knew in Atlanta saw him in worn jeans and a blue plaid flannel shirt that picked up the color of his eyes, they'd be on the next plane out. He'd gone from city slicker to rugged outdoorsman. His casual manner in the woods told her he might actually be a rugged outdoorsman. And she would have never guessed that.

"So everyone"—Melinda glanced around at their group—"tell us three things about yourself, including your occupation. Five miles times two is a long trip, and we seem to have the trail pretty much to ourselves today. I'm including humans and"—she smiled at Jemma—"four-legged friends."

Each person gave his or her three facts. They had a variety of occupations, from lawyer to retail manager to state trooper to plumber and artist. Nathaniel said he was a freelance marketing consultant. Melinda had stepped away from being an elementary teacher to be with her kids. Jemma added her facts last.

"I moved here from Atlanta a month ago, live in a house

my great-aunt left me in her will, and I used to work in the corporate world."

Melinda asked, "What do you do now?"

Jemma glanced over at Nathaniel. Would everyone else see her dreams as he did? She put her shoulders back. No. If she didn't believe in her vision enough to share it here, how could she possibly open a store in a few months? "I flip furniture." At their puzzled expressions, she added, "I take things that aren't beautiful in their present state, and I transform them into something new. A dresser can become a chest, an entertainment cabinet, a bench, etc. I paint them, sometimes with a decorative pattern or stencil. I make a cushion for the bench. Then I sell them at community sales, Friday Fling, etc." She stood tall. "I want to open my own store."

When Jemma stopped, she realized she'd gotten so involved in her dream that she'd talked too long and probably bored everyone else within hearing range. She wasn't prepared for what happened.

"That's so cool, Jemma!" Melinda's eyes lit up. "I'm not artistic, but it sounds like a hoot."

"I've worked with brushes, never with a jigsaw," the artist—Vanessa?—said.

"I am having *a lot* of fun. I love working with power tools." She slanted Nathaniel a glance, and his expression was exactly as she'd expect. Kind of pruney and disapproving.

Nathaniel fought against rolling his eyes. These women actually thought Ms. Harris, Jemma, had a good idea. He could help someone sell new all day long. She had what might be a nice hobby, but she couldn't possibly support herself finding new homes for decrepit furniture. It seemed like a nursing home for furniture. He chuckled to himself and coughed to cover it. He didn't think Jemma would appreciate the joke.

They reached the end of the trail and a peninsula that jutted into the water. A panoramic view of the salt water framed by low mountains extended far to the left and right.

Jemma said, "Wow."

Matt, the state trooper, stepped beside her. "I always think it's a wow, too." He pointed directly across to land. "That's the highway we took to get here. If I couldn't see tiny cars over there, I'd think I was alone in a wilderness. But that's Alaska for you. You can be in the middle of nowhere one day, and I do mean nowhere, then be in a city, having an elegant dinner, the next day."

"That's one of the things I like about Alaska." Nathaniel spoke without hesitating first. Then he paused before saying more. Oh well. He may as well talk to everyone. He'd joined this hike for this very reason, even if he found it akin to torture to spend time with people he didn't know and try to be friendly. "I used to live in Seattle, and I had to drive quite a distance to find anything close to this."

"But you had great sports to watch!" Matt pounded him on the back.

Nathaniel grinned. "That I did. Go, Seahawks!"

Matt chuckled and Melinda leaned over to Jemma to say, "Male bonding" just loud enough for everyone to hear.

When everyone laughed good-naturedly, Nathaniel felt like he'd done well. Maybe he'd found a group he could hang out with.

They sat down on the grassy area, and everyone pulled lunches from their packs that looked like enough to sustain them on the return five-mile hike. Except Jemma. She nibbled tiny bites off a granola bar. She noticed him watching her and turned red. Should he offer part of his lunch?

Melinda beat him to it. "Let me guess. You didn't read the whole description of the hike, so you also didn't bring a lunch."

"Dumb, huh? It must be because I don't have to study things carefully anymore."

Melinda raised one eyebrow. "Please explain." She handed Jemma half a sandwich. "I'll share with you." Then two other people added to her lunch, one with chips, another with half an apple.

"Until a month ago I was a corporate executive assistant. I was the gatekeeper. I had to know everything that was going on at all times and make sure my boss was where he needed to be." Jemma took a bite of what appeared to be a ham sandwich.

Melinda nodded slowly. "Kind of like being a mom, only it's kids I'm doing my best to keep track of. So your brain's on vacation now?"

"It would seem so."

The two women laughed.

As they retraced their steps back to the parking area after lunch, Jemma seemed to purposely avoid him. She talked to each person in the group at one point or another. Everyone but him. For some reason, this bothered him. He'd avoided her company, but now that he knew her better, he actually didn't mind being around her. Pausing at one of the openings through the trees, he let the water and mountains soothe his soul as they always did. When the group's voices receded, he turned and hurried after them. Being alone in the woods, especially with fresh bear scat nearby, wasn't the best idea.

When they arrived at the parking lot, everyone headed back to the vehicles they'd been in before. Part of him felt let down. He would have liked to get to know some of the others better. A small voice told him he'd like to get to know his neighbor, but he pushed the thought aside. She'd probably discuss power tools and remind him of the noise that would begin again tomorrow morning. Gritting his teeth, he climbed into his SUV, the others joined him, and they headed home.

Chapter Four

Driving into Anchorage mid-morning Wednesday, Nathaniel tried to focus on the meeting he had in an hour. Instead, an image of his neighbor kept popping into his mind. He'd been speaking with his caterer a couple of days earlier when, right in the middle of Marcel's assurances that he had everything under control for his business event next Saturday, he'd caught a glimpse out his office window of one of the neighbor's nieces going around the back corner of her house. Then Jemma Harris darted around the front—wearing fairy wings and a tutu.

He'd made a strangled noise that caused Marcel to ask, "Monsieur, are you all right?"

When he gave a standard answer of, "Yes. Everything is fine," he thought to himself that his home life felt less and less that way every day. Everything *would* be fine. He shook his head to get the fairy image out of his mind.

Maybe the letter from his lawyer would scare her. She might not move, but even toning things down would be an improvement. Then again, it wasn't illegal to act like a nut. For Saturday, with current and potential clients coming to his house, the last thing he needed was a crazy distraction. She'd become the topic of conversation instead of how happy they were or could be with his services.

Nathaniel forced himself to focus on driving as he neared the city and traffic picked up. He made his way through downtown traffic to the restaurant where these clients liked to meet and felt like he'd won the lottery when he found a parking space nearby. Since he'd done work for the company before, and they'd seemed pleased with his results, he hoped to make a brief presentation over lunch and secure a new contract today.

Once seated, they made business small talk over ordering and soup, and offered the contract to him with the main course. He read over it, and asked, "Are you able to come to Saturday's party at my house?" as he signed the agreement.

The two men glanced at each other.

Nathaniel set down the pen. "Is there a problem?"

One of the men sighed. "We debated about who would tell you. I lost."

A major contract from the company sat before him. Surely something serious would have kept them from offering it. "Is there a problem with my work?"

The man held up his hands. "Absolutely not. Your work is top-notch. Since you're in the business of making companies look good, we thought you would want to know how people saw you."

Nathaniel tried for a nonchalant expression. "Please tell me."

Dessert arrived just then, and the man took a bite of

chocolate cake, seeming to need whatever fortification it offered. After a quick sip of coffee, he continued. "Everyone I know who's used your services is impressed with the results."

"Good. But? I hear a *but* in there somewhere."

"You're pleasant but standoffish. That's okay here in Anchorage. We can roll with it even though we would like friendly more. I've met a couple of your other clients at business meetings. You're in a community in the Mat-Su Valley that wants to know you better. They want you to be real and one of them."

Nathaniel's brow furrowed. "I can offer advice to others all day long, but I'm startled enough that I don't have any for myself on how to fix this."

The other man cleared his throat. "We thought it would help if you seemed approachable. Having a woman at your side for your party, no matter how old-fashioned that sounds, might make you seem more friendly and open."

Nathaniel left the meeting grateful for the contract but feeling shell-shocked. He'd put his energy into his business, not into a social life. Tapping his foot as he stood at a crosswalk, waiting for the light to change, he realized his lack of a meaningful social life had nothing to do with business. By the time it was his turn to go, he'd realized the real reason was that people, at least people other than his mom and grandmother, let you down. Business didn't. Business could be controlled.

Back at his SUV, he pulled out of the parking garage and drove toward home with his clients' words heavy on his mind. Should he even have this party if people saw him as distant? He knew the event could help him bring in new clients and new work from previous clients.

His business wrapped itself around how people perceived a business. The perception was what mattered. Some might call that shallow, but it worked. A great business or product could be lost behind poor marketing, and a barely functioning business could be masked by great marketing. If people perceived him as distant, he'd change their minds.

He needed a date by Saturday.

Nathaniel leaned on the steering wheel and groaned. This Saturday had taken a turn for the worse. In the fifteen minutes he'd been parked on the road to his house, he could have walked home. And back. Twice. Tonight's party had been on track until now. He'd picked up his suit at the cleaners and three floral arrangements from the florist next door. Everything would have been perfect. Except for the fact that he didn't have a date.

He'd try to remedy that situation earlier today by driving into Anchorage to the furniture store where a woman he'd dated once about a year ago worked. The date had been so-so, but he'd gone through his list of every woman he'd taken out since he'd moved to Alaska, and everyone had told him no. Some, of course, were dating someone else, or even married. One said she was not only married, but now had a baby. Another explained that she hadn't felt like he'd been in the room with her, that he didn't care even a little bit. And they'd gone out three times. Alexis's eagerness popped into his mind, but he pushed her right out. She might be a loose cannon as the hostess of a party.

So, he daily met marketing goals for clients, but he'd failed miserably on his personal marketing goal.

On the drive back up the Glenn Highway to Palmer, he'd

talked to his caterer, Marcel, and the man had wrapped up their call by telling him he had the food under control and everything he'd prepared would be *magnifique*. The often excitable Frenchman was calm.

He shouldn't be. The road just before the curve to Nathaniel's house had a trench cut across it, and a truck now lowered pipe into it. He'd guess the giant concrete pipe was a water main, so his water might be turned off. Even if it wasn't, would his guests be able to get to his house? Nathaniel did a U-turn and pulled into the subdivision that butted against Jemma's property. After parking, he decided to try to walk home, taking his groceries, which could easily be carried, but not the flowers. When he got to the trenched area, the apparent foreman stood off to the side, directing the action, so Nathaniel asked him about his timeline.

The answer would ruin Marcel's day.

"We hope to be done by six o'clock. Seven or eight at the latest. Construction over there"—he pointed toward the subdivision—"damaged one water main, and we'd just recently learned about a slow leak in this one, so we had the crew repair both today."

Nathaniel thanked him and trekked around the trench and through the dense trees and brush that lined the side of the road. The flowers would probably survive in his SUV for the time being, and they'd decorate his house this week.

He pulled out his cell phone to make some calls, first to Marcel, to tell him to freeze whatever he could and to assure him he'd pick up the expense of re-creating his party a week from now. Once inside his house, he dropped onto the couch and called his guests.

At least dinner wouldn't be a total loss. A thick steak had

called his name all day, so he'd stopped at the grocery store to pick one up for lunch tomorrow, and one for the freezer for the next time a ribeye spoke to him. Nathaniel breathed a sigh of relief as he headed upstairs to get a little work done, now that his party was canceled. Social activities weren't his thing, and he'd gotten a week's reprieve on this one. Somewhere out there lived his date for next Saturday. He'd hesitated about asking someone he didn't know at all for a business-related event, one that could impact his future, but he might not have a choice.

Jemma stepped over one of the many fabric projects spread throughout her living room. At the sewing machine that sat on the big old table in the slightly fussy, old-fashioned dining room she loved, Jemma stitched a contrasting piping onto a blue-and-white pillow cushion that would sit on the bench she'd bought from Travis and painted earlier.

She still felt a happy buzz from the first part of the day. She'd taken everything she could stuff into her car to a church yard sale she'd read about. When she'd offered to donate a percentage of her earnings to the church, they'd welcomed her and given her a table. Pillows and table runners made from the old tablecloths had been hits, so sewing up additional products had moved up her list of priorities.

When she turned off the machine, she heard a rushing sound instead of silence, a sound like pouring rain. She loved the smell of a forest in the rain. Break time. Stretching, Jemma stood and reached out to pet Stitches, who had taken up residence on a pile of fabric.

She got up from her chair and wandered out onto the front porch only to find a cloudy sky, but no rain. How odd, considering the sound. When she turned to the right, what she saw made her reel backward, holding on to the railing for support.

A gushing torrent was closing in on her garage, the garage that held her dream inside with furniture and tools. She wheeled around, grabbed her rain slicker off the coat tree in the entryway in the hope it might help keep her dry, and searched for the rubber boots that should have sat underneath. Remembering her nieces had used them for dress-up, she skipped the boots and raced to the garage in her sneakers.

By the time she'd opened the doors, water was creeping inside onto the concrete floor. The day that had begun with a sell-out at the church had taken a significant turn for the worse.

Jemma grabbed saws and other tools, stowing them on waist-high shelves. The bench she'd spent hours painting today using a new technique, three more dressers, the stool she'd bought from Travis, two bookshelves, and some smaller projects seemed to mock her from their positions on or almost on the floor. She had enough money invested in everything in here that her vision of the future could be destroyed in one evening, or at least seriously delayed.

She picked up the stool and raced to her house, setting it inside the doorway. Wiping her hands on her jeans, Jemma saw her array of happy fabrics in a new light. Dragging them to the side so they wouldn't be damaged, she made room for the rest of the furniture. After spreading towels on the wood floor, she raced out for another load.

A half inch of water covered the garage floor. She was running out of time. From the direction of the flow, she knew the water covered the road. No one could reach her to help.

Jemma turned toward her neighbor's house. No one except Nathaniel Montgomery.

Nathaniel flipped on the gas grill on his stove, pulled the steaks out of the fridge, and grabbed a few garlic cloves to crush for seasoning. Just then, his doorbell rang and someone pounded on the front door. With the road closed by construction, Jemma Harris was the only one who could get to his door. Knowing he had no choice but to answer it, he turned off the stove and headed that way.

"What do you want?" he asked a bit less politely than he should have. Jemma stood on his front steps, wearing a rain coat, soggy jeans, and sneakers. What had she been doing?

"Help. Please help me move things out of my garage." She pointed in that direction, then turned back to him with a pitiful expression in her eyes. "I don't know what's going on, but I'm about to lose everything I've worked on."

A raging torrent of water tore through her property, slamming into her garage and rushing by the end of her driveway. Her house sat high and dry on a slight hill, as did his whole property, so the main structures were safe. The odd thing was that there wasn't a creek anywhere near their homes.

An image of the repair crew popped into his mind. "They were fixing the water main. Something must have gone wrong." He held out his hand when he noticed sprinkles splashing on his steps, feeling scattered drops. Now she'd have water from above to contend with too.

Jemma swiped at her cheek, and he suspected it was tears, not just rain, she wiped away. She turned and raced back, slogging through the water where it was shallower, toward the front of her yard, and grabbed something small from the garage that she carried into the house.

The water had risen well above the foundation of her garage, so the floor would certainly be covered. Knowing he had no choice but to help his neighbor, no matter how he felt about her and her junk, he grabbed his coat, slipped on boots, and hurried after her.

One look inside the building told him they had little time. Instead of carrying everything all the way into her house, he opted for setting it outside, but above the water line.

"No!" she cried when she saw him set down the bench. "I just painted this. Even a few sprinkles will total it."

"Paint it again!" he yelled over the roaring water. "Help me move everything out of the garage so nothing will get smashed by the force of the water or wash away. Then we can haul it all into the house." Two inches of water now covered the garage floor, and there was no mistaking the current of the water through it. "This building is old, and the force of the water might push it over."

That must have changed her mind, because she grabbed one side of a dresser, with him on the other, and they hefted it outside.

She leaned near him and said, "I hope you're wrong about the water destroying the building."

They returned for more.

"Don't worry," he shouted. "Insurance should cover it."

"No, it won't. I haven't upgraded my insurance to show that I'm using it for business. I asked the company about that but haven't gotten over there yet."

With the garage emptied, they shifted everything first on-to her front porch, then inside. In her living room, Jemma wiped it all down with paper towels. "Thank you so much, Nathaniel. I can't tell you how much I appreciate your help."

Her praise and the use of his first name warmed him inside so much that he didn't mind, for a moment, that he was drenched and shivering.

Jemma stepped back onto the porch, then called through the open door, "We got everything from here. I wanted to double-check."

Suddenly she strained forward, then motioned him outside. "Hey, come here."

He walked out the door, pushing his soggy hair off his face. "Did we miss something after all?"

"Listen."

Barking. He guessed from very nearby, since he could hear it over the rushing water.

The two of them followed the sound. Jemma pointed, but he only saw brush. "Where?"

"There. See? In the middle of that alder bush."

She was right. A small dog was trapped in the raging waters beyond the garage, caught in the brush and well out of reach. Water poured over him, and he could barely keep his head above it. If anything, the force of the water had increased in the last few minutes. Trying to step into it would probably take Nathaniel to his knees.

"I don't see how we can get to him." He stared at the dog, unsure of any action he could take. "I think he's going to be lost."

"No!" Jemma shouted. "I'll find a way." When she stepped into the water, he grabbed the back of her coat.

"You could be knocked down, maybe even killed by the power of the water slamming you against rocks."

"So will he. I have to try."

Rope Nathaniel had seen hanging in the garage gave him an idea. He ran out there and retrieved it, then tied one end around his waist, looped the other around a hook in the wall, and step-by-step, moved into the water, letting the rope out slowly but keeping it taut. Once, he felt his feet start to slide out from under him, but he stopped to regain his balance, then continued forward. When he'd almost reached the dog, the branches surrounding the little guy began to pull over him. Nathaniel grabbed the dog's back leg just as he was being sucked under and into certain death.

Tugging him close, Nathaniel wrapped his arms around the shivering animal and felt Jemma pulling on the rope, helping drag them both back to safety.

"There you go." He set the dog on the ground and pushed him toward Jemma.

"It's just a puppy." She crouched beside the dog. But when she tried to hold him close, he snuggled next to Nathaniel's legs. "I think you have a new friend."

Nathaniel picked him up and carried him onto Jemma's porch. There was no room in his life or his house for a dog. "I don't think so. Why don't you take him into your house for the night, and I'll haul him over to the pound in the morning."

Jemma glared at him.

He'd fallen back from his earlier role of knight in shining armor, and he didn't feel as happy as he should to be off that white steed. "I don't have a place for a dog." He shrugged. "I don't have a clue what to do with a dog."

"Treat him like any pet you had growing up."

"We didn't have pets. They didn't fit our lifestyle." How could you fit a pet into a chaotic life with an alcoholic?

"Okay. I'll help you."

"Jemma, let's make this easy. I don't want to share my house with anyone or anything. You take him."

"I can't! I'm taking care of my sister's cat while she's on a medical trip to Africa. Just the activity of us going in and out of the house will have chased Stitches under my bed. I can't imagine what a dog would do. And I have a living room full of furniture and fabric spread all over the place. Projects I've created are in almost every room of the house. A wet dog won't mix with any of that."

He stared at the dog, knowing he'd been defeated. "Just for tonight." When he picked the puppy up and stepped forward, Jemma stayed on her porch. He turned to her. "Did you have a dog?"

"Sure. We always had dogs and cats."

"Then you're coming. Help me get him settled."

Jemma's eyes opened wide when she stepped onto Nathaniel's slate floored entryway. The back wall of his house was floor-to-ceiling glass with a stone fireplace set in the center. The view of the forest beyond his house must be spectacular during the day. Medium-toned wide plank wood flooring covered the rest of the floor, including a kitchen most chefs would envy. Glass-fronted cabinets faced a huge, granite-topped island with a six-burner gas stove in the center. She barely resisted the urge to drool.

Nathaniel set the puppy on the floor and Jemma kneeled in front of it. "He's skinny, so I doubt he belongs to anyone. I wonder if someone threw him away."

Nathaniel surprised her when he looked stunned and said, "I can't believe anyone could do something that terrible."

Jemma checked over the puppy and got a tongue across her face for her efforts. Laughing, she said, "He's adorable." When she checked the tail end, she chuckled. "He's a she." She looked up at Nathaniel. "There's another woman in your life."

"Just for tonight."

"As long as they fix the water line."

"I'm sure they will." He took off his wet shoes and socks, and Jemma followed suit. Then he stepped to the sink and turned on the faucet. "This works, so maybe it's already done."

When Nathaniel went over to the fireplace and turned on the gas, the dog whimpered and moved closer to Jemma, apparently wanting the nearest human to help. "Go get a towel to dry her off. Then let's get her fed and a bath." Jemma stood and shivered, rubbing her arms.

"We'd better get on some dry clothes first."

She raised an eyebrow. "You have women's clothing in your closet?"

His neck turned red, and he loosened his shirt collar. Nathaniel must not be the type to have women overnight, information Jemma found endearing. "The clothes are in my guest room and belong to my grandmother. She's stayed here a couple of times."

Upstairs, Jemma found that grandma's taste leaned toward old-fashioned, but not in a hip, vintage way. Choices hanging in the closet included a gingham housedress with giant tulips embroidered down the front, and a sparkly polyester purple top with coordinating pants. Neither fit her fashion sense. Jemma slipped on the pantsuit, realizing when the sleeve's cuffs hit her at three-quarter length and the pant legs fit like elastic-bottomed Capris that the older woman stood quite a bit shorter. After changing into the housedress, and not daring to look in the mirror, she went downstairs, where she found Nathaniel wearing yet one more pair of chinos and a dress shirt, apparently his uniform except when he went hiking, and holding a dark blue towel. He stared helplessly at the puppy, not touching her or talking to her.

Jemma took the towel from him and crouched, rubbing the dog down, then scratching her ear. "Good girl. Thank you for holding still." She stood again, then went into the kitchen to see what she could scrounge up for the puppy. Stitches could share some of his food if necessary, but she wasn't sure if a dog liked cat food. She remembered though that the dogs she'd had while growing up ate anything that wouldn't bite back. The cats had been the fussy ones.

Nathaniel said, "I don't have dog food."

"Obviously. Do you have any meat?"

He pointed to his fridge. "Steak."

"She'll like that." Jemma went over to the fridge and pulled it open. "Your guest room doesn't have furniture. Did you have Granny sleep on the floor?"

"Of course not. She slept in my bed. I slept on the couch."

When Jemma pulled out the steak, Nathaniel stalked over to her. "Hey, that's expensive meat. That's my dinner."

Jemma stared down at the puppy and back up at him.

He raised his hands in defeat. "Okay. It's the only thing I can think of. Does she want it rare or well done?"

Jemma laughed. "She'll take it any way she can get it, including raw." She pulled a knife out of the knife block on the counter and chopped up a steak and put half in a bowl she'd pulled from his cupboard.

The dog lapped it up, then sat down and wagged her tail. Nathaniel reached to give her the rest, but Jemma stopped him.

"We don't know how long it's been since she's eaten or how much water she swallowed. Let's only give her this much for now."

He nodded helplessly.

At Jemma's urging Nathaniel wrapped the puppy in the towel and carried her upstairs for her bath. Trekking along behind him through the master bedroom, she only allowed herself a quick glance at the overall image of dark, masculine colors before stepping into a spectacular master bathroom. Jemma froze. "I've never seen anything like this tub." A huge tub, essentially a modern rendition of her favorite claw foot tub, sat in the corner. After putting down the stopper and turning on the water, she stood back. "I'm not usually into modern, but I can live with this." Realizing how that might sound, she turned to him and added, "Not that I'm planning to live with anything you own, okay?"

Nathaniel raised one eyebrow at the comment, but didn't say anything as he ran water into the tub, then set the squirming dog in it.

Jemma started to bathe the brown puppy, and as the mud washed away, a golden dog emerged. "She's pretty! A good percentage golden retriever or Lab, I guess. Maybe both."

"That means she'll be a big dog." Nathaniel stared at her warily.

"Not tonight." As Jemma rubbed the puppy dry, the little dog wiggled in her arms and licked her face again. "She's a sweetie." Standing, she said, "Now we need a bed for her. Do you have a spare blanket?"

Nathaniel mutely pulled one down from a closet shelf and handed it to her. As they went back downstairs, he asked, "What if she needs to go to the bathroom?"

"That's a good question." Jemma looked down at her little charge. "We don't know if she's potty trained, so I guess she'll either ask to go outside," she said, grinning at him, "or not."

"That wasn't helpful."

"It's all I've got right now." She placed the folded blanket on the floor next to the chair he said he'd sit in to watch TV, found a bowl in a cupboard and filled it with water, then set it beside the food bowl. With her work done, Jemma headed for the door. "I hope someone at the pound loves this little dog."

"Take her yourself," Nathaniel said with an expression that seemed near panic.

The puppy leaned against her as she put on her shoes. "Part of me wants to say yes, but my sister won't be back until the end of the summer, and I doubt her cat's a fan of dogs."

When she opened the door, Nathaniel pushed it closed. "Wait! What if the puppy wants something and I don't know what that is?"

Jemma held up three fingers and folded them down one by one. "Food. Water. Bathroom. That's probably all she'll need. Otherwise, you know where to find me."

He stood at the door as she opened it, visibly trying to get back under control. "The flow of water has stopped. Well, I'm sorry, but it looks like this flood put you out of business."

"No. In the end, I have my inventory. I can repaint it. And I can replace any damaged tools without spending too much."

"What if the garage is damaged structurally or the electric wiring has a problem?"

"Considering the number of storms and everything else the building has survived in its eighty-odd years, I suspect it's sound."

"It's a firetrap."

"In your dreams."

When she stepped through the door, Nathaniel put his hand on her arm. "Jemma, I am sorry about what you lost tonight."

Her eyes started to fill, and he took a step back, wisely wanting to avoid a bawling female. A *yipe* from the kitchen caught their attention, and Jemma blinked back her tears. Laughing, she pointed at the puppy. "I think she's found her first toy."

The little dog sat with his slipper in her mouth, appearing quite pleased with herself.

Chapter Five

Jemma's doorbell rang the next morning. "Oomph." Stitches shoved on her stomach with powerful back legs as he scrambled over her to safety under the bed. Seven fifteen. She'd slept later than usual, but her evening aerobic exercise of running through water and upstairs carrying twice what she normally would had somehow worn her out. As she debated whether or not she should answer the door, it rang again, and Stitches yowled.

"Okay. Okay. I'll get it." Still wearing the big schlumpy sweatshirt and sweatpants she'd put on after a long, wonderfully hot shower the night before, she hurried downstairs and peered around the curtain on the narrow window beside the door. She pulled it open and cried, "Mom! Dad!" before going into their arms for a group hug. "You aren't supposed to be here for another month."

Her parents looked at each other. Then an unspoken response seemed to be that her mother would talk. "Since it's summertime and your father isn't teaching summer classes this year, we could come anytime. Holly said you might need family, so we did some rearranging. You don't like it here?" She gestured to the area around the house.

Leave it to her mother to go directly to the point. "It's beautiful here." Jemma sighed. "I did go on a hike yesterday with a group and met some new people. A couple of them might become friends." An image of her neighbor in his sexy, outdoorsy outfit popped into her mind. *Whoa. Where did that thought come from?* "I've been lonely, but I've been busy with my business. I haven't even had time to redo any of Great-aunt Grace's furniture for myself."

"What's all this?" Her father pointed at scattered debris left behind from last night's flood.

Once Jemma had explained it, her mother suggested they go inside and sit down so they could talk more. As soon as they stepped through the door, her mother said, "Oh my."

Jemma pointed at the mess. "This is where all my projects from the garage ended up."

Her father took charge of the situation. "I rented a minivan so we could take you, Holly, and the girls out. I'm glad I did, because I have room to fit a couple of large fans from a tool rental place in there so we can dry out the garage in a hurry and get everything back in its place."

Jemma felt a burden lift. "Thank you." When she tried to hand him some cash, he pushed it away, then turned and headed back to the van. As her dad drove off, Jemma knew she wanted this in a future marriage, one person helping the other when they were down.

"Tell me what your plan is now." Her mother skirted the project furniture and sat on a wingback chair.

Stitches bumped Jemma's legs, and she reached down to

rub behind the cat's ears. "How'd you know only family was here, so it was safe to come out?" Jemma went through to the kitchen and pulled out a can of food. From the kitchen, she loudly said, "Bree told me he'd bump me when he was hungry, and I get bumped a lot in the morning."

After feeding the cat, she went into her living room and sat in her favorite chair. The scattered furniture in the middle of the room and sewing projects shoved against the wall triggered a replay in her mind of last night's events. Only think of the positive: she'd saved her furniture. Grimacing, she thought, *Nathaniel* and *I saved my furniture.* She owed him. Big-time.

Not one to be sidetracked from her earlier question, her mother narrowed it. "What's your plan for the rest of the summer?"

Jemma sighed and got up, walking around the damp furniture. "I'm trying to put all the pieces into place. My plan currently needs . . . adjusting." Kneeling in front of one piece, she noticed the wood veneer had peeled off in a section, taking with it a day's work of refinishing the wood. She tugged at it and a large area peeled off. The curled, wet mess didn't seem like something she could reattach, so that piece was a loss as is. She'd have to rethink it.

Jemma added, "I'm used to being in charge, but I was always using someone else's money and time. Now it's all mine."

"Does that mean you're giving up?"

Jemma straightened and stood tall. "Never. I worked too hard to save for this business. I do wonder if I made a mistake moving here. Great-aunt Grace's legacy seemed to come at the right time. Work had become . . . challenging."

"I knew you were upset but never knew exactly what had happened."

Jemma instantly regretted her words. She hadn't shared the true situation with her parents. She probably should have. "Sexual harassment."

"What? I thought your boss was a nice old man."

Jemma shook her head. "Not him. I chose to work at that company because of his reputation. He's a good man. It's his twenty-five-year-old grandson who spent a lot of time there. How do you report the boss's grandson?"

Her mother frowned. "You're right. That's an impossible situation. So you leaped at this opportunity?"

"A gift at the perfect time. Just not the perfect place. I've always planned to sell my products at flea markets. Who would have thought the nearest flea market, particularly the nearest one that's year-round, would be fifteen hundred miles away, in Seattle?"

"You're making do, though, right?"

Jemma shrugged. "Sort of. I'm searching for community yard sales and church sales. So far three out of four have said yes when I asked if I could join them. And there's Palmer's Friday Fling. That's been good, but it doesn't have the volume of traffic of a much larger city."

"At least there's time. You don't have to rush into having your store."

Jemma plopped onto her couch. "I wish. If I don't make it this summer, I have to wait until next summer to try again. There won't be many opportunities to sell at yard sales or anything else during the winter."

"Oh my, Jemma. I hadn't thought of that. Can you make it more than a year without a job?"

Jemma wavered her hand. "Yes, but if I do that, I'm left with nothing to restart my life if this doesn't work. I have to get my business rolling along by August and have a store in Anchorage open before the Christmas retail rush."

"You know that your dad and I will help you if you need it."

"At thirty years old, almost, I must stand on my own two feet. I appreciate you—"

"I know. We raised all of you to be independent, and you've not disappointed us. Just remember that we're here if you do need us."

Jemma knew she'd truly been blessed with the parents she'd been given. But she had to make it on her own.

"Aunt Grace wanted you to live here. I know that. She knew you would appreciate her house more than Holly or Bree, that you would help preserve the history of it."

"I love that it's from the 1940s, and that's very old here. You should see *his* house." She pointed across the street. Just then, Jemma heard a vehicle on the street and wondered if Dad had returned already.

"Your neighbor's house? I remember Aunt Grace selling off the land and saying someone built a house. For what turned out to be the last couple years of her life she told us she didn't feel up to company, so we didn't come. I wish we had," her mother said sadly. Visibly shaking it off, she added, "What are your neighbors like?"

"Neighbor. He's a single guy and he's grouchy. He's a marketing consultant. And"—she grinned—"he has a dog."

"A man with a dog can't be all bad."

Jemma chuckled. "He just got the dog. He did help start my van. And drove me to Friday Fling once. And he helped move all of this inside last night." She swept her hand over the room.

"He sounds very nice. Is he young, old, somewhere in between?"

"He's about my age—"

"And gorgeous. *Mr. Gorgeous*, to be exact." Holly pulled open the screen door. "He's driving away right now."

"Gorgeous? Really?" A vulture could have eyed its prey with less enthusiasm. Jemma's mother watched her with an expectant expression.

"He is *not* what you're thinking. Ask Holly."

Her sister laughed. "He is gorgeous. He's also, I'm sad to say . . . well, he might not be so gorgeous inside. He's helped her, but in a not-too-friendly way." Holly sighed. "I wish it was different. Maybe he would be nicer if he was just a neighbor and not having to help Jemma all the time."

"No, he wouldn't be. I decided I had to meet other people, so I found a hiking group online."

"So?" Holly shrugged.

"So, he"—Jemma pointed across the street—"also joined the group for the first time. That's how I learned he's a freelance marketing consultant. He stayed standoffish, even when I tried to be nice." Jemma heard the old swing set squeaking and knew where the girls were.

Holly turned toward his house. "A marketing consultant might be able to help your business succeed."

Jemma opened her mouth to answer that she would not want to work with him when her mother beat her to it. "If that man earns enough from his business to build a house, he would charge more than Jemma can pay at this stage of her business. It does seem to be a very nice house."

Before thinking of the repercussions, Jemma said, "If you think he's gorgeous, Holly, you should see the inside of his house. Slate in the entry, wood floors throughout the rest of the downstairs, with a wall of windows at the back. Granite and stainless are in an awesome kitchen. And the master bathroom off of his bedroom is stunning."

Her mother and sister stared at her with their mouths hanging open.

Oops. Now she'd have some 'splaining to do.

"I need a shower—and tea. Lots of tea." Jemma started up the stairs.

"What? You can't just walk away after saying that!" Holly stomped her foot.

"I can. And I am. I'll give you the rest of the story when I've had that tea. If you want me to talk, you'll fix some hot water. We can have breakfast."

She heard Holly's "Yuck."

Laughing, Jemma said, "I have bagels. I'm not planning to cook, so you're safe." As she turned the corner to the bathroom, she added, "And if either of the two of you are thinking something naughty about me being in his bedroom, don't."

An odd sound startled Nathaniel awake. Groaning, he pulled his pillow over his ears. His neighbor was at it. Again. Rolling over, he kept the pillow tight against his head. *Please.* He needed to sleep more. Last night with the puppy had started out as a nightmare. He hadn't felt that powerless since he'd been a kid, and his dad had come to the dinner table drunk when they'd had company. He still didn't know how they'd gotten through that evening.

When his covers slipped over the side of the bed, he sat upright.

The puppy had the edge of his sheet in her mouth. She dropped it and whimpered. Nathaniel laughed. When the puppy stared up at him and whimpered again, he realized he might need to hurry. He jumped to his feet and put on his slippers. "Are you telling me you need to go outside?"

Seeming to understand, she gave a *yipe* and started for the doorway.

The dog raced down the stairs, with Nathaniel at her heels. When they reached the front door, he paused and looked down at her. "If I let you out, will you run away?" Not waiting for any reply, barking or otherwise, he hurried into the garage with the puppy right behind him. He cut a length of rope for a collar, tied it in place around her neck, then tied on a longer piece to make a leash. When he set her down and hit the button to open the garage door, the pup shot out under it and over to the lawn, pulling Nathaniel along after her.

As soon as she'd finished her business, he reached down and rubbed her head like he'd seen in movies. "You needed to go, didn't you? Thank you for being a good girl." The puppy looked up at him with big brown eyes, and an image popped into his mind of fellow first-grader Chloe Carleton staring at him with very similar brown eyes. Reeling in the rope, he walked over to the edge of Jemma's property, where the puppy had been tangled yesterday. Seeing some fishing line, he realized that's what had held her there.

When Nathaniel turned to go back inside, the dog followed behind him. He chuckled. "You are just like Chloe. She followed me around the playground."

Back in the kitchen, he put out the rest of the steak and

watched her devour it. "You're skinny, but I'm sure someone will adopt you." The dog lay back down on her blanket bed and immediately fell asleep.

He began to plan his day as he sat at the table, eating his breakfast. When he realized what day it was, he hung his head with a sigh. "Today's Sunday. The pound will be closed, so you're mine for one more night." The puppy just whimpered in her sleep. "I don't think I can leave you for church so let's settle in here for the day."

Chloe seemed to take his words to heart because a half hour later, she hadn't moved a muscle. Nathaniel reached down to pet her. She remained still. He could see her chest move up and down slowly. He scratched her ear, with no effect. When she stayed in the same position for another half hour, his worry level ramped up. Had her time tangled up with the rush of water injured her? She seemed fine on the outside, but what if she had internal damage?

He needed a vet.

Small towns shut down on weekends. Palmer definitely did not have an emergency vet—that is, unless you had a vet's cell number because you'd created a new sign for their practice. Nathaniel tugged his phone out of his pocket and dialed quickly.

"Roger?" he said when a sleepy voice answered on the third ring. "This is Nathaniel Montgomery. I rescued a puppy from a flood last night. She's skinny but seemed fine. Now she's unresponsive." He listened as the man replied, and relief surged through him. "Thank you. We'll be right there."

He gathered up the puppy on her blanket, ran out the door, set her on the passenger seat of his SUV, and carefully drove to the office, pulling in just as the vet did.

Inside the clinic, Nathaniel gently set the puppy down on an exam table and stood beside the table while the vet checked her out.

"Did you feed her?"

"Steak."

Roger grinned up at him. "Steak?"

Nathaniel shrugged. "Very expensive dog food. I'd bought it for my dinner."

The dog licked the vet's hand when he checked her ears, and he jumped. Shaking his head, he said, "I think she's simply exhausted. She probably hadn't had a decent meal in weeks. She's so young, probably about eight weeks old, that it's my guess someone threw her away. I usually hear about runaways, and she doesn't match any I know about."

"My neighbor also suggested that. I may not be a dog lover, but I can't imagine anyone throwing a little puppy away."

The vet sat on a stool in front of his computer. "Let me enter her as a patient so I'll be able to compare her results the next time you bring her in."

"I'm taking her to the pound. She'd be there now if it were any day but Sunday."

Roger glanced over at Nathaniel. Then the vet reached out and petted the puppy, something she seemed to enjoy. "She's skinny. She'd have a better chance of adoption if you fed her for a couple of weeks."

Nathaniel tapped his foot. This definitely wasn't going as expected.

"You know that if she isn't adopted, she'll be euthanized."

Nathaniel looked down at the tiny pup. "I can't let that happen." He sighed. "Tell me what to do."

"First, give me her name." The man continued typing, then paused and looked over at Nathaniel.

Nathaniel gave the first name that came to mind. "Chloe."

Roger's eyebrows rose. "The current lady in your life?"

"First grade."

He laughed and entered the information. "There must be a story there."

Five minutes later, Nathaniel lifted Chloe into his SUV. The rope had been traded for a purple collar and a loaner leash. The vet carried a loaner crate for her to sleep in, plus some food samples to take care of her until Nathaniel could get to a store tomorrow.

As Nathaniel put the key in the ignition, the night before replayed in his mind. He turned the key and hurried to roll down the window. "Roger, is there any way to keep her from eating my slippers?"

The vet laughed. "Give her something else to chew."

After changing the sheets on her bed, dusting her bedroom furniture, and vacuuming, Jemma knew she couldn't avoid the conversation downstairs any longer. She turned up the heat on the thermostat at the base of the stairs. Furniture couldn't be repainted until the wood had dried out, so she would keep the house toasty during the day, then turn it off at night so her bedroom wouldn't be an oven.

When she entered the kitchen, she found Holly and her mom sitting at the kitchen table. A pot of tea with a mug and her squeeze bottle bear of honey sat on the table at an empty seat.

"Sit. Speak." Her sister pointed at the chair.

"You need to get a dog. I wouldn't usually respond to

orders, but I've left you hanging long enough." Jemma sat down and took a deliberately slow sip of her tea. "Perfect. The vanilla is a nice touch."

Holly groaned. "Please. Tell me how you got inside his house. Hey, wait. You didn't break in or something like that, did you?"

"Holly, your sister wouldn't do that." She turned toward Jemma. "Would you?"

"Thanks for the vote of confidence, Mom. He helped me during the flood, remember?" Jemma got up and put a bagel in the toaster. As she waited for it, she continued. "The dog he now has is a puppy that got trapped in the rushing water. We rescued her." Jemma told the story of the rescue as she waited for her bagel. Once it had popped up, she slathered on cream cheese and a smaller-than-usual amount of strawberry jam so the others wouldn't make fun of her, and took a bite.

Her mother continued. "She was dirty, and you helped give her a bath."

"Exactly! He never had pets growing up, so he didn't have a clue how to take care of her."

"Wouldn't it have been easier to keep her here?" her mother asked.

Stitches chose that moment to stroll into the room, leading her mother to answer her own question. "I forgot that Bree's cat is here."

Holly laughed. "Remember that time Bree tried to watch a friend's puppy for a night?"

"I'd forgotten!" Jemma added a little more honey to the tea her sister had made a bit stronger than she would. "Didn't Stitches spend the whole night under the bed?"

"Yep. He wouldn't eat."

"I was fairly sure he'd be afraid, so I'm glad I didn't try it. He already mopes around sometimes, so I can tell he misses Bree."

Her mother gently patted Jemma's hand in a way that felt Victorian but somehow suited her. "I'm glad you could just bring Stitches with you when you moved."

The sound of a large vehicle out front brought Jemma to her feet. She hurried outside and instead of her dad found Matt, the state trooper from the hike, unloading a dresser.

"Jemma, I'd been wanting to get rid of this and thought you could use it."

"Thank you!" Now she could keep working. "Your timing is perfect."

"Hey, if I'd known junk would make you this happy, I'd have asked neighbors to donate too. Would you like to have dinner some night?"

Jemma studied him. He seemed like a really nice guy, but she didn't feel even a tiny bit of chemistry with him. "Maybe sometime. I'm spending every spare second working on my business. Yesterday's hike was my one break."

He nodded, then went back to his truck. "No problem. I'll ask again."

When he drove off, she heard Holly ask from beside her, "Who was that?"

Jemma jumped and put her hand to her chest. "Don't scare me like that. I didn't know you'd come outside. Matt's a guy I met yesterday on the hike."

"Wow."

Jemma turned back toward her driveway. Maybe she could fix him up with her sister sometime soon.

Her plans were instantly thwarted. "I'll be glad to have

time for things like dating again. I thought I'd feel good when I got my degree, but now I have to find a job. I can't think about anything else until I have our future secured with steady work." Holly shrugged. "At least I'm free from homework."

Jemma glanced over at their mother standing on the front porch and lowered her voice. "If you and Mom are done grilling me—"

"Yeah. It wasn't anywhere near as juicy as I'd expected. I'm sure Mom will agree."

"The story includes an adorable puppy. Unfortunately, when you saw my neighbor driving off, he was probably taking her to the pound."

"Not on Sunday morning. I know they aren't open."

That made Jemma happy. Maybe the puppy could get some attention before he took her there. Not that he knew what to do with a dog, but still, his house was much better than any shelter. Back inside, Jemma got her second cup of tea, added a good dose of honey, and everyone sat back at the kitchen table.

"You know"—her mother tapped her fingers on the table—"we should check out your neighbor on the Internet. You're pretty isolated here at the end of the road. I want to know you don't have an ax murderer across the street."

Jemma got up and retrieved her laptop from the dining room. "I admit to being curious, but I don't think he has criminal tendencies, unless rudeness is a punishable crime now." As soon as she sat down, she searched for his name.

Holly sat closer. "Click on that one." She pointed to a review. "That client thinks he's worth his weight in gold. She says he almost singlehandedly turned her company around."

Jemma clicked on several other reviews. "All favorable. Here's his website."

Her mother leaned over her shoulder. "My, he *is* handsome!" She watched as Jemma clicked on the pages. "People like him. I'll have to assume he's trustworthy with my oldest." She reached down and gave Jemma a hug.

"Remember, Mom. He's just a neighbor."

They heard activity outside, and her dad called through the screen door, "I'm back."

Jemma went out to help him set up the three fans he'd rented. Leave it to her dad to find someone open on a Sunday morning. As he started to plug one into an outlet in the garage, he paused. "Jemma, is the wiring this old in the house?"

"No. There's a new-looking electric breaker panel, so Great-aunt Grace must have redone it recently."

"I wish she'd done the garage at the same time." He grabbed the tops of the other two fans and walked toward the door. "I'm going to connect these to outlets on the house. I don't want to pull too much electricity from this ancient wiring."

Jemma straightened a few things in the garage while he did that.

Her dad returned with her mom and Holly at his side. He said, "You'll be fine now, Jemma. It's dry outside, so you should be back in business out here in a day or two."

"Are you coming?" he asked her mother.

"Yes. Everything's fine here."

Holly beat Jemma to her question. "What are you two talking about?"

"Your father made reservations for a halibut charter in

Homer tomorrow and a salmon trip two days later. I wasn't sure if I would be needed here. I should have known that my girls had everything under control."

Jemma shooed them away with her hands. "Go on vacation. I'm fine. I was a little sad, but I have some new friends." She heard Holly mutter, "Wow" again and knew she was thinking about Matt. "One brought me this furniture so I have a project to work on. And he's a state trooper, so I'm really in good hands."

"Excellent. We're going on vacation as planned. We're available if you need us."

Her dad closed up the minivan. "I rented the fans for a week, so don't worry about needing to return them. I'll take care of it when I'm here." As always, her dad was Mr. Efficient. Probably part of his science skill set. Her parents got into their seats and drove off, waving just like the girls did when they visited.

Jemma checked her watch when they left. Nine twenty-five. If she hurried, she'd get to church on time. "Holly, you coming to church with me?"

"Yes. If the girls are still presentable."

Jemma hurried inside, her screen door making its trade-mark smack sound when it closed. Probably one more thing Nathaniel Montgomery didn't like about her. Although Great-aunt Grace had used the same door. But she probably stayed inside most of the time he knew her, so it would have smacked once or twice a week.

Upstairs, Jemma quickly changed into a 1970s midi skirt that came to mid-calf and a simple blouse, put on some mascara and lip gloss, combed her hair, and decided that would have to do with the limited amount of time she had.

Holly had a little girl on her lap, a comb in one hand and a ribbon—probably from Jemma's sewing stash—in the other when Jemma came downstairs. While Jemma slipped on her ballet flats, Holly finished up with her girls. With everyone presentable, they headed out the door.

Chapter Six

Sun shining through the window nudged Nathaniel awake. He had slogged off to bed Sunday night after a long day of work, pausing briefly to rub Chloe behind the ears when he walked by her bed.

Rolling over, he touched something wet, and his eyes popped open to stare into Chloe's. She tucked her head into the crook of his arm and snuggled closer. He couldn't remember putting her in her crate, and she was here, so he'd goofed. A good pet owner he was not. When he gently pushed her away, she whimpered, making him pause.

She'd been through so much that he could give her a short time on his bed. "Just a few minutes more. Then we're getting up."

Nathaniel woke up, the clock told him an hour later, to a tongue licking his cheek. Laughing, he picked up the wiggly puppy, set her on the floor, and slid into what remained of his slippers, what could be more aptly called a slipper-and-a-half. "Do you want to go out?"

Chloe raced out the door and down the stairs with him at her heels. At the garage door, he clicked on her leash, then stepped through the door and pushed the garage door opener. Chloe tugged him outside and over to the grass.

Back inside a few minutes later, she barked at her empty bowl. "I guess I should fix us both something." After putting the last of the food from the vet into her bowl, Nathaniel cracked a couple of eggs into a pan and popped a slice of bread in the toaster for himself. Not that Chloe wouldn't like it. He suspected she'd gobble it up.

His eggs scrambled, he picked up his phone to check his schedule while he waited for his toast. "Chloe, I have a business lunch today." He scrolled down and stopped. "And"—he stared down at her for a moment—"I'm taking you to the pound. I'm sure someone will love you and take better care of you than I can. You're very cute." He bent down and rubbed her ears again. "I think you're already gaining weight."

Leaving her lying on her bed, he went upstairs to shower and dress. When he returned, he found the puppy chewing on the corner of her makeshift blanket bed. Shaking his head, he said, "Better your bed than the couch. Or my slippers. Ready to go?" he enthusiastically asked her.

The puppy barked again.

After loading the crate into his SUV, Nathaniel came back for Chloe, picked up the wriggling puppy, and took her out to his vehicle. When she hopped into the crate and licked his hand, his heart sank. How could he take this skinny puppy to the pound? He picked her up again and set her on the garage floor. "Chloe, I can't do this to you."

He popped the leash back on her and took her outside to walk around while he decided how to proceed. Chloe made him grin when she dove headfirst into things she was checking out. As he watched her, his plan came to life. "I'm going to keep you until you're plumped up, just like your vet said. I want to make sure you're adopted."

Nathaniel tied her leash around a tree where he could watch her, then went back into the garage where he picked everything she could get into up off the floor. In less than two days he'd learned that would be almost everything in there. With that task taken care of, he went inside the house, brought her blanket bed and water bowl back out, and put them in the corner. "Once you learn not to seek and destroy, you can stay inside. I'm going to go make us some money at a business meeting. Then I'll buy another pair of slippers."

He backed up his SUV and hit the button to close the garage door. Then, with Chloe in tow, he went in the front door of the house and put her in the garage, leaving the same way himself. She'd be safe. Maybe not completely happy, but she'd be safe.

Standing on his front steps, he paused. Another vehicle must have dropped off furniture at his neighbor's. This time it didn't seem like an actual delivery from an event, more like someone she knew had set a bed's headboard in her drive-way. Jemma's nieces were outside, and appeared to be having an intense conversation in her front yard. They glanced over at him, then talked some more. When he moved down his steps, they raced over to him.

"We have a question for you."

"Okaay." He'd never been good with kids. No, strike that. He'd never been *around* kids, so he didn't know if he was good with them or not. "What would you like to know? My favorite kind of ice cream?"

They giggled and shook their heads.

"My favorite movie?"

"No," one of the matching set said. "We want to know your name."

"My name?" he answered, out of the corner of his eye seeing Jemma running down her steps and over to her nieces.

"Girls," she shouted, "I asked you to stay in my yard."

"I told you so, Ivy," the other girl said, nudging her sister in the side.

"Back home, girls. Ivy, Abbie, now." Jemma looked up at Nathaniel. "I'm sorry they bothered you."

"We didn't bother him, Aunt Jemma. We just wanted to know his name."

"My name? I'm Nathaniel Montgomery." Cute kids, but why the big deal about his name?

Abbie's brow furrowed. "That isn't right. We want to know if your name is Mr. Gorgeous, Mr. Grouch, or The Jerk? We've heard Mommy and Aunt Jemma say all of them. No one has three names."

Nathaniel watched Jemma's face turn a bright red as she ushered the girls away. *The Jerk?* Even though he probably deserved it for some of his comments, the nickname still hit below the belt. He had his nice moments. Then all of the little girl's words really hit him. She'd also said *Mr. Gorgeous.* He whistled as he went to his vehicle. He could live with being Mr. Gorgeous.

As he drove into Anchorage for his meeting with a corporate CEO, Nathaniel's cell rang and he answered. The short-but-sweet call told him that his last possible date, a woman he'd met on a run a year ago, would not come to his party. He wasn't sure if she *couldn't* or she didn't *want* to. His ego chose the first, but he suspected the latter.

The miles passed under his tires as he considered how he could solve the problem. Two clients he trusted had told him what he needed to do. Maybe when he had more than a four-year track record in Alaska, he could get away with being standoffish, as they'd described him, but it didn't seem like that time had arrived yet.

Pulling into the parking garage, he shrugged off apprehensions. Corporate clients weren't his favorite. They reminded him of his days in corporate America. Generally everything was by committee, and good ideas could be lost in the shuffle, only to be replaced with watered-down ideas everyone could agree on. It did pay the bills though.

An hour later he stepped back into his SUV and took a deep breath. An intensive lesson in branding dos and don'ts, couched in a smiling, congenial manner, had convinced the CEO that chartreuse and magenta, though nice colors his wife enjoyed, would not be good colors for his serious enterprise. This one was a win.

Driving through town, he saw a sign for a pet store and whipped into the parking lot. A selection of toys might help curb Chloe's chewing problem.

When he pushed a full cart to his car a half hour later, he wondered what had happened. Sure, food was a necessity, and he knew which ones she liked, so he had a bag of dry and a stack of cans. Then there were the toys. Embarrassment overrode his previous happiness at choosing the toys. Could one dog use all of these?

He loaded them in the back of the SUV. "At least she'll have plenty to choose from when she's considering my slippers," he muttered, catching a curious look from the woman getting into the car parked beside him.

As he drove back home, the party date issue reared its ugly head again. He'd dodged a bullet Saturday, but doubted another water main would buy him time this week. A date needed to appear, and now. An image came to mind of a blonde woman wielding a saw.

Nathaniel jerked the wheel and swerved on the road. Jemma Harris. His neighbor as his date? He could imagine her showing up in a flower power pantsuit from the 1960s. The few facts he'd picked up on the hike made him push that thought aside. He knew she'd mentioned working in the corporate world, so she must know how to dress for work. And there was something about being an assistant of some sort, so she might have attended functions. He wished he'd paid more attention to her words.

He considered the advantages of going down that road. She'd brought chaos to his home. Not only did she make noise in the garage, but people came and went all day long. Kids screeched. Sure, they were only playing, but he hadn't invited any of them into his life; they'd just appeared along with Jemma. Chaos surrounded her house. He turned off the Glenn Highway toward home.

If he traded with her and spent hours helping her succeed, was there a benefit to him beyond the one night? Then he remembered. She'd said she wanted to open a storefront. Oh, yeah. Helping her business thrive meant peace and quiet whenever she was away at her business, which should be al-most every day. Vans wouldn't break down at dawn because everything related to her business would move far away from his house.

He would definitely ask Jemma Harris to be his date.

Grinning, Nathaniel swung his vehicle into his driveway and reached for the door's remote. Then he remembered he had a puppy inside his garage so he parked and entered the house through his front door. Chloe ran over to the garage door as soon as he walked into the garage, ready to go outside. He clipped on her leash, hit the button for the door, and she was out. She might have been abandoned, but somehow she'd learned to go outside, and he'd forever be grateful for that.

"Would you like to go for a walk?" He scratched behind her ears where he knew she liked it. Standing back up, he surveyed his domain. He'd chosen a beautiful location for his house. If it could only be peaceful and quiet again.

Heading down the driveway and up the road, Chloe pranced along happily. "Maybe we can take a couple of breaks during my workday and go for walks. Weather permitting, of course." Chloe looked up at him with what he thought was a happy expression. "Montgomery, you are talking to a dog now. And seeing a reply." He shook his head. "You need to get out more." A few steps later, he grinned and added, "And not talk to yourself."

Today's question: *did he really want to ask Jemma Harris to be his date for Saturday's party?* Considering the unavailability of every woman in the state of Alaska that he'd previously dated, his options were limited. The object of his imagination turned on a power tool, what sounded like a drill, in her garage. Chloe tugged him that direction, probably to check out the source of the noise.

He held the puppy back at the entrance to Jemma's garage. Today she wore old-fashioned overalls over a pale pink blouse, he guessed both circa 1955. Jemma glanced over and set down the tool, her focus on Chloe as she walked over. "Hi, sweetie. How are you?" She stooped down and wrapped the puppy in a hug. "I'm surprised you're still here." She looked up and gave him a curious expression.

"I decided to keep her to fatten her up and make her more adoptable." He cleared his throat. "The vet recommended it."

"Vet? Is she okay?" When she held the dog's head still and studied it, she got a tongue across her face. Laughing, she sat down on the garage floor and pulled Chloe into her lap.

"She's fine. I thought something was wrong Sunday, but it was exhaustion."

"You're better now, though, aren't you?" Jemma ruffled the puppy's fur and got another lick for her efforts.

"Chloe felt good enough to eat most of a slipper."

Jemma grinned and her eyes sparkled. *Whoa.* She had transformed from vintage pixie to adorable. And where did that thought come from?

"Chloe?"

"She needed to have a name. While I have her."

"Uh-huh." Jemma nodded.

"There's something I want to ask you."

"And that would be . . . ?" She changed from happy to wary.

"I'm having a party for business associates Saturday, and it's been suggested that I should have a date for it."

She leaned back. It was a bad sign when a woman moved away from you when you used the word "date." A business event wouldn't mean they were *dating*.

"I wondered if you would be available Saturday from about six to ten."

Jemma's mouth dropped open, and she froze for longer than he would have expected. Closing her mouth, she studied him.

Had he been so horrible to her that this was impossible? Replaying a video of their various encounters, he had to conclude yes.

Chloe jumped to her feet, apparently ready to continue their first walk together.

When Jemma stood, shaking her head from side to side, he wasn't sure if it was to clear her head or to say no. Neither seemed good.

"Before you say no—because you are going to say no, aren't you?"

"Yes, I am."

"I have a proposition for you."

She turned her head to look at him sideways, with one eyebrow raised.

"Bad choice of words. Proposal. I have a proposal for you."

"That's more interesting than a proposition. To a girl like me, anyway. Does this mean you're proposing to me?"

"No! Never!"

"Mr. Montgomery, be careful or you'll turn my head."

How could this woman make him act like an idiot, or a sixteen-year-old boy? In his case he'd been an idiot around girls when he was sixteen, so it was the same thing. Why her? He chose the right words for clients every day.

"I know you want your, um, business to succeed. I propose—see, that word doesn't always mean what you expected—that if you help me on Saturday and maybe one more event if needed, I will create a marketing plan for you and help implement it. I have a long track record of success so, in short, I'll help you succeed with what you're trying to do."

Jemma stared at him with a not-too-friendly expression.

"I'll help you meet your goals."

Jemma had been ready to tell Mr. Nathaniel Montgomery no. His last sentence stopped her. Did he know about her goals? For just a second she wondered if her mom or Holly had put him up to this. Then she realized that was ridiculous. If he *could* help her meet her goals, and what she'd seen online made her think that was more than likely, what would it matter if she spent a few hours with him? Even if he could be a pompous jerk.

"Miss Harris?"

"Totally a business arrangement, right?"

He nodded his head vigorously.

She put out her hand. "Shake on it."

When he took her hand, electricity passed between them, a stupidly cliché thing she'd read about in romance novels. But it had never happened to her before. Not even close.

Nathaniel stared at his hand, so she wondered if he'd felt it too. He lifted his head and stared into her eyes. He had gorgeous eyes, blue, rimmed with long, black lashes, girly-long lashes that somehow still suited him.

Chloe darted between them, circling Nathaniel's legs with the leash and bringing him to his knees. Jemma crouched and held her still while he unclipped the leash and set himself free. He held Chloe by her collar as he reattached the leash, and she snuggled against him. For just a second, he seemed to hug the puppy.

Grateful for the moment to compose herself, Jemma

wondered if she felt something for her neighbor. A replay of their previous contacts ran through her mind. Arrogant jerk. She was just tired. Or something.

While he was here, though, he could help solve a problem.

"I think the furniture's dry enough now to work on. Could you help me haul it back to the garage?"

When Nathaniel checked his watch, Jemma figured he'd find a time-related reason to say no. "I can't do it right now."

Just as she'd expected.

"But I can come back in a couple of hours and help you. We can talk briefly about your business goals so I can start thinking about how to help you."

Relief rushed through Jemma, and a little bit of liking him came with it. Could it be that he had a nice side, that they'd simply gotten off on the wrong foot?

She watched as he directed Chloe—what a cute name for a dog—back to his property and around the back of the house. There was something between him and the puppy that made her think he had a permanent addition to his life. She wouldn't tell him though, so he wouldn't notice the relationship growing and stop it. The puppy obviously adored him, and he seemed to have a soft spot in his heart for her. That surprised Jemma, because before this she hadn't thought Nathaniel Montgomery had a heart.

Jemma attached the last drawer pull to the dresser she'd rehabbed into a baby dresser and changing table. She'd decoupaged the drawer fronts with a garden scene. The finished product was whimsical, fun, and she suspected would sell well at Friday Fling, with its elements of a farmers' market. After grabbing a stool from the house, one of the few things she could carry on her own, she checked it for damage and did a happy dance. She'd only have to give the stool a light sand and a coat of poly to revive it. If the rest were as easy, she'd be ready for the events she had planned for this week with no problems.

As he finished up his last call for the day, Nathaniel stood at his office window. His neighbor had just brought a stool out of the house, set it down, and danced around it. Weird. Could he work with her? It was probably against the odds that they could be less alike. Of course, he'd worked with all types in the corporate world and even now took on clients that he wouldn't want to spend an evening with. If he thought of her as just a client, this arrangement could work. But what was that zing he'd felt when he'd held—no, he corrected, he'd *shaken* her hand? *Held* and *shaken* had different connotations when it came to hands.

He put on his business persona and went across the street. "Miss Harris, I can help you now."

She rolled her eyes. "This isn't 1952. You can call me by my first name. J-e-m-m-a." She said it slowly, as though he wouldn't understand otherwise.

He felt his business relationship dissolving. Taking control again, he said, "I want to treat you as I would any client. It's best if I call you Miss Harris."

"Do you call any of your clients by their first name?"

He ran through a mental list of clients and realized he called all but two by their first names, and they were from an older generation that saw his use of Mr. or Mrs. and a last name as a courtesy. "Well, no, but—"

"Jemma. Or if you have trouble with that, Ms. Harris. I'm a modern woman." She grinned up at him.

Something about her grin always got to him. "Jemma works. Let's get your furniture. Then maybe we could discuss your business goals."

They worked together to bring everything back out to the garage. As they set the final piece down, she said, "As I considered this during the last couple of hours, I came to the conclusion that . . ."

He felt dread course through his system and her words faded away. She'd changed her mind.

"Mr. Montgomery? Hello?"

He blinked. "I'm sorry. I was in another place. Please repeat what you said."

"I came to the conclusion that I felt rushed, that I like to consider everything overnight. I want to be able to tell you my goals in a concise manner. Then you will be able to help me with a plan and with features and benefits."

Her marketing-speak completely caught him off guard. What had she said she'd done before moving here? "Okaaay. Can we meet for lunch the day after tomorrow? We both work from home, so we need to take a break then anyway. Maybe noon at your house?"

Jemma blushed, and he wondered how he'd embarrassed her. She asked, "Do you have anything you could fix?"

Was she too poor to share food with him? That had never occurred to him. She had the house, but maybe she was short on money for groceries. A new drive lit him. He would do all he could to help this woman succeed. "Let's eat out. My treat as your consultant."

They'd settled on a restaurant in Wasilla for their first meeting. Jemma had insisted on keeping everything businesslike, and Nathaniel had wholeheartedly, maybe a tad bit too enthusiastically, agreed to those terms. Since she had eaten at all of the restaurants in Palmer multiple times by now, she wanted to try a new one. Atlanta and the surrounding area offered a seemingly endless choice of restaurants for the cooking challenged, but the choices in a small town were finite. Nathaniel recommended a sandwich shop, and that sounded like something that would fit her budget since she wouldn't let him pay.

Arriving before him, Jemma ordered iced tea and flipped through the slide presentation she'd put together the night before so she could show him her plan. When she paused, a slide presentation of sorts played in her mind, as it had every time she thought about her agreement with Nathaniel Montgomery and their meeting.

This could be a huge mistake. But it might also be one of the best things to ever happen to her. Having a marketing expert of his caliber work on her business could turn it from an unknown booth at local markets into the retail store she had planned for while working long hours the last few years.

Sliding her tablet back into her briefcase, she took a sip of the iced tea set before her and grimaced, sputtering as she grabbed packets of sugar and poured them into the liquid. Nathaniel stepped up to the table as she dumped in the third packet, and the littered remains of the other two sat beside the glass.

He raised an eyebrow. "Like sugar, do you?"

She shuddered. "It came unsweetened. It takes quite a bit of sugar to make it right."

As he sat down, he gestured with his head toward the waitress. "She didn't ask, 'Sweet or unsweet?'?"

Jemma grinned. "How did a guy from Seattle—isn't that where you said you'd lived?"

"Yes. I moved to Seattle for a job and lived there for quite a while."

"How did you ever learn about sweet tea?" She took a sip of the perfected beverage and sighed.

"The company I worked for sent me to Nashville for several months a few years ago. One hot summer day I saw the waiter bringing tea to everyone, so I ordered it. His next question was 'Sweet or unsweet?'" I had to gradually work up to sweet." He grinned and it totally transformed him from gorgeous to magazine cover–worthy.

"Alas, sweet tea lives only in the South. Other places make you add your own sugar, and it doesn't dissolve the same way. In the South tea is just . . . better."

He laughed and she jumped. Not only had she never heard him laugh; she didn't know he *could* laugh. And his laugh had an earthy, almost sensual quality that made her shiver in delight. That was bad. Nathaniel Montgomery was the last man on earth she wanted to feel any attraction to. Besides, all-business had become the only route she wanted to take after James. She wouldn't get attached and wouldn't get hurt.

They ordered, she a veggie salad and he a chicken sandwich he said they did wonderfully, with just the right amount of garlic and a great aged Swiss. She said a silent prayer of gratitude that she hadn't offered to have lunch at her house. If Nathaniel's lunch expectations lingered in the range of garlic perfection and the right aged cheese, a sandwich with deli meats from the grocery store wouldn't be a good idea. She did toast a good bagel with cream cheese, but that just didn't cut it for lunch. Unless she told him she'd made brunch, so the bagel would seem more special. Yep. She could do that. Some fruit and microwaveable bacon would make it more of a meal.

Nathaniel shifted into a more formal business manner that made her quite grateful. She wanted to steer clear of the charming man she'd caught a glimpse of earlier.

As they ate, he said, "So Ms. Harris, Jemma, tell me why you believe this business idea of yours will succeed."

Jemma pushed her salad to the side and prepared to ask him to stop maligning her idea when he raised a hand and interrupted her.

"Don't get your hackles up. I ask that of every small business I work with. I need to have the owner or manager, whoever has been assigned to the job, able to tell me why the business is a good idea. That helps me communicate it to customers."

Settling her blood pressure down, she took deep, even breaths then ate more of her salad. "To begin with, I'm not the first person to have a business like this."

"Really?"

"Really. Flipping furniture, repurposing, upcycling, whatever you want to call it, is popular. Have you ever been on Pinterest?"

"Briefly. I'm considering using it for a couple of clients and need to spend more time there."

"Women love seeing these kinds of projects on Pinterest. That's where I first saw the photos of pieces of furniture like I make. My dad raised his girls to be competent with power tools and to take care of whatever needed to be done around the house. He's a very analytical and orderly professor, so he taught us well. Anyway, when I saw a photo of a dresser someone had turned into a bench, I said, 'I could do this.' I tried it, had fun, and thought—"

"You thought, 'This could be a business.'"

"Exactly." She signaled the waitress and mouthed "to-go box," then continued. "During the next year, I made a new project every time I had time off, went to flea markets to see how others did business, and finally decided that I could have a successful business that supported me."

Jemma piled what would become her dinner into the container the woman brought. As Nathaniel ate his last fry, she said, "Now that we're both done, let me take you through my presentation."

When Jemma reached beside her chair and lifted a brief-case onto the table, opening it and removing a tablet computer, Nathaniel leaned back in his chair and marveled. She'd shifted into a business mode that he hadn't seen before. Jemma worked on the computer for a moment, then placed it between them. "I created this to show my plan and the steps I believe I need to take in order to succeed."

He sat watching while she moved a couple of slides.

"I set my goals several years ago. I keep revising them, but I'm having problems now."

He started to speak, but she interrupted him. "Let me go through this before you say anything."

She took him step-by-step through her plan. As she spoke, he stole a glance at her. For the first time he noticed that she didn't have on her usual clothes from earlier decades; she wore a navy jacket, matching dress pants, a white blouse, and low heels. She looked conservative.

"What's this?" he interrupted, pointing at her.

"Huh? Did I spill something?" She brushed off her lap.

"No. Instead of old clothes, you're wearing a conservative suit."

She raised an eyebrow.

"I meant *vintage*, not old."

"The last corporation I worked for was *very* conservative, so this is the business wardrobe that's in my closet. And this is a business meeting."

He couldn't argue with her logic. He just wasn't sure why that same logic didn't apply to many other events that saw her in crazy outfits. For a few seconds, he envisioned her coming to his party in something appropriate. Then he brushed off the idea. Not likely.

She continued her presentation. "I knew how much I needed to save to stay in the Atlanta area. I wanted to have enough to get by for a year, not struggle but maybe not buy new clothes." She glanced over at him and could tell he wanted to comment. "Hey, clothes matter to a girl." She shrugged. "At least they matter to me."

When Nathaniel didn't say anything, just clamped his lips together and pointed at them to show he wasn't going to talk, she continued.

"About the time I reached the halfway point for my savings, I was also interviewing for a new job. Then I learned Great-aunt Grace had left me her house in Palmer. Maybe I should have thought things through better, but I'd spent many vacations in Alaska growing up, so it wasn't unfamiliar. I grabbed at the opportunity and ran with it. My sister Holly has lived here for two years, but the life of a college student is totally different."

Jemma's voice thickened and he thought she might start

crying. Then she straightened her shoulders and carried on with her story.

"I had always planned to take a year from beginning my business to opening a storefront. I would go to flea markets most weekends year-round to build a clientele." She glanced over at him. "See the problem?"

She had such pretty eyes. Blue. He thought glacier blue, almost chuckling out loud at what she'd say of the Alaskan description.

"Nathaniel, do you see the problem?"

He cleared his throat. "No, I don't see a problem." Because he had only a vague idea of what she'd just said.

She sighed loudly and in a way that seemed to indicate a lack of faith in his business acumen and general intelligence.

He thought he'd heard something about flea markets. "I don't remember seeing any flea markets in this area."

"Thank you. And I can't sell beyond a few months in the summer here."

He sat back in his seat. "Because of the climate. Yes, and in Atlanta—"

"I could sell year-round at the flea market there or in any number of other flea markets within a few hours' drive in Georgia and surrounding states."

"So we need a new plan for you."

"No. I have a new plan. It's the only thing I can think of, and this is where you come in. I need to make a success of my business before it gets cold."

"Jemma, you know that's September?"

"My research tells me it might be as early as August. Palmer's Friday Fling runs through the middle of August."

"And some years it does frost in August. Once kids are

back in school, everything changes." He tried to process the timeline she'd set up for him. "It's early June now, so that gives us maybe three months to take you from near obscurity to having enough of a following to justify a retail storefront in Anchorage. Do I have that right?"

She huffed. "You don't have to make it sound impossible." She pushed back from the table. "From your reputation, I figured you could take this on and succeed. I'm going to have to find another way to do it." When she started to stand, he put a hand on her arm.

"Please sit down and let's finish our discussion. This is business, pure and simple. I need for all parties to understand every aspect of it before we move forward."

Halfway to her feet, she eyed him. "Are you saying you'll help me meet my goals?"

Staring up at her, he felt pulled into those blue eyes that pleaded with him so passionately. Knowing he might be taking on his first impossible job, he said. "Yes. Let's do this."

"Then come along with me to Friday Fling. Let me show you what I've got."

How could he turn down an offer like that?

Chapter Seven

Jemma wandered through her garage, picking the pieces she planned to take to today's Friday Fling. She'd done well last week but had learned that, with a few exceptions, small pieces sold better there. Smaller pieces also meant she could fit everything in her car and not have to ask Nathaniel for help.

Why did he choose to use the full version of his name? Nate would be so much shorter. And it suited him. At least it had suited him on the hike. There he'd seemed like a Nate. Here in town he seemed so stuffy. Maybe she was wrong and the full version of his name somehow made him happier. She shrugged as she added another piece of furniture to the stack in front of the garage. Who was she to decide the name a man should use? Someone had once called her Jem, and that hadn't sat well with her at all.

With a stool, bench, and nightstand in front of the garage, Jemma went back in for a couple more things, then added fabric projects from the house. Ten pieces in all should be about right. At least that's what her very limited experience told her.

After so many years of being the one directing the various parts of an event, it felt odd to be doing it alone, not relying on expert opinions and workers, and responsible for every aspect of it. She found it much easier to be the foreman.

Before she set anything inside her car, she checked her trunk to make sure her standard items were there: folding table, chair—no, make that *chairs*. She ran back into the house and returned with a second folding chair.

Lifting up the table, she verified that her business sign lay under it in the trunk. Check. Loading the car, she filled up the backseat and trunk, popped a bag filled with pillows on the passenger seat, and stood back, pleased with her efforts.

A garage filled with dressers and other large pieces of furniture stood open before her, and she chuckled. She'd definitely need a truck sometimes. Ready to go, Jemma turned back to her car just as Nathaniel brought Chloe outside. He glanced at his watch and loudly said, "I'll be over in a few minutes."

When Nathaniel walked over ten minutes later instead of pulling up in his SUV, Jemma pictured her passenger seat. "Are you riding with me?"

He shrugged. "I thought it would be easiest since we're going to the same place." He glanced in the front passenger window. "I may have to rethink this."

"I have to stay all day."

"I know it begins at ten. I assumed it ran about two hours and that was it."

"No. All day."

He paused and seemed to be going through something in his mind. "I would like to be there most of the day—so I can get a good sense of what you do."

"I'm going to a church sale tomorrow, and that's just a few hours."

"That won't work. I'm having the party tomorrow night, so I have things I need to do. I do have a few clients within walking distance of Friday Fling. I can also step away to make some calls." He nodded as though he'd made a decision. "I'll spend most of the day with you."

Something about the way he said that made Jemma's pulse race. An entire day with Mr. Nathaniel Montgomery. She might have a good day. Then again, she could see so many ways this could go wrong.

He pulled out his phone, and she focused on his words. "The vet said he had someone who could help out with Chloe if I needed him, a tech that wouldn't mind running over here at lunchtime. I don't see another way to make this work."

"Wait." She put her hand on his arm, then pulled it back. That felt way too personal. "Put her in my fenced backyard. Give her water and she'll be fine for the day."

By the time they'd arrived at the Friday Fling parking lot, Nathaniel knew what it felt like to be a sardine in a can. When Jemma pulled into a parking spot, she glanced over at him, and he could tell she was biting her lip to hide a laugh. She hurried out and around the car to his door, opening it and standing there. He still couldn't get out. Only his forehead and eyes stuck up over the bag of pillows she'd wedged on his lap. When she tugged on the bag, it fell sideways onto the parking lot.

Nathaniel rolled his shoulders and wiggled his fingers. "Everything had started to fall asleep." He stepped out of the car. "I sincerely hope I don't have to ride home that way."

"I hope not too, for both our sakes. I certainly expect to sell some things today."

"Good point." He grabbed the bag and a stool from the backseat. "Show me what you've been doing."

Jemma popped the trunk and offloaded everything down to the folding table, setting things on the ground. Finally, she pulled out the table.

He held out the bag of pillows. "Here. Trade me."

"I've been carrying all of this by myself, Nathaniel. I can manage a table and chairs."

"I know, but the macho male in me can't let you do that today."

She chuckled. "Okay. I'll let you be a man."

Once at her space, he set up the table, placed the chairs behind it, and went back for another load. With everything eventually set up, he sat down and watched her. When she started to arrange a lamp and the pillows on her bare table, he stood.

"Did you forget the tablecloth?"

"No. I don't have one." Jemma stepped back, obviously pleased with the display. Moving on to her larger furniture, she placed the bench to the side of the table.

He didn't want to get her riled up, so he quietly asked, "Why don't you have a tablecloth?"

She pointed to several of the booths around her. "They don't. I copied what others did."

He went to see the booths she had pointed to and returned with a bunch of daisies he'd apparently bought that he proceeded to tuck into her display. "I would say that someone selling fresh produce and flowers was in a different category from a woman who's trying to make a success of a retail business in a few short months."

"Don't exaggerate. They aren't all selling produce. Some have products they've made. That's what I have." She waved her hand over her table in a game-show-hostess way.

"I stopped and talked to one business owner. She has a cottage industry that she believes will always be in her home. She simply wants to have fun doing something she enjoys and make some extra cash."

Jemma sat down. "I've tried so hard, but I haven't been seeing this from the right angle, have I?"

He positioned his chair to face hers and sat down. "I don't think you have. We have to pull out all the stops and do a thousand percent more than anyone else. I should have asked about your background, what credentials you have. That will help me work."

"I didn't bring that up because you were listening on the hike, right? You know my background . . ." She left the sentence hanging.

He blew out a long breath. "I have to admit that I heard what you said but don't remember it. I know you worked in corporate America, and you said something about being an assistant."

"Yes, I was the executive assistant to the CEO of a major corporation."

"So you were in charge." He grinned.

Jemma shrugged. "You're joking, but there were times when I was. He signed documents, of course, but I made many of the day-to-day decisions. I planned events for as few as a dozen, or thousands. I worked with every department in the company."

"What education brought you to that career?"

She paused long enough that he glanced over at her.

"This is a sensitive issue," Jemma said at last. "And a long story. I have a degree in international business. Close to graduation, I researched companies, found one I thought I'd like to work for, and applied to their management training program. When I didn't hear back, I applied for every open position at the company, and my computer skills landed me a job as an administrative assistant. I thought I could get into the company's management trainee program from anywhere. That never happened, and I ended up stuck in a direction I hadn't intended to go. Others may enjoy the work and even thrive on it, but it wasn't what I wanted."

The desire to reassure Jemma rose up in Nathaniel, catching him off guard. "You did well for yourself."

She continued, "Not in my family. I have a father with a PhD, a sister who's a doctor, and another who's just completed a bachelor's degree while being a single parent to two young children. They've achieved the goals they set for themselves. I haven't. But I plan to."

Her passion to succeed felt intoxicating, like he'd had too much to drink, and he never touched a drop of alcohol. "You have the drive I've found is necessary for small-business success. Now I'm going to run over to the chain store and pick up a tablecloth. We haven't had time to talk about colors you might like to use in your business. Do you have any ideas?"

She shook her head. "All of this came about so suddenly that I haven't had time to consider everything. I thought I'd have more time."

He took a couple of steps toward the car, then returned. "Two things: I want you to think about whether or not you want to do this business this summer. What happens if you don't succeed?" She gave a single emphatic nod. "And"—he held out his hand—"I need your car keys. I forgot I didn't drive."

Grinning, she handed them over. Every time she smiled like that, his heart did a flip. Jemma Harris must charm every man she met.

As he drove away, Nathaniel replayed Jemma's revelation about her work life and the strong desire he'd had to hug her, to comfort her. He had never, not once, in his life felt a desire to comfort someone. Yesterday he would have said it wasn't in his DNA. Sure, the pro bono work he did for charities made him feel good inside, but even then it felt distant, not personal. He found Jemma's determination compelling, and it touched something inside him. The cards were stacked against her. Excellent marketing ideas needed to come to him, and now. He wanted to help her make this dream come true.

Nathaniel roamed the aisles and found the tablecloths, settling on white because the others had patterns. He suspected they'd have time today between customers to talk more, so maybe he'd have a better idea of how he could help her by five o'clock.

Back at the outdoor market, he assisted Jemma with taking all of her inventory off the table, putting on the tablecloth, and replacing everything. When he walked around the table to sit down, Jemma picked up a long piece of paper and paused in front of the table.

"What's wrong?"

She looked everywhere but at him as she attached it to the front of her table with tape. Knowing something wasn't right, he came around to see. 'Vintage Furniture'?"

"Rules say there must be a sign."

"Jemma, this isn't helping. It doesn't say anything about what you do. Sit over here and let's make a list of ideas for your business name."

She brushed him away. "I actually have a name for my business. Vintage Cozy. But I thought I'd save it until I knew what I was doing. I didn't want to taint it with early business stupidity."

"I see."

"I know. I know. I don't have the luxury of time." She stomped off, leaving him to man the table.

A woman bought two of the pillows, giving him cash that he made change for from out of his wallet, and she was considering adding a lamp to her purchases when Jemma returned, smiled broadly, and quickly closed the deal on it. This was the moment when Jemma needed to hand the woman a business card that had a website on it. They could eliminate the cost of brochures if he built a website for her.

He knew her business needed something special though, something to quickly generate interest. The idea would come to him. It always did. But would he have the idea and be able to implement it in time to help Jemma succeed? What would she do if she failed? He'd made this deal with her to have a date for tomorrow's party, but he felt the weight of more than her business riding on his ideas.

Jemma drove away from Friday Fling by herself after a

surprising twist near the end of the day. An attractive woman spoke with Nathaniel, and he left with her, saying it was business. Then he called and said he wouldn't need a ride home. Jemma felt slightly abandoned. Who was the woman, and what was her hold on Nathaniel? Knowing it was none of her business didn't help.

This meant that Jemma could do whatever she wanted on the way home. She'd seen a bookstore but never taken the time to stop.

Hurrying past the romance and mystery sections, her favorite places in any bookstore, she went straight to the business section. She searched through several books on starting a business, bought the one she liked best, and headed home.

Nathaniel had made her realize something very important, something that made her feel like an idiot for not seeing it before. She may have a degree in *international business*, but she needed to study *small-business* basics. Having a dream was one thing. Making that dream come true took a fair amount of knowledge.

As she left the bookstore, she noticed the tourist information office where she'd met the other hikers. It seemed counterintuitive to go to a tourist office when she wanted to feel like she lived here, but it also sounded like a good way to see what activities were available. The helpful woman inside showed her the array of choices. Jemma picked a handful of brochures and headed home. She'd flip through them when she had time. *If* she had time.

She was in her driveway, unloading the things that hadn't sold, when Holly pulled in behind her. When the twins got out and immediately ran into the backyard and to the swing set, she was glad Nathaniel had texted earlier that he'd removed Chloe's "deposits" from the yard.

Her sister went around to Jemma's trunk and picked up a couple of things. "How'd you do today?"

"I sold most of what I brought." Jemma pointed at the items her sister held. "Please take those into the house."

When Holly returned, Jemma had just closed the trunk.

"Catch me up on what's been going on. Have you seen Mr. Gorgeous lately?"

"Um, things have changed." How would Holly react to the changes? She thought she could guess.

Her sister's brow furrowed. "What's changed? He moved? You finally got so mad at him that you broke his windows?" She turned to check out the house across the street. "Nope. They're intact." Holly slowly spun around, her eyes widening as she stared at Jemma. "You're dating him, aren't you?!"

"No! Don't be ridiculous. He's helping me with marketing for my business. That's all."

"Whew. I wondered how everything could change in just a few days. That seems like a nice thing for him to do. And he didn't seem nice before. What gives?"

"It's his way of paying me back for a favor. A business associate told him he needs to appear more approachable. It was suggested that having a date for his own party this Saturday might help." She smirked. "I got the impression that all of the women he knew turned him down."

"Ha! This is easy for you. You must have attended hundreds of functions for your job."

"So many. Nathaniel's helped me with my business already, but in a surprising way. I hadn't realized I'd focused almost completely on learning my craft—that whole trash-to-treasure thing—but I hadn't studied how to run a small business. My long-term plan included classes, but everything went into overdrive when Great-aunt Grace left me the house. Now here I am, with no serious business skills, and a few short months to make this dream into a reality."

"Ouch. He is right. So this makes a shift to the plan."

She hadn't seen it that way, but it was a change to her plan. "Tonight I'm reading this book." She reached into the car and pulled it out. *Small Business 101.*

Holly yawned and patted her mouth with her hand. Laughing, Jemma swatted her with the book. "I'll call you about midnight when I'm starting to nod off reading it."

"Hey, if you wake up Abbie and Ivy, I'm bringing them over here. Those girls are cranky when they wake up. Just like their Aunt Jemma."

"They need tea." She grinned. She turned and headed toward the house. "Do you want to stay for dinner?"

"Dare I ask what you're planning to have?" Holly asked, trailing along behind her.

"I picked up a salad and a frozen lasagna. And I'm not *that* bad in the kitchen." The screen door smacked behind her.

Holly followed her inside. "Yes, you are. I've had any number of meals prepared by your hands that I felt lucky to survive."

"Now you're exaggerating."

"Remember the scrambled eggs with black bits? I assumed they were coarse ground pepper until I took a bite and discovered it was burned egg. It took a day to get that taste out of my mouth. Maybe the leathery steak, so chewy it couldn't be swallowed, served with crunchy baked potatoes, is more memorable. Or—"

Jemma turned on the oven, then sat down at the kitchen table to wait for it to heat. "Okay. You're right. I should never cook anything myself."

"No." Holly peered out the window in the back door and must have decided the girls were safe because she sat at another of the kitchen chairs. "You just need practice. You worked from dawn until dusk, and later than that most days. When were you supposed to learn how to cook? Of course, it might have helped if you'd let Mom teach you growing up, but you were too busy studying and being the best student in school."

"And look where that got me."

"You may not have been in the position you expected, but you had great jobs, jobs that many would love to have. And your income was way higher than most."

"There was that. It's a good thing, too, since I was able to save enough to get through a year with little income. I feel like a whiny baby. I need to be grateful. I've been given a gift, the gift of starting my own business."

"What you need is a day off. Step away from your business so you can appreciate it again."

"Yeah. Maybe see more of Alaska so I can learn to appreciate it too."

"I kind of hoped you'd stay in Alaska forever with me and the girls. I love it here and don't want to leave. But I have a feeling you'd go back to the Lower 48 in a heartbeat if you had that option."

Jemma leaned back in her chair. Holly had nailed it. She hadn't even realized that she'd jump at the chance to head south. "I'm still lonely. Even with Nathaniel in my life."

Holly raised an eyebrow.

"Bad choice of words."

"Really bad," Holly muttered.

"Let me rephrase. I'm lonely even though I now have a human being to talk to who isn't related to me." She picked up the stack of brochures from the tourist information center and flipped through them. "Which of these trips should I go on in the next step of my quest to learn to love the Last Frontier?"

Holly pulled one from the stack. "Here."

"Why this one?"

"You'll like it."

Jemma stared at the brochure in her hand. Seeing a glacier up close did sound very Alaska-ish. It might even be fun. Jemma picked up her phone and made a reservation for a trip on the next Saturday. When she hung up, Holly was biting her lip, obviously hiding laughter.

Her sister asked, "What are you going to do?"

"What do you mean what am I going to do? You chose it. I'm going to see Matanuska Glacier a week from now."

"That sounds like fun." Holly giggled. "I had no idea what I'd chosen. I figured anything would be better than spending the whole day alone in your house or garage. You need to get out among people."

The stove chimed that it had reached the right temp, so Jemma rose and slid the lasagna out of the box and into the oven. "You know, I think I've had so much fun being creative with my projects instead of sitting at a desk most of the day that I may have blocked out the business side of things. Other than my plan, of course."

"We can't forget the plan, can we?"

"Hey, the plan got me Nathaniel. If it weren't for his

mentioning he'd help me with my goals, I would have sent him walking."

"So, what's he like one-on-one?" Holly got a glass of water and sat back down.

Jemma could once again feel the zing that had hit her when he'd touched her hand. She fought the smile that she knew her sister would pick up on. Holly would never let her forget it and forever be pushing her toward him.

"You got a goofy expression on your face. You aren't falling for him, are you?"

So much for successfully fighting the smile. "Pleease! He's surprised me by being nice. He helped me before. But he's been nice since we made our agreement."

Holly softly said, "Gorgeous, helpful, and now nice?"

"Don't put on rose-colored glasses about him. He drove to Friday Fling with me today and left with a woman."

"Ooh, that isn't nice. I guess you do need to stick to business. At least he's being nice while he helps you."

"My thought exactly. I was angry at first when he took off, but I decided to just be grateful. He's already helped me and made me realize I have, or had, a gaping hole in the middle of my plan."

They went out the back door and took turns pushing the girls on the swings. When the lasagna was almost done, Jemma went inside to get the salad ready and set the table. Then she called everyone in when it was time.

The girls froze when they stepped through the door, their gaze going from the table to Jemma and back.

Ivy asked, "What's for dinner, Aunt Jemma?"

"You too? It's a frozen lasagna."

Abbie sighed with obvious relief. Always the peacemaker,

she wouldn't have said anything but apparently didn't want to experience her aunt's cooking either. Maybe Jemma needed to invest in cooking lessons. She'd check into them once her business was up and running.

When Jemma was alone again, after dinner, she picked up her new book and lay down on the couch. Beginning on page 1, she read straight through the book, stopping only long enough to get ready for bed before picking it back up.

The next thing she knew, sunlight was streaming through her window. Joined by light from her lamp, it all made for a bright morning. Blinking, she moved and felt something on her hip. The business book. Moving slowly, Jemma thought over the book she'd read as she climbed out of bed and went downstairs, with Stitches trailing behind her. He watched her as she made and then took a sip of her tea. As the hot drink woke her up, Jemma felt a grin start and grow wider.

Then she did a happy dance across the room, startling the cat, who responded with a fat tail and fur rising on his back. "It's okay. I'm not crazy." When she reached to pet him and he scooted away, glaring at her, she got a can out of the cupboard, which he stared at with interest. "Would tuna make up for scaring you?" She took his meow as a "yes."

After fixing his food, she sat at the table, and sipped a second cup of tea. "You see, Stitches"—he stopped eating long enough to look her way—"I felt comfortable reading the book last night, and it wasn't until this morning that I realized that's because I know this stuff. I've been in business for a decade. I didn't realize so much would be the same in the corporate world as it is for a small business."

She stood and happy danced over to the toaster, the cat

warily watching her. "I'm not an idiot. I know business. Sure, I need help with marketing, but together Nathaniel and I can rock this thing. I will be a success!" She popped some raisin bread into the toaster, spread on cream cheese when it came out, and drizzled honey over the top. "I may not be able to cook, Stitches, but we're doing okay, aren't we?"

He put his face into his food bowl and ate the rest of a meal he appeared to approve of wholeheartedly.

Chapter Eight

Hearing the door open, Nathaniel glanced up. A vision in red stood before him. The neckline of her short cocktail dress scooped low enough to hint at more, the length above the knee just enough to make an innocent but seductive combination. She had her long, blonde hair piled on her head, with strands escaping. The total package was one that drew him toward her. Blue eyes focused on him with confidence.

She must be one of his clients' "plus one." Whoever she was, he wanted to—make that needed to—meet her. Coming toward him now, she had a smooth gait, slightly sexy but casual at the same time.

She glanced down at herself and spoke in a familiar voice. "I thought this fit your dress code for the evening, but the way you're staring at me makes me wonder. Did I miss the mark?"

The sandwich in his hand dropped to the counter, bounced, and hit the floor, cucumber cream splashing in a wide arc.

"Jemma?" he croaked.

"Would black be better? I knew that would be safer, but I like this dress. Let me run across the street and change." She waved and turned toward the door. "I'll be back in a sec."

"Wait."

She stopped.

"You look"—he sought a word that would keep them on a solid business footing but come close to how she looked—"great." Yes, that sounded like something a business associate might say.

She turned slowly to face him. "Whew. There for a second I thought I'd made a mistake." She waved her hand over her front.

He stepped closer. "No mistakes."

"*Oui, mademoiselle.* You are a vision in red."

"Exactly, Marcel."

Jemma started. She apparently hadn't noticed the small Frenchman setting things up at the dining room table.

Nathaniel asked, "Isn't that from a well-known designer?"

"Yes. Isn't it stunning?"

She turned full circle, and Nathaniel's heart leaped into his throat. It fit her like a glove from every angle, a very expensive glove.

"I'm trying to figure out how to ask this. I hadn't realized you'd been that high up in the corporate world salary-wise."

She laughed. "I needed to look expensive when I was out with my boss."

Nathaniel choked and coughed. She patted him on the back. When he stared up at her with a stunned expression, her eyes widened.

"*Not* what you're thinking. I was a corporate executive

assistant. I planned and attended events of all sizes and had a clothing allowance. In my last job I had a *very* generous clothing allowance."

Nathaniel sat down on the couch. Jemma had an easygoing manner, and that was a good thing. Another woman might have stomped out of the place if he'd acted this way, basically accusing her of selling herself. "I apologize. I shouldn't have thought that."

She grinned. "Instead of this dress, I did briefly consider wearing a 1950s formal with crinolines that pushed the skirt"—she held her arms wide—"out to here. Admit it: that's what you pictured."

He shook his head slowly and dramatically from side to side. "No, you're doing me an injustice." When she hesitated, he added, "I pictured you in a flower power jumpsuit from the 1960s."

Jemma giggled, then snorted laughter. Her hand flew to her mouth. "Oh, sorry. I've tried to fix that all my life."

He leaned back on the couch and laughed. She sat at the other end of the couch, apparently keeping her distance.

When Chloe jumped onto the couch between them, he stood up, speaking to the puppy. "I know you won't like this, but it's time to go to the garage for the evening."

"Run her over to my backyard again."

"Chloe and I thank you. I didn't want to have to leave her in the garage with all the noise from people in the house and her wanting either to get in to join the party or protect me, but I don't have a fence. Be right back." He stepped into the garage for her leash, returned and attached it. Then he headed toward the door.

"Take a water bowl."

He hit his forehead with the palm of his hand. "We're glad someone understands dogs, aren't we, Chloe?"

Jemma watched as the dog looked up at Nathaniel with nothing short of hero worship. She hoped talking to his dog was a sign that he'd bonded with her, and Chloe had found her forever home.

Marcel spoke when man and dog disappeared out the front door. "I had not realized Mr. Montgomery had a girl-friend. He is a nice man, no?"

"No. I mean, yes, he seems to be a nice man, but we're business associates. I'm his client. And his neighbor." She pointed across the street.

Marcel nodded in that very French way that said he knew more than she did.

She asked, "May I help you? I'm just a little nervous, and it would be better if I were doing something."

He looked up at her, seeming to take her measure. "I'm sure Mr. Montgomery would appreciate that. Are you a good cook, mademoiselle? I have one thing to sauté at the last moment."

Jemma glanced back at the door to make sure it remained closed. "I know food. And I know how to set up events and work with caterers. But I can barely make a scrambled egg, and only attempt it when I'm desperate." She shrugged. "I spent years too busy to do anything but buy takeout." She heard Nathaniel opening the door. "But let's keep that our secret, huh?"

Marcel raised one eyebrow but nodded.

She pasted on a smile as she turned to Nathaniel. "Chloe happy?"

"A squirrel thought it would cross the yard as Chloe entered, so he or she is keeping her happy right now. When I left, her playmate was chattering at her from a tree."

Marcel took Jemma's prompting. "Mademoiselle, would you mind setting up the rest of the shrimp cocktails while I sauté some mushrooms?" He winked.

"I would be happy to."

"Are you sure, Jemma? Marcel usually takes care of everything himself for an event this size."

She hurried over to the table. "I want to help."

He shrugged. "Fine."

As she worked, light classical music came on in the background, an interesting choice from Nathaniel. When she glanced up, he nervously cleared his throat and adjusted his tie. Maybe he wasn't as comfortable in social situations as she'd assumed.

Then he checked his watch and hustled over to his coat closet. "I just realized that I haven't made a place for coats, if anyone chose to wear one. I meant to clear everything out of here." He pulled a handful of coats out—the man must like outerwear—and carried it upstairs.

Jemma busied herself with the hors d'oeuvres as her mind wandered. Marcel had assumed a relationship between her and Nathaniel. Everyone else attending probably would too. And she couldn't say she was his neighbor and was just helping him out because he needed a date to look good to clients. Or that they'd traded marketing for a date. That might be even worse.

When the doorbell rang, Nathaniel took the last half of the stairs two at a time and pulled the door open. Jemma moved to his side and greeted guests as they arrived. More than a few raised eyebrows met Nathaniel's introduction of her, which he managed with the words "my date for the evening." Since the majority of his guests fell into the business-only category, she figured there were few who actually knew his dating history.

A woman came through the door that made Jemma's breath hitch. The mysterious woman from Friday Fling who Nathaniel left with would now have a name. Since Jemma had no ties to her marketing expert, she considered her emotions to be pure curiosity. What was the name of the woman who had caused him to abandon her during their day together, or rather, their day *working* together?

"Natalie, I'm so glad you could make it," he greeted her with what Jemma estimated to be a bit too much exuberance.

"I'm so glad I could come. Herb's out parking the car."

Did Natalie have a husband? Jemma forced a smile and remained in her proper position at his side instead of poking her date in the ribs, as she'd have liked to. Shame on him for fooling around with a married woman.

As Jemma listened with half an ear to their conversation, she caught a glimpse of herself in a mirror hanging over a table off to the side. The red was a bold choice but one she knew he appreciated. Then it hit her; she'd chosen this dress to please him, not herself. At least not her new self. She did have vintage outfits she could have worn, but she'd chosen a striking dress that fit her perfectly and would draw his attention. She, Jemma Harris, had dressed to please Nathaniel Montgomery. This was a welcome wake-up call.

Nathaniel directed Natalie to the buffet table and returned, seeming to settle in as he waited to greet his next guest, who didn't take long to appear. First a couple, then a man alone, probably Herb, the sucker married to two-timing Natalie.

When several people from their hiking trip arrived, Jemma's smile became genuine. Leaning close to Nathaniel, she said, "Possible clients?"

He answered in a near whisper, "Everyone who owns a business or works high up in a business is a potential client." In a normal voice, he asked, "Would you like a drink?"

"That would be fine. Whatever you're having." He raised one eyebrow when she said that, then walked away and returned with what appeared to be champagne. Until she took a sip of it. "What?" She pointed at the glass.

"Sparkling cider. I don't drink alcohol, and you said you'd have what I was having."

"I'm honestly not much of a drinker myself, so I'm fine with this."

He pointed toward the door. "Most of my guests have arrived, so you can mingle if you'd like." Then he wandered around the room, stopping to speak to a couple of different people before he ended up at Natalie's side.

Jemma surveyed the group that now included about thirty people. Maybe she could have a party for clients this fall. She'd need something not-so-elegant for her business' more casual *brand*—a new word from Nathaniel reinforced by her business book. Jemma wandered over to the table, assembled a plate of food for herself, and stood off to the side. She dipped a shrimp in cocktail sauce and took a bite. Sighing she took another bite. Alaska did fresh seafood well.

When she went back to the table for more shrimp, Melinda walked over. Gesturing toward Nathaniel, she said, "I never would have guessed the two of you would be a couple."

Jemma laughed. "Because we seemed to hate each other?"

Melinda grinned. "Well, yes!"

"We have moved ahead in our relationship, but only to the point that we can carry on a conversation. We're neighbors, and he's helping me with my business. I'm helping as his date." Jemma hoped that didn't give away too much of their agreement.

Marcel gathered up some things and appeared ready to leave. As Jemma ate yet another shrimp, she turned to face the door in case another guest arrived. The Frenchman stopped at Nathaniel's side, and the two shook hands before the caterer left.

Melinda stood beside her. "That's right. You said you were neighbors. I've thought about the furniture you talked about several times since the hike."

A woman she'd met earlier—Mary?—must have overheard because she asked, "Do you make furniture?"

"No, I rehab old furniture into new pieces."

Mary's eyes sparkled. "I've seen that done on TV."

Melinda waved an hors d'oeuvre. "I'd love to see what you do."

"Me too."

"What's going on?" Another woman approached. Melinda introduced her as Anna, a woman she knew from church.

Mary explained, "Jemma rehabs furniture and makes it into something new. I told her I'd love to see what she does."

"Ooh," Anna said. "I've pinned projects like that on Pinterest. I want to do it but haven't found the right piece of furniture. Maybe I haven't found the nerve." She grinned.

Now Jemma was having fun. She glanced over at the party's host. Nathaniel seemed busy speaking with a small group. Maybe he wouldn't mind if she took a second to plug her business at his party. "Almost any piece of furniture, no matter how bad of shape it's in or how seriously ugly, can be turned into something wonderful."

Another woman joined their group. "Did I hear you mention fixing old furniture?"

Melinda nodded. "That's Jemma's business."

The woman's eyes lit up. "In case you can't remember from our brief introduction, I'm Jennifer. Now that the niceties are over, can you turn a changing table I used with my son, who's now in college, into anything I can use? We put it in the storage shed when he stopped needing it, and I ran into it the other day when I was searching for a rake. Literally." She rubbed the front of her leg.

"Absolutely. And when I make changing tables, I always make that part removable so it can be used as a dresser later."

The woman said, "I'd love to see some of your work."

Jemma opened her mouth to say she'd be at Friday Fling, but Melinda spoke first. "Jemma lives across the street. I seem to remember you saying you worked from home, right?"

"My workshop is in my garage." She popped yet another shrimp in her mouth.

"And you have a light in it?"

She hesitated, hoping Melinda's thoughts weren't taking her where she thought they were going. "A rather weak light. But I can see where I'm going."

"Ladies, let's go across the street so we can see Jemma's furniture."

"But," Jemma sputtered, "we should stay and enjoy Nathaniel's party. And I'm at Friday Fling every week."

Anna answered. "We won't be gone long. Many of us are

Nathaniel Montgomery's clients already, so we won't be missed. He's handled the marketing for my law firm for about two years."

"That's good to know," Melinda said. "My husband's employers are considering using Nathaniel's services."

When the group moved toward the door, Jemma felt it had a power all its own. She smiled weakly at Nathaniel as they got closer to him.

Melinda said to him, "Jemma's been coerced into showing us her workshop. Don't worry about us. We'll be back to eat some more of your delicious food shortly."

The husbands took notice of the goings-on when the women neared the door. Melinda once again explained, and they joined in.

Jemma glanced back as they stepped outside and saw a slack-jawed Nathaniel staring after them. She suspected every guest was with her and felt a bit like Noah leading everyone two by two across the street. If the water main broke again, the scene would be complete with flood.

While everyone waited in front of her garage, she raced to her house, at least as much of a race as she could manage in heels, and came back with the key to the door's padlock. Once open, she pulled the chain hanging from the light and nervously stepped aside. Would they like what she did? Other than close friends in Atlanta and family, she hadn't personally known many people she'd shown her projects to.

Words like *cute, aww, love it* flew around the small building. Jemma wished she could save them up for a time when she wondered if her business would make it. By the time everyone seemed ready to return to Nathaniel's party, Jennifer had promised she'd bring the changing table over in the next few days and Jemma had sold two pieces. She felt like she was floating on air as she turned back. Natalie and Herb caught her eye. They'd bought a dresser-turned-bench for the front hall and *seemed* like a happy couple.

Chloe barked, a bit delayed as a security alarm, but maybe she'd been busy with her squirrel. Herb immediately headed toward the barking, and Natalie said, "He's a vet. He has to meet every dog we see. Or in this case, hear." She went after him and Jemma followed. Everyone else stayed put, probably enjoying the evening outside. She hoped the mosquitoes didn't discover them.

"What kind of dog is it?" Herb asked as he neared the fence.

"She seems like mostly golden retriever or yellow Lab. She's Nathaniel's dog, but I thought she'd be happier here than in the garage during the party."

"Chloe?" He put out his hand and she ran over to lick it. "I'm her vet. I knew Nathaniel from work he did for our practice."

Natalie said, "Nathaniel's also going to do some work for my temp agency. I guess he was with you yesterday when I talked him into coming to our house for dinner to talk about it." She laughed, and Jemma felt mortified at the thoughts she'd had. If she'd felt bolder earlier, she might have accused Natalie of cheating on her husband, and that was totally out of character. Why would she care so much about what her neighbor was up to?

Feeling thoroughly chastised for her thoughts, and more than a little embarrassed, she led the group back to Nathaniel's house. When she opened the door, she found a surprising scene. It seemed a single guest had arrived while they were gone, a rather stunning guest dressed in the classic little black dress, with a marketing expert attached as an accessory. Jemma pulled the door slightly back and adjusted the strap of her shoe, hoping her neighbor would take the moment to peel the woman off of himself.

When she pushed the door open, Nathaniel came toward it, and the woman stood off to the side of the room.

Herb said, "Sorry to leave you alone, Montgomery. Your neighbor is doing some interesting work."

Nathaniel gave a slight smile. "I agree. Her projects are interesting."

Why had it sounded so much nicer when Herb used the word *interesting* than when Nathaniel did? When she moved to Nathaniel's side to play her role, the woman in black did what Jemma could only describe as pout. He got her wrap out of the closet, gave it to her, and said something that had her appear very happy when she left. Jemma didn't want to consider what he might have promised to earn that expression from her.

Jemma waited until the last guest left before she headed for the front door herself.

"Thank you, Jemma!"

She kept moving. "This was a good group, so I didn't mind being here."

"No, thank you for helping with Alexis."

She stopped and spun around. "The woman you played around with at your own party?"

Nathaniel blushed and that startled her. "No playing involved." He rubbed his right hand over his face. "At least not on my part. She's worked for me for a couple of years, and I hoped we'd come to terms to be only business associates.

With everyone gone, she took it as an opportunity to give me a sample of what she'd like to do."

Jemma smiled in a who-are-you-kidding way. "And yet she seemed quite happy when she left."

He ran his fingers through his hair, making the waves deliciously messy. She shook herself at the direction of her thoughts and focused on his words. "I told her we would discuss our future together." Shrugging, he added, "She took it as I hoped she would so she'd leave and not make a scene. We have no future, and I will call her in the morning to tell her that."

His expression was so little-boy cute that Jemma melted just a bit, then caught herself.

"I must admit you ticked me off when you talked every-one into going outside with you."

Jemma sputtered. As soon as she thought he might be a nice guy, he went directly back to Mr. Jerk without passing "Go." She continued out the door and over to her property. Nathaniel could seem so nice one minute. But then . . .

A vehicle came around the bend in the road, and Jemma assumed it was someone related to his party, maybe Marcel returning to clean up. As she took a step toward her house, the minivan pulled into her driveway. She lunged to the side to dodge being hit.

"Jemma!" Her mother got out of the car. "You stepped right in front of us! Are you okay?"

She wanted to say, "You mean on top of being angry with Nathaniel?" Instead, she forced a smile. "Just a bit shaken. I wasn't expecting you tonight. Are you staying the night with me?"

With her arm around Jemma, her mother steered her

inside. "Yes. We have fresh salmon for dinner tomorrow night. I thought we'd invite Holly and the girls—if you clear off the big dining room table."

"I think I can do that. For salmon." Being with her family *usually* made her happy. She hoped this visit would be one of those times.

Chapter Nine

The phone rang in the middle of a project Nathaniel was trying to sneak in after church, breaking his general policy of not working on Sunday if he could avoid it. He glared at the persistent device and turned back to his computer. Whoever it was could leave a message. When the ringing stopped only to start again a minute later, he checked the caller ID and grabbed his phone.

"Grandma! How's everything in the desert?"

"Hot. That's all I can say about June in Arizona."

"Come visit me. We'll go wild and hike Resurrection Pass." He offered his standard greeting and chuckled, knowing that at seventy she could still do the thirty-eight-mile trail if she chose to. He wasn't sure what he'd say if she did agree, since he'd have to set aside his work and take most of the week off.

When silence greeted his remark, he felt the hair raise on the back of his neck. "Grandma, what's wrong. Is someone sick? Do I need to catch the next plane out?" He kept his phone to his ear and turned back to his computer, one-handed typing in Anchorage-to-Tucson flights.

"Calm down. Everyone's healthy. It's just that I thought I should let you know that your mom's been seeing someone. You're so far away that you wouldn't know that. She hasn't said anything, right?"

Nathaniel folded up into his chair. Mom and a man? To his knowledge she hadn't dated anyone since his father. He couldn't even *think* of that man as Dad, simply as the man who'd fathered him. "No. She hasn't said a word about it. Come to think of it, she's been busy a lot when I've called this year. I know her law practice can be hectic, so I assumed the world needed her services more than usual."

"That isn't it." The tone in his grandmother's tone raised his blood pressure.

"There's a problem with this man, isn't there? Don't tell me no, because I can hear it in your voice."

"The man might be okay. I don't want to say more about it because it's her business. I may be having a hard time with it because of all she went through with your father."

A childhood with a raging alcoholic left scars that opened wide at moments like this, scars that would be difficult to un-do. Especially since his father hadn't wanted help, hadn't wanted to heal so he could share a life with him and his mother. "Thank you for calling. It helps knowing this much so I won't behave badly if she tells me." He turned the conversation back in a direction he could handle. "Now, are you sure you don't want to visit? It's in the upper sixties today."

His grandmother's sigh told him she'd let go of the other subject as well. "I dream about weather like that. Do you have a girlfriend to introduce me to? Someone special in your life?"

She'd shifted from his mother's love life to his. "I've told you I'm happy with my life."

"I'm going to tell you something I should have said years ago. With everything coming to a head with your mother, it needs to be said now. You have the kindest heart I've ever known. But you've built a barrier around it so secure that it makes the Great Wall of China look like my doggy door."

Nathaniel stared at his office wall, torn between commenting on the horrible analogy and her sweet words.

"Kind of got you with my comparison, didn't I?"

When she chuckled, he realized that she'd set him up. He'd been pulled out of his earlier thoughts, and she'd planned that very thing.

"Think about what I said. Your eyes twinkled with laughter before everything that happened with your dad shut you down. I'd like to see them twinkle again."

"Okay. I'll think about it." Pushing away emotions he didn't want to explore, he asked, "So when will you be arriving?"

"Did you get a bed for your guest room?"

They had this conversation every time she thought about visiting. "You know you love the view out my bedroom window. The guest room's view isn't anywhere near as good."

She sighed. "I just hate having you sleep on the couch. By the way, I was thinking about that housedress I forgot last time. Would you box it up and send it to me?"

He pictured Jemma wearing that dress the night of the flood and realized she still had it. He stood and went to the window. She hadn't started working in her garage yet today. "Uh, sure. I'll get that to you."

"Is there a problem?"

"No. Absolutely not. I need to mail something tomorrow, so I'll try to get it out to you then."

As they said their good-byes, Nathaniel noticed a minivan parked in Jemma's driveway. Great. She had company, and he had to ask for the outfit she'd worn home from his place. Even a text could turn embarrassing.

Getting back to work, he struggled to push the image of his mother and a man out of his mind. The last man in her life hadn't treated her very well, so he hoped this went better. For both their sakes. As a kid he couldn't do much when his drunk father went on a rampage, never hurting anyone but always scaring. Now he could, and that terrified him.

Chloe leaned against him, seeming to know he needed comforting. After a few minutes she gave a short bark, what he'd come to know was her "I'd like to go outside now" sound. When they stepped through the garage door and outside, Chloe ran to her favorite area, pulling him along. While he waited for her, he turned toward Jemma's house. He'd gone over there last night after Jemma had left and retrieved Chloe, who hadn't wanted to leave. The puppy seemed to like being outside, and who could blame her? He liked the outdoors too. In fact, he needed a break in the next couple of days. Maybe Chloe was ready for her first hike.

A woman stepped out onto Jemma's front porch. Noticing him, she waved and came in his direction. Chloe bounded over there, probably believing another person might pet her. The woman didn't disappoint her. She cooed over Chloe before greeting him.

"I'm Jemma's mother, Maggie Harris. Her dad and I are visiting, and we'd love to have you join us for a salmon dinner tonight. We just caught it on the Kenai River."

Nathaniel tried to find a polite way to refuse dinner across the street. He certainly couldn't say he had other plans unless he actually wanted to leave the house.

Then a man who must have been Jemma's father came over as Mrs. Harris added, "We're going to get some fresh produce at a roadside stand this afternoon. Dinner should be delicious."

Mr. Harris, or he guessed it should be Dr. Harris since Jemma had told him her father was a professor, said, "Yes, please join us. Jemma has told us how you've helped her and are working to make her business a success. We aren't going to take no for an answer."

That ended that. Nathaniel didn't know how to respond other than by asking, "What time should I be there?"

When it was time to leave for dinner, Nathaniel started to put Chloe in the garage but realized she'd probably be welcome in Jemma's backyard. Flashbacks of family life flipped through his mind as he crossed the street, and he fought against the panic that tried to seize him. He gulped and kept moving.

Family events were to be avoided at all costs, and here he was, stepping into the middle of one. Wondering if he could get out of it by not feeling well—because he was feeling worse with every step—he immediately decided he had no choice. Neighbors needed to get along, especially neighbors who sat alone at the end of a road. He and Jemma had started out so badly that he could sacrifice one evening to make her happy.

Nearing the backyard, he heard children's voices. Of course, Jemma's nieces would be here, and the yard would be full of kids. Well, two kids who were racing around, playing with their grandfather, a man who looked up just as Nathaniel considered taking his dog back home.

"Nathaniel, welcome. I was spending quality time with my grandkids. Bring Chloe on in here."

Nathaniel held tightly to the leash. "I'm not sure how she'll do with kids running around."

Dr. Harris brought the girls over and asked them to be quiet and still while Chloe got to know them. The puppy bumped them with her nose and took off running, with the twins behind.

"I guess I worried for nothing."

"You didn't know. I like a man who's cautious around kids."

Nathaniel watched him, seeking signs of a father playing matchmaker and wondering if the evening could go into an even worse tailspin. When the older man didn't say anything else, he felt himself relaxing.

The girls squealed with delight as they played with Chloe. "Grandpa, Abbie and I need a puppy! Can we have this one?"

Could finding a home for Chloe be that easy? He could have order back in his life—and left and right slippers from a single pair. When he pictured them driving off with the puppy, he felt something inside twist.

"Ivy, the dog belongs to Mr. Montgomery." Turning to Nathaniel, Dr. Harris said, "Knowing my wife, dinner will be ready in ten minutes. She's very exacting about these things. Kids," he called, "let's all go inside and get cleaned up for dinner."

When Nathaniel went toward the back door, the older man put out his hand to stop him.

"That goes through the kitchen, and with three women—well, really two—in there, racing to make a meal, you don't want to go there."

When they walked around to the front, Jemma waited on the porch for them, wearing one of her crazy outfits. She'd stepped out of her comfort zone with their business meeting and the party last night, but it was back to the usual Jemma, with today's look a midi-length skirt and yet one more peasant top. She seemed to favor them, which probably made her seem a little less quirky to other people because they wouldn't look close enough to know Jemma's were slightly different from today's peasant tops, and decades old. For some reason her vintage look didn't bother him as much as it used to.

She let her family members pass but, glancing around, put a hand out to stop Nathaniel. "I have to warn you," she said in a raspy whisper that reminded him of something from a detective movie from the 1940s.

He almost—almost!—tried a Humphrey Bogart imitation when he answered. "Of what? Your dad's very nice."

She spoke in the same whisper. "They're *all* nice. I think this is a setup. B-e-w-a-r-e," she said slowly.

He swallowed a chuckle as the conversation continued to sound like it had come from an old detective movie. "I don't think so. Once in the backyard, I thought your dad was targeting me as a future son-in-law, but he wasn't."

Jemma raised one eyebrow. "Just consider yourself warned."

She turned to go inside, but realizing he might not get another chance for privacy, he put his hand on her arm and whispered, "My grandmother wants her housedress back."

She grinned. "It didn't look good on me anyway."

"No. It didn't." That dress had made her vintage outfits look good.

As he stepped through the door, she added, "Oh, one more thing. Holly thinks you're gorgeous."

Nathaniel froze. He could still feign a headache or even twist his ankle on a porch step if need be. A little physical pain might be better than the way this evening could go. Jemma held the door open, and her smile said that she truly had warned him. He sighed and entered the fiery furnace.

Instead of the grilling he'd expected, Jemma's family welcomed him with open arms. He felt like family and not like prey, more like a very welcome guest. One of the twins—who could tell them apart?—pulled on his arm, tugging him over to a bathroom on the ground floor, insisting he also wash his hands. He obliged.

When he stepped out, Mrs. Harris called, "Dinner's ready."

Checking his watch, he saw exactly ten minutes had passed. The man knew his wife well. So far, so good.

They seated him with Jemma to his left and Holly across the way. One of the little girls sat on either side of their mother, so also next to a grandparent, who took up each end of the table. This was obviously important to the grandparents because each hugged the child next to them before sitting down, something he wasn't used to seeing in a family. The scene made him happy but sad at the same time because it seemed so natural to them and completely awkward to him.

Jemma said, "In case you notice that the corners of the room are cluttered, I want you to know I'm not messy. My workspaces may sometimes seem chaotic"—she glared at him—"but they're organized. This is my office and studio, but Mom insisted we eat here."

"And where would we eat otherwise?" Mrs. Harris asked in a tone that would bring a small child quaking to her knees.

It didn't faze Jemma. "Outside. Or we could sit in the living room, with plates."

"Eating with mosquitoes dive-bombing us, or having four-year-olds eating on upholstered furniture. Hmm. Those are nice options."

"You're right. You're always right."

Nathaniel cringed as the fighting began, and he slipped back in time to when he was eleven or twelve and his father, who had started drinking earlier in the day than normal, had started a fight at the dining room table. That was the last dinner he remembered them sharing.

Her mother grinned and broke the spell.

He reached for the glass of ice water someone had provided and took a big gulp.

Mrs. Harris continued, "In case you think we're arguing, Nathaniel, we're not. Jemma's gone on all day about this room looking bad for company. She appears to be concerned about your opinion of her housekeeping. For your information she is neat and takes good care of things." The woman gave him a knowing glance.

Jemma went bright red and leaned closer to him, muttering, "I told you so."

Prey, just as he'd originally thought.

Holly laughed and winked at him. He grinned back because he didn't think she saw him as prey, just *gorgeous*.

Platters and bowls of food were passed around the table, salmon, small potatoes with butter and parsley, peas, and rolls. "This looks delicious," he said as he served himself a generous portion of fish.

"That's king salmon Michael caught yesterday. He's always been an excellent fisherman."

"Thank you, Maggie. And my lovely wife makes delicious food, like these rolls." He buttered a roll, bit into it, and sighed. "I've enjoyed our thirty-five years together."

Jemma's mother gave a casual nod in her husband's direction, obviously used to his compliments. "So, Nate, have you been married before?" she asked casually as she forked a piece of salmon.

After recovering from wincing at the shortened version of his name that he despised, he answered. "No ma'am. I've enjoyed my freedom." That reply had spared him from further matchmaking in the past.

Undaunted, Mrs. Harris continued, "Neither has our Jemma. Her job kept her too busy for much of a relationship. I imagine it's been the same with you."

"Mother!" Jemma sputtered. "I don't think Nathaniel needs to hear about anyone from my past." This time the glare she gave her mother wasn't as kind.

As Nathaniel considered how to continue, Jemma's father stepped in and diverted the track his wife had been on. "Jemma tells us you're a marketing expert. That's completely outside my experience as a biologist. Can you tell us about your work?"

Nathaniel gave him a look of gratitude and received a kindly smile in response. He could imagine college students liking him because he could read between the lines of a situation. Not that his wife had been any too subtle. "Yes, sir. My career in marketing was quite accidental. I joined a management trainee program after college and spent time in each department. During my week in the marketing department, the marketing manager's assistant went into labor, a startling experience for a twenty-two-year-old man to witness, I must add. The manager handed me that woman's work as the ambulance wheeled her off screaming during a contraction.

"He liked what I did that day, so he asked me to fill in. The new mother decided not to come back to work, and I was in marketing. I earned a master's degree in it at night and worked in various corporations. When I moved to Alaska, I started freelancing."

As he stopped speaking, he realized that everyone, except the twins, had stopped eating and was watching him. Embarrassed, he added, "I'm sorry. I'm sure that was much more information than you wanted."

Dr. Harris waved his comment away. "No, son, it wasn't too much. It was interesting. If you tell everyone else's stories in a similar manner, I can see why you're successful at marketing. Jemma, you've picked a winner here."

Nathaniel wasn't sure if the last comment meant he'd do a good job for her business or that Dr. Harris had joined his wife's cause.

Mrs. Harris asked, "Nate, are you familiar with working with such small businesses?"

He completely ignored the nickname this time. If the woman wanted to stay on safe ground and discuss business, he'd join her there.

"Yes, ma'am. I actually prefer to work with small businesses."

Dr. Harris examined him very carefully, much, Nathaniel

imagined, as he would a specimen under a microscope. "Can you share one of your ideas for Jemma's business?"

"I've given the matter quite a bit of thought. I know she needs a website, and I've sketched out some ideas for it. She also needs business cards, and I'm about ready to submit the order for them. We need a way for people to remember her later."

Jemma set down her fork. "You plan to order business cards without my seeing them?"

He hoped this wouldn't all go badly. "Um, with your short timeline I thought I'd go ahead. I think you'll be happy with them. If not, I'll pay for them."

She seemed to consider her options, then said, "That part sounds great." Jemma grinned, and he felt her smile warm him inside.

"We can get together to go over some additional details."

Her mother spoke up again. "So that means you'll need to spend time with Jemma?"

He cleared his throat. "Yes, ma'am. But I'll come up with ideas first so the *business meeting*," he emphasized, "shouldn't take too much of her time."

Mrs. Harris left the room, making him wonder if he'd insulted her. Eating dinner with his parents and having someone suddenly leave the room had usually meant something unpleasant had just happened. His blood pressure returned to normal when she returned with a three-layer cake decorated with strawberries.

"Holly made this. She's been busy with her studies for years but has time again to bake."

She handed him a slice, and he took a bite. "Delicious. What did Jemma make?"

Everyone, including the kids, went silent and stared at Jemma. What had he said wrong?

"It's a secret," one of the girls, Abbie he thought, said.

Jemma took a sip of water but didn't answer his question. When everyone focused on their cake but didn't eat any, remaining quiet, she said, "Okay. I can't cook. There. I said it. Don't let me in the kitchen."

Jemma's mother stared at the ceiling. Apparently the secret was out, and she figured the wedding was off.

The whole situation made Nathaniel chuckle. He tried to stifle it, but laughter bubbled up and overtook him. "I'm sorry. I shouldn't laugh, but I think it's funny that *this* is Jemma's deep, dark secret."

Dr. Harris joined in, and then everyone else, including Jemma.

Jemma wiped her eyes. "Thank you for that. They treat me like I'm some sort of pariah."

Her mother shook her head. "It's just that *someone* should be able to cook in a house. Frozen dinners get old."

Nathaniel accepted another piece of cake. "I'm going to have to take a long walk with Chloe tonight to walk this off." After eating another bite, he said, "You wouldn't know this, of course, but I've been called a gourmet cook, so it doesn't matter to me if someone else can cook."

Mrs. Harris smiled. "Why, Nate, that will be such a good thing whenever you settle down."

Back in the fire. He'd struck that match himself.

"Dr. Harris, you've always been surrounded by women, first your wife, then two daughters, and now two granddaughters. I don't know how you've survived."

The older man chuckled. "There's some truth in that, son,

but I've actually been blessed with three daughters. Bree isn't here."

"I just assumed this was the whole family."

The other twin, this time he thought Ivy, said, "Aunt Bree is helping save lives."

Nathaniel turned to Jemma, waiting for her to interpret the four-year-old's words into something that made sense.

"Ivy's right. Bree is in Africa with a medical mission group, and she is helping save lives. Dr. Briana Harris just finished her residency, and instead of taking a well-earned break, immediately set off for Africa. That's why I'm watching her cat. I was going to Alaska about the same time she was going overseas for a couple of months, so it worked out well for me to just bring him here instead of boarding him somewhere. Not that he doesn't miss her."

Abbie said, "Stitches is under the bed. He's always under the bed when there's company."

"Stitches? Oh, that's a perfect name for a doctor's cat."

After dinner, the adults sat around the table and played a board game. He couldn't remember when he'd had so much fun. People argued good-naturedly but didn't get angry. When he stood to leave, he felt warm and fuzzy inside.

"Thank you, everyone. I appreciate the meal that Maggie and Holly prepared, and also that Jemma did *not* help." Everyone laughed. "And I'm glad I won at least one round of backgammon."

He moved toward the door. Everything felt so relaxed here. So *this* was normal family life. He'd seen it in movies and read about it in books, of course, but until now he hadn't believed it existed outside of fiction. This wasn't a fantasy world, so he imagined they got mad at each other occasionally, but he could tell they'd patch things up pretty quickly. He could definitely get used to it.

Jemma stood and Dr. Harris started to rise, but Nathaniel watched his wife put her hand on her husband's arm and shake her head. They'd wrap up the evening as it began: in matchmaker mode.

Stepping out on the front porch, he held the door open for Jemma, and she went out onto the porch with him. She grinned and motioned him with her head away from the screen door and windows. "I told you so."

"You have a great family. Matchmaking or not."

"I am blessed. Why didn't you correct my mother when she called you Nate? You winced every time she did it."

"Ah, well, my mother raised me to be respectful. And since I probably won't see your mother again, it was a battle I didn't need to fight."

"You mentioned your mom, but what about your dad?

He muttered, "My parents divorced when I was in high school." Then he gave more information than he'd ever done before. "He was an alcoholic, and I don't have a relationship with him."

Startled at revealing his past, he was even more startled when Jemma gave him a brief hug before turning toward the backyard and Chloe. For just a second, he wondered if she'd thought her mother's attempts at matchmaking had proven successful. Then he pictured the kids with their grandparents. No, they're huggers.

When he opened the gate, Chloe raced over. He scratched beside her ears and asked, "Did you have fun?" receiving a licked hand in reply. Laughing, he clicked on her leash, and

Chloe bounded around on it. "I would have thought she'd have the bounce worn out of her, but she must have been sleeping back here. Walk with me."

As Chloe led them up the street, he swatted at the mosquitoes that had homed in on him, and Jemma turned the conversation to something safe, a visit to a glacier that she'd signed up for.

"I've never gone on a trip like that, but it does sound fun," he said. "I wonder if they have room for one more."

As soon as the words left his mouth, he wanted to recapture them—particularly since Jemma had gasped. Standing in the middle of the road, he wondered what he should do.

Had he really just said he wanted to join her for her trip to the glacier? He saw her watching him out of the corner of her eye, probably well aware that he regretted his words.

Finally, she said, "I'm sure you're too busy to go on a trip that takes more than half a day."

"No, I'm not." Nathaniel brushed almost absentmindedly at a mosquito on his arm that had taken advantage of his stillness. "I don't have anything on my schedule for Saturday, nothing that can't be moved anyway."

Jemma swatted at her arm, so a mosquito must have tried to make a dinner out of her too. She said, "You and Chloe have a good walk. Neither of us has mosquito repellent on, and I don't want to spend tomorrow scratching."

He surprised himself again when he offered, "Speaking of tomorrow, I can't meet then to talk about your business, but I can the next day. I shouldn't have ordered business cards without your, 'the client's,' approval. Why don't you come over about noon Wednesday for lunch."

"I can do that." She waved as she turned back.

Nathaniel watched Jemma walk toward her house, wondering what had gotten into him. Chloe seemed to sense his mood and tugged him toward home instead of on her usual preference of a longer walk.

Inside his house, Nathaniel settled into his favorite chair and picked up what had been a compelling thriller, but every time he tried to read it, he thought about Jemma. A short time remained for him to make a success of her business or she would be gone from Alaska, probably forever. It might be selfish of him, but he'd gotten used to having her as a neighbor and didn't want to have to break in another one.

Setting down his book, he instead headed over to his office to work, his method of clearing out all thoughts he really didn't want to have, and Jemma fit into that category. Choosing to put some time in on a home decorating company, he worked on branding the husband-and-wife team's business. They mainly found clients by word of mouth but wanted to appear high-end to potential and even present clients.

Grinning as ideas popped into his mind, he opened a design program. Thinking about graphic design made him think about Alexis. He knew he *should* stop right now and find a replacement for her so he could ask his designer to give him ideas instead of doing it himself. If he didn't, he'd have a huge work slowdown in his immediate future that could translate to his bottom line.

Instead, an idea came to him that would help Jemma *and* this decorating business.

Right after he and Chloe had breakfast the next morning, Nathaniel picked up his phone and placed a call to the owner of that business.

"Marina? Nathaniel Montgomery here. I'm working on your business and another one right now, and it's just occurred to me that you might have something in common."

She said, "I have about three minutes. Then I have to grab some samples and head out the door."

"No problem. My other client transforms"—he rather liked that word and would have to use it again—"furniture and accessories. She takes older pieces and turns them into things you would never guess had started life any other way."

"I don't know, Nathaniel. We specialize in high-end. We use new or valuable antiques. This sounds like a step away from junk."

Nathaniel cringed when she used the last word, since he'd once said the same thing. "She has an artistic touch. Much of it is hand painted or has other treatments. A bench will have a custom seat. I'm sure she could work within whatever color palette you chose."

Silence met his words, and he wondered if he'd pushed too hard. And when had he decided that Jemma's furniture—and former junk—had merit?

"Never mind. I shouldn't have suggested this. I don't normally ask one client if they would work with another."

"Well, I might like to see some of her pieces."

"I admit I have a personal connection with Ms. Harris."

"Ahh." A feminine note to her voice told him she had the wrong idea.

"Not what you're thinking right now. She's my neighbor."

"And probably twenty years older than you and married."

He cleared his throat. "No. She's my age, attractive, and single."

Marina laughed.

"I'd like to give Ms. Harris a boost with launching her business. Can I offer to pay for a piece of furniture as an incentive? That would minimize your risk."

"I've never done this before, taken money from someone to try a vendor, but it does take away some of the risk for something that seems very different from our usual style."

Nathaniel felt a grin spread from ear to ear. He'd helped Jemma. "Thank you! I'll get the check right out to you."

"Just take it off my bill. Your services are as expensive as mine."

"Ha! Will do. One more favor with this. Please call Ms. Harris and talk to her about what you want. My guess from living across the street from her workshop is that she could deliver in a few weeks." He gave Marina Jemma's contact information.

Jemma hung up the phone, dazed. She needed to tell someone about the phone call she'd just received. Checking the time, she knew Holly would be busy, and her parents and Bree were traveling. Movement out the window caught her eye. Nathaniel was walking Chloe, the dog who had stolen his heart, the heart she wasn't sure he knew he had before that puppy washed up into his life.

"Nathaniel!" she yelled as she stepped onto her porch. He turned toward her, and Chloe bounded over for some puppy love.

"You look happy. Glowing, actually. Good news?"

She crouched down and wrapped her arms around Chloe. "You're so adorable." Standing, she said, "Yes. An interior designer just called. The company heard about my business and placed an order for several large pieces of furniture."

He got a strange smile. "What was the name of the business?" When she gave it, he said, "I've heard of them, and they do high-end work. Did she order that sort of furniture?"

Jemma thought over the conversation. "Yes, I was told to make pieces of furniture that were hand painted, in certain colors, and nothing 'too funky.'" Jemma shrugged. "I can do that. I'll have to search around to find exactly what was ordered." She sighed blissfully. "I sure hope this can work out. It *never*, not once, occurred to me to contact local interior designers."

"It might be something to consider. Your business plan is about reaching individuals. That could have worked, and worked well in Atlanta, but the short season for events limits that here. Perhaps you should also show some of your photos of pieces around to shops and see if they'll take something on consignment, or better yet, outright buy a few pieces like this person—a woman did you say?—wanted."

She hadn't said it was a woman . . . Oh well. It was probably an easy assumption.

"I'm glad for you that this happened," Nathaniel said. Just then, Chloe barked.

As Jemma looked down, she saw the dog pulling on her leash.

"I think my puppy wants to explore new places." Then he added, "I'll see you for lunch at noon."

She watched Nathaniel and *his* puppy hurry off. She hoped he'd let his mind acknowledge his love for Chloe before he gave her up to someone else. His heart would be broken if he didn't.

Chapter Ten

Jemma felt excitement rush through her. Nathaniel was about to reveal some of what he had planned for her business. She could hear the clock ticking on getting it up and running this year. She hated to admit the possibility of defeat existed, but she'd come to realize she might have unrealistic goals, even for someone with Nathaniel's obvious talents with marketing.

As she dried her hair after her shower, she went through a mental checklist for the meeting. She needed to *feel* business-like, so a suit would be a good choice again. A suit made her feel a little more formal and remote, and anything like armor between her and Nathaniel Montgomery would be a good thing. She'd started to like him as a person, and she hadn't expected that. At all. Ever.

When she reached for the drawer with stockings in it, she pulled her hand back. Suit, yes. Stockings, not unless she absolutely had to. She put on higher-than-normal heels, telling herself she did that because she wanted to be feminine but businesslike. It had nothing to do with being attractive to him. She grabbed the briefcase she'd already loaded with paper and computer tablet, then picked her way down her driveway.

Jemma tapped on Nathaniel's door.

As soon as he pulled it open, he rushed in the other direction, saying, "I'm in the middle of cooking the chicken breasts. Come in, take a seat at the table, and rub behind Chloe's ears. She likes that." He grinned as he stood at the stove.

When Jemma stepped into his house, she heard the same classical music playing in the background again—at least she assumed it was the same; she was no expert—and a fabulous scent surrounded her. "Mmm. That smells divine."

"Thank you. I added some shallots and fresh basil to the chicken. I also made a balsamic vinaigrette to dress the salad. It's experimental, but I think lunch should be good."

Note to self: never invite him to eat anything at my house. Not unless I've bought it somewhere that makes delicious food or had the meal catered.

When she sat down, Chloe came over to her, and Jemma rubbed her as instructed. The dog leaned against her legs with glee. The man knew his dog. When he kneeled as he set down a bowl of food for the puppy, Chloe ran over and licked his cheek. Laughing, Nathaniel petted her.

He placed a salad topped with sliced chicken in front of Jemma and at the placemat next to her, then set a bottle of dressing between them. "I made a special beverage for you." He held up a glass pitcher of a golden-colored liquid.

"Tea?"

"Not just any tea."

Jemma leaned forward.

"Sweet tea."

She sighed. "Sweet tea and pecan pie are two of my favorite things from the South. You don't have a pecan pie tucked in the kitchen somewhere, do you?"

"No." He laughed. "But I'll remember that for a future meeting."

After filling two glasses, he placed one at each seat. Jemma picked up her glass and took a sip. She rolled her head back. "I've missed you, sweet tea. Thank you!"

Once Nathaniel had sat down, Jemma took a bite of the salad. Covering her mouth with her hand, she said, "Oh . . . my! This is so good." She took another bite and closed her eyes as she chewed. "You're going to make some woman very happy when she marries you." Then her eyes opened wide and she felt her face go hot. "I'm sorry. My mouth disconnected from my head." She waved her fork. "That was inexcusable for a business meeting."

He set down his fork and grinned. "I can't be offended. I believe you just gave my food high marks."

"The best. I need to remember that even though we're neighbors, right now we're business associates."

"Let's switch to business. We talked about your goals. Tell me what brought you to this business idea." He picked up his fork and began eating again, giving Jemma a moment to gather her thoughts.

She shook herself mentally, sat up straighter, and moved into business mode. Nathaniel was a business associate, and she needed to act appropriately. She took a bite of her salad and her mind emptied of all thought. "This salad is so good. I'm going to finish it. Then I can think again."

"Good idea. Since I slaved over a hot stove for you."

Laughing, she speared another bite of her lunch. Then she sat still, vowing to keep Nathaniel Montgomery at arm's length. It was getting harder and harder. Sometimes she wondered why she should. Then she remembered all the times he'd been rude to her and the distance at which he held people. She wasn't sure he was capable of a real relationship.

He seemed to be attempting small talk when he said, "I see you're back to business suits."

She shrugged. "This is a business meeting. I thought I might feel more businesslike in a suit."

"And?" He took a bite.

"I think it helped put me in the right frame of mind." She finished her tea and stood. "More?" He pointed at the fridge, so she went over and refilled her glass. "I've gotten very casual lately. I'm not used to being that way."

"Vintage clothes are naturally casual."

"Actually, they aren't necessarily. Some things from the past are quite formal."

"If that's the case, remember Alaska is a very casual place. You'll fit in just fine."

"I've noticed that, and that may explain my transformation." She sat down with her glass of tea. "Atlanta likes to dress up more. But maybe that's my perception through the corporate lens." The excitement for what she had to talk about today bubbled up inside her. She forced it down so Nathaniel could finish his lunch. When he'd taken the last bite of his salad, she said, "You asked where I got the idea for this business."

Nathaniel held up his hand to stop her. "I have dessert. You'll want to hold off a few more minutes." He got up and went over to his fridge, returning with bowls filled with shortcake topped with raspberries and a dollop of homemade, freshly whipped cream. She might not cook, but Jemma knew the good stuff when she saw it. She took a bite from the bowl he set in front of her. "More deliciousness. I'm going to gain weight eating like this."

"You'll work it off in that garage of yours. Speaking of the garage, you do know it's uninsulated, so you won't be able to work there during the winter, right?"

She nodded as she spooned up more of the shortcake. "I've thought of that. I can do fabric projects inside. I've also thought of having a workshop attached to my store. That would be ideal."

"We'd have to ask a commercial real estate agent if anything like that is out there."

Jemma paused with her spoon in midair. *We?* A warm feeling flowed through her. Part of her wanted to argue that he shouldn't be stepping so deeply into her business. Another part, the part that won the battle, felt relieved that she no longer walked the business road alone. Nathaniel Montgomery was right beside her. She gasped and almost choked on her dessert. Reaching for her tea, she took a long drink. He was walking beside her in the best definition of a *business* consultant.

As soon as she'd taken her last bite, Nathaniel lifted the dish from in front of her. "You gave me your business plan earlier. I need to create the website for you, so knowing where you got your business idea will help me at the very least with the About page.

She studied him, looking to see if a sneer lurked underneath the question. He hadn't viewed her business in a happy light before, but he seemed to be kinder about it since he'd started working with her. At times he was charming and likable, but this could be *his* business mode. He accepted her business at face value because she was a client. She liked the idea that he didn't treat it with scorn, but she also wanted him to be genuine.

He ran his fingers through his hair. Wouldn't he make beautiful babies? The image of a toddler with his dark, wavy hair and green eyes popped into her head. *Don't go there, Jemma.* This was a man who had proven time and time again that he wasn't nice inside. Even if he'd been nicer lately, she had to remain wary of him in case his beauty was truly only skin-deep.

Taking a deep breath, she pushed personal to the side and shifted to business. "I'd known for three or four years that the career I had would never make me happy, and I wanted to have my own business. There aren't any entrepreneurs in my family, but that's what I wanted to be. As I said before, I'd come home after a long, sometimes very long, day and have fun pinning projects I'd like to do on Pinterest. When I began to notice from my pins that I loved the *idea* of turning an old piece of furniture into a useful, new, often fun, thing, I put paper down on my condo's deck and spent two weekends reworking my childhood head-and footboards into a bench."

She grinned. "I had fun, and the bench was so cute when I finished it that three different friends offered me money for it. When I put in seventy hours at work in each of the next couple of weeks, I thought back to the fun I'd had and started to wonder if that could be my business." She leaned back in her chair. "You know the rest. Great-aunt Grace left me a house, I wanted to change jobs, and here I am."

"In Palmer, Alaska, drinking sweet tea, talking about that very business."

"And doing my best to fall in love with Alaska."

His brow furrowed. "You don't like Alaska?"

Jemma wondered if the two of them should move this far from business. Why not? She'd met people on the hike, but she hadn't taken the time to connect with them again—outside of Nathaniel's party—so she still didn't have any friends here other than family. "It's stunningly beautiful. Gorgeous. The view from my front porch is awe-inspiring. But I've stepped so far outside of my comfort zone that I can't even find it anymore. Here I am, starting a new business, striving to meet the goals on my plan in a hurry, so I'm working every second I can, and yet I also need people."

Nathaniel watched Jemma smile as she ended her sentence, but there was something behind her words and her smile. And she thought *she* was outside of her comfort zone? Having a personal conversation and having it slip into needing people was something he didn't have any reply to. He felt most comfortable by himself. But being with her did make him surprisingly happy too.

He jumped to his feet, knocking over his glass of iced tea, rescuing it before the liquid could pour onto her lap. As he sopped it up with his napkin, thoughts raced through his mind. He felt comfortable being around Jemma, even talking to her. He'd felt comfortable being with her family. He'd spent years in therapy after his dad had left; his mother had made him go. In the end the therapist had said he'd do okay, and eventually he'd be happy to be with people again. That had happened, after all these years, with Jemma.

He might have a friend. But to say that a conversation about that subject went way over the line between business and personal would be a massive understatement. Backing away, he said, "We need a way for you to have time to relax and still succeed. I hope I can help." He gave his pleasant business smile, the one he knew calmed clients down. "Now, let's get down to serious business. I thought of one thing I'd like for you to do if you haven't already. I mentioned photos of your furniture before. Are you taking photos of it?"

"Yes. Before and after photos. With the hope that one day I'll have time to post them online, either on a blog or social media."

"Excellent. Print out those photos and bring them to every event. Let's see if it sways people if they can see more of your work. Of course with some, it might be best not to mention that it used to be a wreck." He smiled to soften his words.

They spent the next hour talking about colors to be used in all marketing materials. Jemma liked blue and yellow. Nathaniel suggested making them faded, more vintage-looking colors, and adding brown to ground them.

"I'm going to build your website myself and do your design work. I have the skills, but my business has gotten to the point that I generally have a graphic designer handle that portion so I'm freed up to work on other aspects of the marketing. Unfortunately, my graphic designer and I parted ways Saturday night."

"The night of your party? Ah, the woman in black."

"I need to hire someone who understands that I don't want a personal relationship." Here he was, having another intimate discussion with Jemma. What on earth had happened to him?

"I'm glad I know the truth." She rushed her next words, probably because she felt uncomfortable about such a personal subject. "So I didn't have the wrong idea about you. I know it's silly to many, but I actually want to like and respect my marketing expert, and anyone I associate with for my business."

Nathaniel leaned back in his chair. He agreed. "I think that's it for now. I had thought about showing you some options for your website, but I learned some things today that will change the direction a bit, so I'll do that later this week." He stood. "About what you said earlier . . . I love living in Alaska. You aren't happy here?"

When she didn't immediately answer, he realized he shouldn't have brought up the subject again. "I'm sorry. We're business associates, and that was personal."

"No. It's okay. I've tried not to think about it, to just focus on the business. It's probably a good idea to tell someone other than Holly." She sighed. "We visited Alaska several times when I was a kid. We went fishing and camping, did fun kid things. I hadn't come here since I got out of high school so I didn't have a grown-up take on living here."

"Do you have anything in mind to help you fall in love with this great state?"

"The trip to Matanuska Glacier I told you about."

"Right. I'd forgotten about that." At least he'd tried to forget about it. He still didn't know what had made him suggest going.

"The trip isn't cheap—nothing like that is—but I'm trying to bond with Alaska. A guide takes us out on a glacier, and we walk on it." She grinned. "I chose the trip randomly, but it sounds fun. And very Alaskan."

"It sounds like a nice trip. A little—"

"Touristy? I know."

Nathaniel once again felt his lips moving and words coming out of his mouth before his brain engaged and stopped them. "Why don't I drive you around instead? Show you some of my Alaska?"

As he considered how to take back those words, she said, "But you aren't from here either."

He laughed. "Jemma, a huge percentage of Alaskans aren't from here. We come to Alaska and fall in love with the state. Some of us, like me, stepped off a plane for a vacation and never wanted to go home. I came for a ten-day trip, and knew that first day that this would be my forever home. I went back to Seattle just long enough to pack up and move to my new home, Alaska."

"Well, that's such a nice offer that I hate to say no. A glacier does sound awesome, but it will be better right now to save the money. I should pay you for gas if you're driving me around." She bit her lip and watched him, maybe waiting to see if he'd grow three heads since his words were so different from those in the past. "And I don't want to take you away from your work."

He thought about it for about two seconds before deciding. There was something about Jemma Harris that made him jump in with both feet and help. "We'll avoid a lot of the crowds if we go on a weekday, and working for myself, one day is pretty much the same as another. I know I don't have any appointments on Thursday. Let's spend the day enjoying Alaska. If you can take the day off."

Jemma stared at him, not saying anything. Right when he expected her to tell him no thank you in no uncertain terms, she said, "I think I'd like to do that. I'll work Saturday instead. I probably would have anyway. Where are we going?"

Now it was his turn to stare dumbfounded. Where *were* they going?

"I'll make that a surprise. I know I want to get an early start, maybe about six o'clock."

Jemma's eyes widened. "Do you make good tea?"

"Yes, I do."

"Bring me some. You're going to want to pour some tea into me if you expect me to be awake that early."

The next morning, Nathaniel leashed up Chloe and went out the front door. Going up the road toward the highway, he worked off some of Chloe's energy and thought about Jemma's business. He needed something unique, something eye-catching that would bring people to her. Nothing flashy, because she wasn't, and it wouldn't fit what she was doing. Coming up dry, he purposefully moved on to something else, hoping an idea for her would come to mind if he didn't work so hard at it.

His grandmother's call still haunted him. He wasn't a little boy who could guilt his mother into staying single. She was an adult, and more than fifteen years had passed since the fateful day when she'd asked his father to move out. After years of unpleasantness, she'd had enough, no matter what promises his dad gave to clean up his act. She deserved happiness. Maybe a card that said he was thinking of her would be a nice touch. He'd pick one up at the store when he went to town and drop it at the post office to get it on its way.

As the image of the card came to mind, he froze. He envisioned a postcard with the sort of words you'd have on a "thinking of you" card—with Jemma's logo and address on the back. When he went to take a step, he almost fell. Chloe had wrapped her leash around his legs. After getting her untangled, he hurried toward Jemma's house to tell her his idea and ask if she'd thought of anything new overnight. He could, of course, e-mail or call, but he always preferred the personal touch with clients. It just wasn't usually so personal that said client lived across the street.

Still overflowing with puppy energy, Chloe needed to walk more before she'd sit still long enough for them to do more than say hello. Nathaniel turned back toward the highway, and a car passed him with two little girls waving at the back window. By the time he went around the curve to his house, the girls were running in the front yard, and Chloe wanted to join the fun. She dragged him over to them, and they squealed in delight.

"Can we take her home with us?"

Nathaniel fought a surge of panic. He squatted in front of them. "Girls, I think we need for her to grow bigger before she's ready to live with anyone else."

"Are you sure?"

"I am. You may need to wait awhile for a puppy of your own."

When Abbie's eyes filled with tears, Nathaniel quickly added, "But I can bring Chloe out for you to play with her sometimes when you're here."

Abbie wiped the tears away and beamed at him, showing him she'd inherited her smile from Jemma's side of the family. Chloe chose that moment to roll over, and he showed both girls how to rub a dog's belly, something he'd just learned himself. He glanced over at Jemma's house. Maybe instead of telling her the idea, he'd bring the printed cards and show her. This project would be hard to describe without having the visual in front of her.

Jemma and Holly watched through the screen door. Holly spoke first. "He's gorgeous and great with children."

Jemma sighed. "He is." She continued watching him.

"Hold it! You told me you weren't falling for the neighbor, the Jerk, Mr. Grouch."

"Of course not. But he is easy on the eyes, and he has his nice moments. I think he has some baggage from his past that he needs to offload before he's ready for any kind of decent relationship."

Chapter Eleven

True to his word, Nathaniel had a thermos of tea waiting for Jemma when she got to his SUV Thursday morning. He also had that ruggedly handsome look going on again, with his faded jeans and plaid flannel shirt, this time one in red and black. Before she could climb inside, he asked, "Do you own a camera?"

"Sure. The digital SLR I use to take photos of each of my projects."

"Great. I didn't know if you were using your phone or tablet. Go get it. I think you'll want some quality photos of where we're going."

She hurried off and came back with her camera. After she'd stepped into the vehicle and closed the door, he handed her a homemade breakfast sandwich he called an egg Montgomery muffin. She unwrapped hers and bit into it when they pulled onto the highway. "Oh, my. So much better than the ones I drive through and buy."

He turned and raised one eyebrow, but didn't say a word.

The man had probably never been near a fast-food restaurant. Not with his cooking skills.

"How did you know I needed breakfast?"

"Seriously? You groaned when I said I wanted to pick you up early and warned me to have tea. I'm just happy you got up early enough to take a shower." He grinned.

Jemma reached a hand to her still-damp hair. "I thought you'd rather I didn't smell like paint and stain." When stopped at a light, she poured a cup from the thermos. After another bite of the sandwich and half a cup of tea, she started to feel human. "I wondered if you'd bring Chloe."

"No. I'm teaching her how to act in boats by having her sit in my canoe in the garage, but I think there's still too much puppy in her. The woman who cleans my house every week moved it to today, and she's going to spend some extra time doing a deep clean so Chloe will have someone to let her outside. They've met before."

She now knew Chloe would forever be with Nathaniel. The care he'd taken with the puppy touched her heart. He was such a mess of contradictions. She took another bite of her sandwich. "So, Mr. Montgomery, where are we going?"

"I thought about heading up the Parks Highway to Talkeetna, or even just going nearby to Hatcher Pass." Carefully driving—he seemed to do everything that way—he bit into his sandwich.

"Not going to either one of those?"

He swallowed. "No. I wanted to give you a truly unique Alaskan experience, to immerse you in Alaska."

Jemma stopped eating. "This isn't going to be dangerous, is it?"

"It shouldn't be."

"And I am going to enjoy it, right? I mean, that's the whole point of this trip."

He took a sip from the cup of tea she'd poured him. "I guess I should ask one question: do you like to be in boats?"

She shrugged. "I haven't been in very many, but I don't have a problem with being on the water."

Nodding, he said, "Excellent. This is a bit long for a day trip, but neither of us can spare more than that. We're taking a trip today that you will enjoy—I'm going to be positive about it—and I know for certain that you will never forget this place."

"Your hopes for the day might be hard to live up to."

"I'll ask tonight if I succeeded."

As they pulled out onto the Glenn Highway, he put on music. "Do you like Bach?"

"I have no idea. I enjoy classical music, but don't know one composer from another."

A few minutes later, Jemma felt her eyelids growing heavy. She yawned and forced her eyes to stay open as they left Palmer behind and rolled into the less settled area, all of it beautiful. The always raging, wide Matanuska River, the same river she regularly crossed in Palmer, stretched to the right of the road.

"How long of a drive is it?" As soon as the words left her mouth, she chuckled. "That sounds like what Abbie or Ivy would say." Leaning her head against the window, she yawned again.

"You seem tired."

"I wanted to finish a project before I took a day off. I don't even know what time it was when I turned off the sewing machine. I trudged upstairs and fell onto the bed." She turned toward him. "Then an alarm clock, which I had the foresight to set earlier, woke me at 5:30."

"We have a two-and-a-half-hour drive ahead of us. Take a nap."

Jemma shook her head. "Huh-uh. Then I'll miss the whole trip and ruin the day you have planned for me."

"The real trip is what we find when we arrive. Besides, it's Alaska in June, so it will be light later, and you can see the same scenery when we drive home."

"True." She leaned her head against the window and felt her eyes close, opening them when she heard a turn signal and felt the vehicle turn left. "Where are we? You aren't an ax murderer taking me to my final destination, are you? In movies, a killer usually takes victims down deserted roads, and I don't see another car." She glanced around them at the wilderness that extended as far as she could see.

"Not . . . an . . . ax . . . murderer," he choked out, his laughter growing until he had to fight the wheel to keep going straight. Wiping his eyes, he said, "Jemma, thank you. I haven't laughed that hard in . . . well, I don't remember when." He cleared his throat. "To answer your question, I have never noticed any ax-murdering tendencies in myself, so I think you're safe. This"—he waved his hand at the area around them—"is the road to Lake Louise. It's in good shape, and it won't be long before we arrive."

"I think I can assume your surprise is at Lake Louise?"

"Yes and no. You'll have to wait to see the full surprise."

When she opened her mouth to ask more questions, he held up his hand. "I couldn't do this justice with words, so I'll have to show you why I brought you here." Smiling, he added, "And don't worry. There are no axes involved."

When they pulled up in front of a beautiful lodge, Nathaniel went around to the back of his SUV and popped it open, hauling out a small backpack and a cooler. "You may want to come inside with me and use the restroom. You won't find another one that flushes out there." He grinned as he pointed at the surrounding area.

Jemma nodded. "That sounds like a very good idea. I used an outhouse once when I was a kid and don't want to repeat that experience if I can avoid it."

He laughed. "An outhouse is pure luxury when the alternative is bushes."

They entered the lodge and Nathaniel pointed her toward the restroom. When she came back out, he stood in the entry.

He asked, "Ready for the adventure?"

"I'm curious about what can be near here that we can go to in a day, and is *better* than this."

She walked beside him as they left the lodge and went down a slight incline to the water's edge. The landscape differed from anything she'd seen before. The lake stretched in front of her for what seemed miles. Trees and brush lined the shore on the edges she could see. "This is stunning. You're saying this isn't the surprise?"

"This is Lake Louise. There's more. Now we get into a boat." Nathaniel ushered her over to a dock. "One of my clients mentioned he had a boat here that I could use if I wanted to. I never took the time off before, but he was happy to loan it to me today. I thought I'd better let the lodge owner know so no one would think I was helping myself to someone's property."

He stepped into the boat first, then held out his hand to assist her into a boat with two bench seats across. After pulling out a life jacket for each of them to put on, he sat at the rear, started up the motor, and pointed the craft to the left across the lake.

Jemma was grateful that she could see the shoreline. It seemed like they were going to land the boat, but a narrow stream opened in front of them, and Nathaniel slowly took them in. When they came out into another lake, this one narrower but stretching open in front of them, she felt like she'd stepped into another world. "Thank you for my surprise! It's beautiful here."

"This is Susitna Lake. We haven't arrived at your surprise yet, Jemma. I've only been to our destination once, but I've never forgotten it."

Jemma marveled at the landscape streaming by them as they plowed through the water and up the lake. They saw an occasional cabin, and she guessed she might see another boat on the weekend, but today they were alone. Time seemed to stand still as they continued. The lake narrowed, and they seemed to jog to the left. Then the waterway widened again, but it was different, shallower perhaps, since there were areas of lily pads.

"Now we're at Tyone Lake."

They continued for a short distance more until Nathaniel pulled the boat up on the shore, got out, and helped her onto land. She felt like they were the only two people on Earth. The quiet was broken only by the rustle of a bird taking off from a bush. Nathaniel seemed to belong here. Did she? Would she ever feel she belonged?

He moved to stand beside her and waved his hand over the surroundings. "*This* is Alaska. A nothingness, stillness, sense of awe and wonder. Alaska."

Jemma slowly turned in a circle as she took it all in. "I see what you mean. I've only been in places in Alaska you could drive to, and most of those right off a highway." This was a moment out of time, a place she wouldn't forget no matter the location her life took her.

"It's my opinion that to truly know Alaska, you have to leave roads behind. You had a taste of that on our hike, but you weren't far enough off the beaten path to get away from people. I've tried to describe this feeling to someone from the Lower 48, but they don't have a point of reference. You have to work very hard there to find a place that leaves you truly alone, with vast open nature surrounding you. Notice how quiet it is."

At that moment a small plane flew overhead and he grinned. "With the occasional airplane. It is Alaska. Relax and take off your life jacket." Nathaniel set his down, then pulled the cooler out of the boat, opened the backpack, and took out a blanket which he spread on the ground. Before he sat down, he also pulled out binoculars and checked out the area.

Jemma took photos in every direction. There was such a sense of space. She settled on the blanket, feeling like a cross between a queen being cosseted by her servants and an early explorer.

"In Alaska we can start the day in civilization and move as far away from it as modern mankind can. Today we began in small-town Palmer, but we could have just as easily come from big-city Anchorage with a short drive more. And now, we sit here in God's country."

Nathaniel spread a picnic in front of her. She would always remember this day, the view, the lunch—homemade salmon salad sandwiches, a brownie, and more sweet tea.

"Did you make the food?"

He said, "I can't take credit for the brownie. I didn't have time for that. But I made the sandwiches from a salmon I caught last month."

She stared at the sandwich in her hand. It certainly tasted good, but . . . "Last month?"

He grinned. "I froze the leftovers."

"I'm glad, because I'm enjoying it."

Every once in a while, Nathaniel stood, studied the area around them with the binoculars, and sat back down. At first she thought it might be because he'd been sitting for so long. She knew she felt like stretching her legs too, but when he kept doing it, she started to wonder. The next time he stood, she got up too. "You're doing that because . . . ?"

"I was concerned that we might not be alone out here."

"I don't see another boat, in fact, nothing else that indicates other people are anywhere near us."

Dropping the camera strap over her head and putting the life jackets in her hands, he shouted, "Run for the boat!"

Jemma froze for a few seconds. Then she forced herself to start running. When she leaped into the boat, Nathaniel was just a step behind her. He threw the blanket he'd carried under an arm and the cooler he'd grabbed by one handle onto the floor of the boat and pushed it into the lake, jumping in as it started to float again. As he pulled the cord to start the engine, a massive brown bear raced onto the shore near where they'd been.

Jemma put her hand to her chest and felt the camera. She lifted it and started snapping photos. This would be once in a lifetime, for sure. Her heart raced, but she took a slow breath. "At least we're on the water, so he can't get us."

"Have you seen photos of bears standing in a river, fishing for salmon? They aren't afraid of water."

The engine caught and the boat began moving as Jemma's heart went into overdrive. Grateful, she saw the bear stop at the exact place they'd been sitting on their blanket and eat the half of a brownie she'd dropped. The animal watched them move back up the lake.

Nathaniel looked over his shoulder. "That was a fairly good-sized brown bear."

Jemma sat still in her seat, wondering if she should scream, shake, faint, or laugh. Laughter won. She giggled, the sound seeming to startle Nathaniel.

"Are you okay?"

She tried to stop giggling, but couldn't. "Yes." She gulped air. "I think this is just my reaction"—she wheezed—"to almost being eaten by a bear." She gulped air again.

"We weren't in danger of being eaten. I have a feeling he wanted our salmon sandwiches. I had bear spray, so I think we would have been fine."

Jemma let his words wash over her, and her giggling slowed down, at least to the point that she could breathe regularly again. When the words "I think" settled on her, she fought to stay calm and prevent what she felt was imminent hyperventilation.

Nathaniel watched Jemma and wondered if he should stop the boat at the first dock he came to. He navigated out of Tyone Lake and into Susitna Lake. A dock might be private property, but in Alaska, no one would mind if he used it in a medical emergency, and he was starting to think he might have one on his hands. "Jemma," he said loud enough to be heard over the engine, "you're safe. You don't need to worry about bears or anything else."

She nodded, but he wasn't sure his words were really getting through to her. A sense of relief rushed over him when he spotted a dock. Stopping the boat, he tied it to a post and moved forward in the boat until he was right behind her. "It's okay, Jemma." At that moment, he wanted to pull her close, wrap his arms around her to reassure her it would be all right. He stuffed his hands in his pockets.

"Thank you for stopping." She gasped for air. "I think I needed to catch my breath in a place with no bears." She whipped her head around, he was sure to see if there were any bears staring down at her, but it put her face, and lips, close to his.

He leaned back. "Don't worry. I'm watching. We can get out and walk around if you want."

She took a deep, calmer breath. "I can make it now. I don't want you to think Mr. Brown Bear took away my joy in that place. Nothing will ever take away my happy memories of Tyone Lake."

"That's exactly how I felt. This was the first place I felt that. I've been in others now, but this was the first." He moved back to his seat by the engine, started it up, and then headed them toward Lake Louise.

What on earth had come over him? She wasn't a date; she was a business client. And a neighbor he'd have to be around even if the relationship didn't work out. And it wouldn't. He'd never felt emotionally connected to a woman, and always cut ties before she could get hurt. At least he hoped he'd always done that in time.

After the bear incident, he was glad Lake Louise was as

calm when they returned through the channel as when they'd come. He'd heard stories of a wall of waves greeting people and hadn't even wanted to contemplate what that would do to Jemma right now.

Jemma stepped tentatively from the boat onto the dock. "We made it! I want to do a happy dance, but I'm sure people are watching from the lodge."

He grinned. "Probably."

"Okay. Then just hand everything to me."

He glanced at her.

"I won't break. I'm sorry about the meltdown. I've never had that happen in my life."

He passed the backpack to her, scooted the cooler onto the dock, and hefted himself out of the boat.

Glancing once again at the lodge, she put her shoulders back and walked over to his SUV. When they started down the road, Jemma asked, "Have you been that close to a bear before?"

"Almost. Alaska is beautiful, but it can honestly be dangerous too. Sometimes people forget that. It isn't a wildlife refuge. Here, the animals belong and we're the trespassers."

Jemma seemed content to sit quietly, so Nathaniel put on some low-key classical music and drove toward Palmer.

"I missed a lot on the drive here." She pointed at the mountains framing the road.

"It's exactly the same on the way back, so no worries." He felt like he was taking a child on a tour as Jemma pointed out everything she saw. She finally went quiet, and he glanced over at her. She'd fallen asleep again and probably needed it after the bear scare. But she might not be happy if she missed much of the drive. He glanced at the clock. They only had an hour left, so Jemma could easily see this section of road any day.

She mumbled in her sleep and leaned toward him, resting her head on his shoulder. Her hair smelled of coconut—must be her shampoo—mixed with the outdoors. He couldn't imagine a more provocative scent. He should probably stop somewhere for dinner, but he hated the thought of waking her.

When they pulled into his driveway, he nudged her shoulder. "Jemma." She muttered something in her sleep. "Jemma," he said louder, and her eyes blinked open. "We're home."

She sat up, glanced over to his shoulder when she realized where she'd been sleeping, and yawned. "Did I miss anything important?"

"Nothing you can't see another time." He hoped he'd be able to go with her that day too.

"I want to thank you for today. I saw a part of Alaska I'd never seen before, both a new place and a new feeling. I'll keep that with me wherever I go."

An image of Jemma packing up and leaving flashed through his mind. She needed to stay here, and he would be the one to help her see that. He didn't have very many friends, none from adulthood, and Jemma had started to feel like one. "I could hardly leave you to dislike Alaska when I'm working so hard for your business."

She stared at him in a semi-angry way. As he thought back over his words, he couldn't find anything that should have caused that.

"Thank you, again." She got out of the car and crossed to her house.

Chapter Twelve

Friday morning Jemma stepped out her front door and onto a narrow box. Lifting the box, she found a note from Nathaniel taped to it. "Your business card order came in yesterday's mail, but I didn't see it, of course, until after you'd gone home and could have been asleep. Pass these out to everyone who shows even a small amount of interest as they walk by. They're inexpensive." She opened the box and squealed. Running inside, she picked up the phone and called Holly. "Nathaniel's amazing!"

"Excuse me? This voice sounds like it belongs to my sister Jemma, but Nathaniel is the name of the man who annoyed her yesterday."

"Only at the end. I replayed the scene in my mind when I was lying in bed last night—awake for hours as I thought about it—and I'm not sure he said anything that should have made me angry."

Silence greeted her words.

"He's my marketing expert."

"Jemma, is that all he is?"

"Of course! You saw how nice he was during dinner with Mom and Dad. He can be nice. I think he's starting to be a friend. Anyway, stop by my booth today at Friday Fling and I'll show you what he dropped off."

Holly promised to do that before hanging up. Jemma danced through the house, put the box on the dining room table, and removed what she thought would be more than enough cards for the day.

The morning went pretty much as expected, right up until her phone rang. Watching a scene play out in front of her with a screaming child and an exasperated mother, she absentmindedly reached into her purse to pull out her phone as the mother picked up the child and marched toward the parking lot. The number was one she knew well. "Hello, Mr. Morrison. I hope everything is going well in Atlanta."

Her former boss made a frustrated sigh. She couldn't remember hearing him do that before.

"Is Mrs. Morrison okay, sir?"

"Everyone is healthy. I am calling to offer you your job back. With a raise. I know you wanted to be in the management training program, so if you would agree to spend a year with me first and find the right replacement, I will guarantee you are in the program."

Jemma felt like the air had been sucked out of her lungs. A long-held dream lay before her on a silver platter. Taking a deep breath, she glanced around at the other tables and the people slowly walking through in a pace different from her old life. Someone nearby laughed. A woman stopped at Jemma's booth and knelt to examine a table. "I've built a life here, Mr. Morrison. I want to make a success of it."

"I suspected you would say that, but I will not take no for an answer. Not yet. Your replacement has not replaced you. We are conducting a search and do not expect to fill the position for three to four weeks. Please call if you change your mind."

"I'm—" She realized he'd hung up. Her old life had many moments like this. Could she even consider his offer? She leaned back in her chair and stared up at the mountains. No, she couldn't.

About noon, Holly and the girls came by with lunch for Jemma. Her sister's eyes went wide when she showed her the business cards. "You're right. I love the colors and this logo he made for you. He managed to make your business look vintage and cool at the same time."

"I know. With each sale I've felt a little bit more like I'll succeed. Right now, I'm able to believe my business will make it. I had something happen earlier—"

Her sister interrupted. "What? Has Nathaniel done something stupid again?"

She shook her head. Jemma gave her sister a play-by-play of the phone call with Mr. Morrison.

"That's everything you said you wanted. Were you tempted?"

"For a millisecond. I want to succeed in my own business, not go back to a place where others control my work life. Actually, my job controlled my entire life. Working seventy to eighty hours a week didn't leave time for much more. I got excited when I was able to squeeze in my furniture rehabbing a couple of times a month."

Holly took over her booth while Jemma ate her sandwich and talked to her nieces. The rest of the event went pretty much as usual. She sold some things and brought some things back home with her. At least she'd learned to take lighter items when she drove herself.

The next morning Jemma woke up excited about the day, but with a bit of apprehension. She had high hopes for sales today, and Nathaniel had told her he had a surprise for her. She hoped he'd finished her website because she thought it could be good for her business. She'd told people yesterday when she'd handed out cards that her website would be up soon.

He backed his SUV up to the garage, and the two of them loaded first the furniture, then the small things into the back. "So what's today's event? You said this was the next one I should attend, that it was different so it might help with my marketing ideas."

"I have high hopes for it. An Anchorage women's group is having a craft fair. I paid a small fee for a table and will give them 5 percent of the profits for their charity. They're supposed to have advertised it in the newspaper, on the radio, and on social media. I'd love to have a sell-out."

"That must be why we'll barely have room for us inside this rather large vehicle."

Jemma picked up a couple of small things she'd made from bits and pieces and searched for a hole to put them into. Not finding one, she tucked them under her seat. "Perhaps. I like to be prepared. If everything I bring sells, I want to be able to replace the inventory and keep selling."

"You're thinking like a retailer. Good going!"

His praise touched something inside her. She spent so much time on edge, wondering if what she did or was trying to do was right. Every once in a while it was nice to have some validation.

As he drove them into Anchorage, they chatted about the trip to Lake Louise and her business.

"Did you bring the before and after photos?"

"Yes, sir. I try my best to do everything my marketing expert tells me to do."

"I have a couple of surprises today."

"What?"

"I'll tell you one. I have a sign with your company name on it."

Jemma sighed. *Company name* had such a nice ring to it. She pushed aside thoughts of what the sign cost. It wasn't optional, and from seeing the business cards, she knew he'd done a great job on it. "Wonderful. I've noticed that in some places I can hang it behind my booth, and in others I'll have to hang it off the front of the table."

"This will work for both."

"What's the other surprise?"

"The key word here is *surprise*. The other one is best shown once we're there. I think it turned out great."

Jemma was certain he meant her website.

Once they arrived at the craft fair, Nathaniel helped her set up. He swirled ribbons in her business' colors artistically around items on the table and even on some of the furniture. They gave a perfect vintage feel to her booth. Between those and the sign, her area looked both professional and festive. The ribbon wouldn't cost much, but she tried not to clench up a when she once again thought about the sign's bill.

The doors opened, and people began streaming through, everyone here for this charitable event. She quickly sold two small items, a stool, and a wooden box, reinforcing her thoughts about the size of items she brought to events. Nathaniel stood and hovered near the outside of the booth. When a man walked by without checking it out, Nathaniel touched his shoulder, offering him a business card, which he took. These were a great idea, and she knew business cards didn't cost much, so she only felt a little twinge when someone took one.

Nathaniel suddenly placed cards the size of small postcards on the table. She glanced at the stack. The artwork and ribbon tied onto it screamed big money project, the kind of project her corporate boss wouldn't have batted an eye at. Checking under the table, she found a box full of them, and her heart sank. These must have cost her quite a bit, and she didn't have the money to spare right now.

Nathaniel handed one to a woman who had spent a few minutes thoroughly checking out Jemma's booth, including some of the larger pieces.

The woman read one side, flipped it over, and cooed. "What a wonderful idea! Can I take another one for a friend?"

"Of course." As he handed it to her, Jemma wanted to grab it away. She couldn't afford to give people who hadn't bought anything from her even one card, let alone two. After the woman left, and the booth was momentarily empty, Jemma said, "Please explain why you did something again for my business without asking me first." She pointed at the cards.

"Why do you seem angry?"

"*Cha-ching. Cha-ching.* They look expensive."

"Exactly." When she tried to interrupt, he sat down and motioned for her to sit beside him. "But they aren't."

Whatever they cost, they were outside of her comfort

zone right now. She had asked him to help her, though. "I don't want to throw a thousand dollars at fancy promotion materials."

"I've done my work well if something *looks* expensive but isn't. These came in at less than a tenth of that. I added the ribbon myself."

Jemma fought and lost the battle of smiling at the image of Nathaniel working with ribbon.

"I'll show you how to do it, and maybe your sister can come by to help you." He leaned back in his chair and watched her. "As for what you just said about these being expensive, I thought you had enough money set aside to survive for a year."

"Yeah, well, I have a bad idea that my house might need some serious plumbing repairs. Melinda recommended a plumber, and he's coming out next week."

"Ouch. Don't worry about what I've done. Nothing has been expensive. Did you actually pick up one of these cards?"

She shrugged. "No. I figured it's a postcard, and that's a large business card. The ribbon is a nice touch."

Two women approached her booth and looked at a few items. Nathaniel offered the cards. They each read the front and flipped it over. "Thank you!" said one of the women. "I'll definitely use mine." She held up a pillow. "And I'd like to buy this."

With the transaction completed and the ladies on their way, Jemma picked up a card. The front read like a "thinking of you" card. Flipping it over, she found the only advertising was a small logo and her contact information in the lower right corner. Nathaniel had tied a ribbon through holes in the corner so it was beautiful, useful, and would be remembered by pretty much everyone she gave it to. It was nothing short of brilliant marketing.

She began doing as Nathaniel, her marketing expert extraordinaire, suggested and passed out business cards to passersby and postcards to anyone who seemed truly interested. When the woman he'd given two cards to earlier returned with a friend to see the larger pieces of furniture, Jemma held her breath.

"I love this"—she pointed at the most expensive piece Jemma had brought, a small corner hutch she'd spent a ridiculous amount of time painting with tiny leaves and vines in golds and dark greens—"but—"

Jemma deflated in a whoosh. This couldn't be good.

"I need it in different colors for my house. Do you make custom furniture?"

Did she make custom pieces? Jemma decided in a heartbeat. "Yes, I do. But each of these is a transformation from a vintage piece, so it won't look exactly the same. Why don't you tell me what you like about it, and if there's anything you don't like, I should know that too."

The woman pointed, and Jemma took notes on a notebook she'd brought not for this purpose but for any marketing gems Nathaniel imparted. As they talked, Jemma became more and more confident. "I'm sure I can make something you'll love."

The woman beamed. "I'm so glad. This hutch is stunning. When will mine be ready to pick up?"

Again Jemma paused for a heartbeat. "As long as I can find the right hutch to convert, a month should be fine. It might be sooner. I will need half down, though, if you don't mind."

"Martha," the woman's friend asked, "I love this exactly as

it is. It sounds like yours will be so different that no one will know we have something similar, don't you think?" Her eyes pleaded with her friend.

The woman, now identified as Martha, something Jemma immediately noted in her book, smiled. "Feel free. I might have to pick up that tray, too. And maybe something else." Pursing her lips, she put her finger over them and considered Jemma's display.

Jemma bustled around, gathering the items the women chose, bagging the smaller pieces in turquoise bags, which Nathaniel pulled from under the table, a higher-end extra she'd never considered. He was good at this. When they asked if they could take a few of her "thinking of you" cards to their friends, Jemma didn't hesitate. She knew Nathaniel had a home run and hoped this was enough to take her business over the edge.

She slanted a glance at her neighbor. He'd moved to stand in front of her booth and was handing out her business cards. As he handed one to a woman, he looked up for a moment, and she felt warmth move though her body down to her toes. She sighed, then caught herself. *Jemma, don't you dare even consider falling for this man! He doesn't have a warm and fuzzy side. He won't ever let you get close.*

Knowing her instincts were right, she pushed the warm fuzzies away and decided she felt gratitude for his marketing skills. Certain she was right, she continued working and crouched down to check out the pieces she'd kept to the side for later. Adding a few, she moved things around to fill in the gaps resulting from the women's purchases.

Nathaniel proved her earlier decision about distance between them right when he mentioned a dinner he was going to tonight—and said he'd managed to find a date for this one! Whew, her heart had a near miss there.

A short time later, the day took an unexpected downturn when she almost came to blows with one of the event's attendees.

A man stopped in front of her booth and looked from side to side before saying. "This is junk. How did you get into this show with junk?"

Jemma took a deep breath. "Sir, this is my craft. I rework old things into new things."

He scoffed. "Junk is always junk."

Jemma could hear similar words coming from Nathaniel.

"This"—the man pointed at a lamp—"is probably something someone gave you when they *didn't* sell it at their garage sale."

Her mouth dropped open. How could anyone be so cruel?

Nathaniel stepped forward. He probably agreed with the man. Maybe she could sneak away and avoid the ugliness that was sure to occur in a few seconds.

"You're right, sir." He smiled broadly at the man.

Jemma considered ripping the smile off Nathaniel's face.

The man was caught off guard. "You agree it's junk?" His expression seemed to add, *But you're sitting at this booth.*

"I know the process each of these pieces goes through." Nathaniel shook his head. "Much of it begins as something that should be hauled to a dump"—he leaned closer to the man and dropped his voice to a whisper just loud enough for her to hear—"and stays that way for quite a while."

The man stood tall, knowing he had an ally.

"But Ms. Harris spends hours, sometimes days, transforming each of these items into a work of art." He gently pulled on the man's elbow. "Let me show you what I mean." Nathaniel then talked in detail about the piece she'd been working on when he'd last visited. And she hadn't thought he'd paid any attention to what she was doing. "So you see, each of these is unique and special when she's finished with it. All of the fabric pieces are handmade, so there's attention to detail throughout."

The man nodded. "I can see that now. Once I stepped closer, I could tell my wife would like that." He pointed at a bench Jemma had made elegant with metallic gold painted trim and a crushed velvet seat sewn from old drapes, Scarlett O'Hara–style.

While Jemma stood by, too stunned to move, Nathaniel took the man's money and helped carry the bench to his car. Shaking her head slowly, she watched them walk away. Nathaniel had turned straw into gold.

The clock, her Alaska clock, was ticking toward cold weather and the time when her business could make it through a long winter. Or not. This sale, the earlier custom job, and the order from the designer gave her hope that people could like her things and be willing to pay for them, enough people that she'd succeed.

Chapter Thirteen

Nathaniel savored his dream as he woke: he was lying on a sandy beach with waves gently lapping against his cheek. When a wave crashed over his face, he opened his eyes, sputtering. Chloe stared at him from beside his pillow and swiped her tongue across his cheek. Standing, he headed across the room and down the stairs to let her out, rubbing at his cheek. Not waves. Dog spit. That would have really grossed him out not long ago, but this dog was clean, so he figured it must be okay.

Taking the steps, he once again went over his conversation with Jemma about his *date* Saturday night. What had made him say that? The word conjured up images of romance, but that couldn't be farther from the truth. His date was an interview over dinner with a promising graphic designer, one he learned was not only happily married but also had three children ages twelve through sixteen. He'd learned years ago that casual interviews worked better because eventually most people relaxed and you saw them as they truly were, not just the interview persona they put on. By the end of dinner at a non-romantic chain restaurant, he'd decided to give her the small job of a client's business card. He suspected she'd be able to handle it with ease, then move on to more complicated jobs. And the help couldn't come too soon.

When he neared the garage door, he changed his mind, deciding to first pop out the front door and grab the newspaper so he could read the headlines while he stood out back with Chloe at the end of her leash. He opened the door and had just taken a step outside to pick up the paper when Chloe shot by him, down the steps and up the road.

"Chloe!" he called. "Come back here right now."

Instead of turning around as he'd expected, the puppy kept going.

"Chloe! Here, Chloe!"

She vanished out of sight. Scrambling, he grabbed some shoes out of the coat closet and ran after her. Once around the curve, he stopped. "Chloe!" There was no answering bark, no rustling in the brush. Just the whooshing sound of a few cars on the highway.

He turned slowly in a 360 but saw nothing new. "Chloe!" He ran up the road into the subdivision, slowing to a fast walk as he looked from side to side, hoping she'd stopped to catch her breath. When he found nothing, he turned back toward home, went inside for his keys, and hopped into his SUV.

He drove slowly, hoping for a glimpse of a golden puppy going around a corner or up a street. An hour later, he returned home and walked around the outside of his house, calling her until he was hoarse. Finally, he sat on his front step, head in his hands, and a tear fell, first one, then another, and soon it was as though a dam had burst. He hadn't cried when his father left, when the divorce was finalized, when his grandfather passed away two years ago. Now, he couldn't seem to stop crying.

"Nathaniel?"

He felt a gentle touch on his arm.

"Can I help you?"

He shook his head and rubbed his face, hoping to remove signs of tears. Gulping, he tried to focus on the step in front of him. Focus and push all other thoughts and emotions away. He could do that. He was a master at pushing emotion away.

"Chloe ran away," he rasped in his hoarse voice, but in a measured tone that removed all emotion, at least it would have if he hadn't sniffed at the end.

"Tell me what happened," Jemma said in the same gentle tone he'd heard her use with her nieces.

"I went out to get the paper, the door was barely open, and only for a few seconds. She shot out the door and up the road." He described everywhere he'd gone looking for her.

"Okay. Let's go inside." She helped him up. "I want you to go upstairs and get dressed."

He glanced down and realized he was still wearing his pajama bottoms with no shirt, and he had on running shoes with no socks on his feet. Upstairs, he pulled on jeans and grabbed a T-shirt out of his closet, one he'd been given at some event or another. If—no, *when*—they found Chloe, she might be muddy or wet.

Downstairs, Jemma waited with a mug of coffee in her hand, so she'd found his emergency stash of high-end instant coffee. He started to feel human again about halfway through the hot drink.

"I remember you saying the vet keeps track of strays. Did you call him?"

Nathaniel pulled out his phone and got the vet on the line. Nothing. He fought against tears again as he pushed the phone back into his pocket.

"Hand me your keys, and we'll look for her some more. You had to drive and look. This time you can focus on watching for her."

This sounded like a plan he could get behind. "Thank you." He took a deep breath. "Let's go."

They spent two hours cruising around Palmer, everywhere he could think of within a few miles. They didn't see a single stray. When they pulled into the garage, he leaned his head back against the headrest. That little dog had charmed him, and he didn't want to have to live without her. Climbing out of his SUV, he went outside and called, "Chloe!" one more time. He could hear Jemma calling from over by her house.

"Come over here, Nathaniel!" she shouted from beside her garage.

He raced over there. "Did you find her?"

"*Woof.*" The brush rustled.

Jemma stayed beside him as he parted the alders, revealing Chloe caught in the brush again, almost in the same place where they'd found her the first time. She was muddy but didn't seem injured. Jemma pulled on one side of the branch while he lifted her out and sat down on the ground with her in his arms. Holding the puppy tightly to his chest, he said, "Don't ever leave me again, Chloe!" The puppy replied with a lick across his cheek.

* * *

Laughing, Nathaniel got to his feet with Chloe in his arms. Shifting her to his right side, he wrapped his left around Jemma and hugged her. "Thank you for helping me."

When he leaned back slightly, Jemma looked into his eyes, and he pulled her close for a kiss. Nathaniel's lips touched hers and her toes curled as she sank into his kiss. Pressed against him, she felt his heart racing to match hers beat for beat. When he put his fingers into her hair and deepened the kiss, a *yipe* from Chloe pulled them apart.

Jemma tried to make eye contact with Nathaniel to see what he felt, but he seemed to be looking every direction but hers. "You might want to take her to the vet to make sure she's okay."

"Good idea. You drive again and I'll hold her."

They got into his SUV, and Nathaniel held the puppy close.

She slanted a glance toward him, feeling the heat rise in her cheeks. Now that she'd had time to think about it, she had to admit kissing him was pretty terrific. What did it mean? Did it mean anything at all? Or would he have happily kissed any woman who was standing there when Chloe came home?

The vet pronounced the puppy healthy but dirty, and they came home. As Jemma pulled into the garage, Nathaniel clipped on the puppy's leash, then stepped out and set her on the ground. He stood there shifting from foot to foot as Jemma climbed out of the SUV and came over to him. "Jemma, I was so happy to see Chloe that I did something I shouldn't have. I apologize for kissing you. I hope you won't hold it against me."

Jemma stared at him. An apology was not what she'd expected. "No worries. Friends?" She held out her hand.

He stared at it for a minute, then clasped it for just a second. "Friends. That sounds good." He reached down to rub Chloe's ears. "Let's get you inside, get a bath and have a nice meal. You must be exhausted."

As Jemma turned to go home, she had to admit to herself that while an apology sat at the bottom of her list of things she thought might happen when they got home, a passionate kiss or two sat at the top. She'd thought of Nathaniel from the beginning like one of Alaska's many mosquitoes. She kept swatting at it, and it still came by for another pass, if only to annoy her. If he truly was a friend, she had to like him, right? Maybe a kiss was okay between friends.

Jemma's phone rang as she stepped onto her front porch. Pulling it out of her purse, she answered and learned the plumber was on his way. And how had she managed to forget that? She pushed away the little voice that said, *Nathaniel's kiss.*

The man quickly arrived and set to work checking out the house's plumbing. Jemma took inventory in her garage while he did that, sorting through what she had and what she still needed. She might be new to owning her own business, but she wasn't new to being organized, something she knew made a huge difference in her life. As she made notes, she considered what items to shop for. An auction late this afternoon—she checked the time on her phone—might get her some deals that would make up for at least some of the plumbing bill. The notice had mentioned a houseful of furniture, and she needed a hutch to rework for her custom order and some other pieces for the interior design company.

About ten minutes into her project, the plumber sought her out.

"That was quick. You didn't find any problems?" Jemma held her breath as she awaited the answer.

"The opposite. I'll have to take apart quite a bit of the plumbing in the kitchen and bathrooms. Some of it's original to the house, and what isn't is decades old and a little oddly done. It might have been a homeowner who did it himself thinking plumbing's easy." He smiled to soften his words.

Her dream might be vanishing before her eyes, or she should say, going down the drain. Hiding a nervous chuckle with a cough, she held her head up high and asked, "Do you have an estimate of the cost?"

He quoted her a figure that took most of her savings. Once she'd given him half down, he went inside to begin the job, saying he'd work from room to room so she'd have a usable bathroom most of the time.

Jemma's choices for the future evaporated on this pretty summer day. She now had to make it before the cold weather arrived or get a full-time job. She couldn't go through a whole winter otherwise. And who knew what else the house might need? She'd hold on to enough for a plane ticket and apartment fees so she could return to Atlanta this fall, or wherever her next job took her.

Chapter Fourteen

Nathaniel leaned back on the couch and stared out the windows at the backyard with Chloe curled up at his side, soundly sleeping off yesterday's journey. What had he been thinking to kiss Jemma? Sure, he'd been relieved, excited, happy to see Chloe, but he'd never kissed someone for a reason like that before. He expected panic at the thought of those emotions to strike him, but it didn't. It felt safe to be near Jemma, but maybe that's what friendship meant, a safeness.

Of course, her lips had been soft and she had felt good in his arms; well, arm, since the other had held his puppy. He couldn't come up with a decent reason why he'd done it, other than he'd wanted to. And he wanted to kiss her again.

Chloe made a sleepy sound and rolled over. By returning to him, the puppy had shown she trusted and loved him, both emotions he'd been short on as an adult. Thinking about Jemma left him confused; the puppy was something he could handle. Chloe enjoyed being in his backyard and in Jemma's fenced yard. He pulled out his phone and searched for fencing companies, checked reviews, then called one and set up an appointment for someone to come out and give him a quote. Reaching over, he petted Chloe. This puppy had worked her way into his heart from day one. Looking back, he could see it happening bit by bit.

It felt good to love something and have it love him back.

Thinking about love reminded him of the people who loved him, his mother and grandmother. Should he call his mom, or wait for her to call him? He strummed his fingers on the couch arm. Going upstairs, he left Chloe to sleep. After working for a while, he stretched his arms in front of the window and noticed a plumbing truck in Jemma's driveway. When a man stepped down from the back of the truck and carried an armful of pipe inside, he groaned. She'd been hit with the dreaded plumbing bill, and judging from the fact that the man was already returning to his truck for more materials, he guessed the bill would be a few cents short of the national debt.

After evaluating the contents of his fridge and freezer, he left his house and crossed the street to her workshop, aka garage, which had loud sounds emanating from it. Glancing up from her work, she grinned and set down the power tool of the moment.

"The garage seems more full than I remember."

Jemma nodded vigorously. "I really scored yesterday."

That could certainly be misconstrued.

Obviously forcing a smile, she added, "I got some great deals at an auction. They partly make up for—" She pointed at the plumber's truck.

"Big job?"

Jemma rubbed her arms as though she was cold on this sunny day. "I'm a little overwhelmed right now. Let's just say it was twice what I'd thought, and about twenty times more than my best-case scenario."

"Has he started on the kitchen?"

"He said he should be able to complete one bathroom and start on the kitchen today."

"Since you can't cook—"

She cocked one eyebrow. "That was a given."

He chuckled. Having a sense of humor at a time like this was a good thing. "Rewording. Since you won't have clear access to your kitchen to defrost and cook or reheat something, I wondered if you'd like to have lunch with me and Chloe."

The grin this time spread from ear to ear.

He hoped she didn't read more into this than he meant. "As friends and neighbors, of course."

"Of course. And it doesn't matter what you cook. I'm sure it will be delicious."

When Jemma finished her meal and pushed back her plate, she sighed. What this man could do with a piece of meat and a few vegetables. "That was, as always, wonderful." She stood and gathered their plates. "I'll do the dishes."

"You're my guest."

"No, I'm your friend, and friends don't mooch off friends. I have to do my part."

His phone rang as he opened his mouth to protest again. Checking it, he saw his mother's name and picture on the screen. She'd called to tell him.

"Mother! How's everything in San Diego?"

"I'm at the airport, on my way to Alaska to see you."

He wanted to say, "Great!" as he usually would, but knew from his grandmother's call—nay, warning—that this visit had a purpose. "Will you be staying long?"

She sighed. "Nathaniel, I have to tell you something, something you don't want to hear."

"Okaaay." Was this somehow worse than his grandmother had indicated? Maybe a man with a record or something equally nasty?

"I'm bringing a man with me, someone I care about."

"You're an adult, Mom. That's fine with me."

"You don't remember your father before he became addicted to alcohol. He was a good, kind man and an excellent father. I loved him dearly and haven't found anyone like him in the last fifteen years."

"It sounds as though you have now. Congratulations, Mom!" His mother sounded happy, so he was happy. He smiled in Jemma's direction and gave a little wave as she finished putting dishes in the dishwasher. Silence lingered so long he checked his phone to see if the call had dropped. "Mom? Is something wrong?"

"Actually Nathaniel, everything's right for the first time in a very long time."

"Good," he said cautiously. Something told him there was a big *but* here and that he might not like it.

"Your father contacted me about a year ago. He stopped drinking a decade earlier, hasn't had a drop since then. He started a construction company about five years ago, and it's thriving."

Nathaniel remained silent. His father's history shouldn't have any bearing on his mother's present situation.

"We got together every once in a while just for old time's sake, and after a while we both admitted we're still in love with each other."

He gasped.

"Haven't you ever wondered why I never remarried? Never had a lasting relationship with another man?"

Nathaniel felt ashamed to admit that he hadn't. She was his mother, and he never saw her as a normal woman, and particularly not one who was still in her prime.

She continued, "I didn't want another man in my life. Your father is the only man for me."

"Okay. I understand you, I think. So you're seeing Dad"— he choked the word out—"on a regular basis."

"Your father and I remarried last week. I thought it would be easier on you if it was done and you didn't have to think about the what-ifs. We'll arrive in Anchorage late tonight and would like to drive up to see you in the morning."

Nathaniel gasped for air.

Jemma hurried over as he started to see stars. "Breathe, Nathaniel."

He sucked in air. Jemma pushed his head onto his knees. Somehow, she knew what he was going through. He could hear his mother's voice in the distance. He breathed deeply and managed the words, "I'll see you then" before setting the phone on the table. Resting his head in his hands, he wondered what he should do.

"Nathaniel, are you okay?" Jemma sat in the chair next to him and scooted closer.

He sat up again and leaned his head back. "Yes. You aren't going to have to do any emergency medical treatments. That was my mother."

"Bad news?"

He gulped. "The worst." He blurted out, "She remarried my father."

His childhood poured out, stories he hadn't shared with anyone, some not even with his mother or grandmother, about his father when he'd had too much to drink. "The saddest thing of all is that I remember him before he became an alcoholic. He was a great dad, and even after that time he was a good man—when he didn't drink. But I trusted him less and less. Finally when I was fifteen, Mom had enough one morning and told him to pack his things and be gone by the time she got home from work. He was, and I haven't seen him since."

Jemma stared at Nathaniel. Here she'd had an idyllic childhood, and he'd had nightmare after nightmare. Today's news about her plumbing seemed insignificant. Expensive but a blip on her radar that would be unimportant years from now.

"I'm surprised he never contacted you."

"I didn't say that." A forlorn expression crossed Nathaniel's face and made *her* feel like crying. "My father sends cards for my birthday and Christmas. He writes letters. I just—"

"Don't open them."

"I remember who he was, Jemma." He stood and paced back and forth across the room. "I don't want to see him again. Ever." He leaned his forehead against one of the tall back windows.

"While that's certainly your right, and you have good reasons for that, I have one question for you, though: do you want to have a relationship with your mother?"

He paused. "Of course, but—"

"Their lives are now intertwined. You can try to stay away from him, even push him away, but that will only hurt your mother. I don't think you want to do that."

He rubbed his face. "I don't want to lose her too."

She took his hand. "Nathaniel, take steady, even breaths. Time is on your side. You can sort this all out in your mind and be ready when the time comes to see your dad again."

He made a strangled sound. "They're on their way," he said evenly.

"As in, coming here?"

"Here." He pointed with his free hand to the floor. "To Alaska. To visit my house. Now. She called on the way to the airport."

"Did she say where they were staying?"

He shook his head. "No. I didn't give her a chance." He gave a sideways smile. "I had a bit of a meltdown."

She smiled back. "A bit. You could ask them to stay here."

"Never!"

She raised one eyebrow.

Exhaling, he rolled his eyes heavenward and tapped his foot. "I don't know what to do. Yes, I do. I want everything to stay the same."

"And yet, few things stay exactly the same forever." She shrugged. "I think that's probably for the best. This one's a biggie, but you're a strong person. You've held up all these years filled with pain. Now you might be able let some of that go."

"Jemma, I don't think I can let them sleep in my bed. That feels too . . . personal."

"You have a beautiful guest room with a private bath."

"I know. The architect said he needed to add a guest suite for future resale. I probably should have fixed it up for my grandmother."

"Let's do it today."

He checked his watch. "Jemma, it's 2 p.m. It's a big, empty room. Carpet and paint are its only accessories."

"They aren't knocking at the door right now. We have time." She moved toward the stairs and started up them. "I'm sure you have a tape measure somewhere. Would you bring it upstairs and help me take some measurements? And bring paper and something to write with." Feeling somewhat bossy, but also that Nathaniel needed someone to take over right now, she took her chances with their budding friendship by adding, "You should call your mom and see what time their flight to Anchorage arrives. Oh, and have them cancel their hotel reservations."

Jemma stood in the corner of the room and pictured what it would look like with a bed in it. She heard Nathaniel speaking on his phone and moving closer.

He tucked his phone into his pocket when he entered the room. "They'd planned to rent a car, but I told her I'd pick them up. In Mom's words, 'We'll be landing at Ted Stevens Anchorage International Airport at midnight. Are you sure you want to drive out there in the dark?' I reminded her it would be close to daylight the whole time." He stood in the doorway. "I cleared my schedule of appointments for the next three days. That part was straightforward, but Jemma, I don't see how we can get this room ready in less than half a day. We have to leave here by eleven to pick them up."

Jemma held the smile inside when she heard him say "we." Apparently she was in this the whole way. And she didn't mind. She liked having Nathaniel Montgomery as a friend. He stood there with an adorable, helpless expression.

"Your house is beautifully decorated. How can you not be good with home decor?"

"I paid a designer. She became a client. This isn't my kind of design work." He slowly shook his head from side to side, each movement seeming to add to his helplessness.

"Okay." She didn't leave him any room to waffle on decisions. "We're going to buy a bed. Do you have rope or straps to hold it onto your SUV?"

He nodded. She grabbed his arm and pulled him out of the room. "We don't have a second to waste. The soft yellow in the room gives us colors to work with. I guess the designer chose that too?"

"Yeah. I approved everything, but she chose all of them." He grinned. "I only argued one point. She wanted to paint the master bedroom a gray so dark it was almost black. She called it masculine. I know gray is in, but I didn't want to live in a cave. We settled on a blue she called 'restful.'"

As he drove to a furniture store he knew of, Jemma went over everything they needed in her mind. Bed, of course, but also nightstands, lamps, dresser, and the room was large enough to have a seating area with a chair or loveseat and another table. She felt like they were standing still. Glancing over at the speedometer, she saw they were going the speed limit, and maybe a mile or two over.

Inside the store they quickly checked out the mattress section. Nathaniel pointed at the least expensive bed, but Jemma said, "We want them to be comfortable, not tied in knots the next morning. We may need to spend a little bit more. Lie down on it."

Nathaniel flopped onto it. Rolling a bit from side to side, he moved his shoulders like they hurt, then got to his feet. "You're right. It isn't very comfortable." Moving quickly to the most expensive bed, he lay down. "Now, this one is great."

She laughed. "I think we can get something in between." The salesperson came over then, and Jemma explained what they needed. The woman took them to a bed. "We sell more of this model than any other. It's comfortable but priced in the middle between the low and high. Try it out."

Nathaniel lay down. "You're right. I can move on this one, and it feels good."

The woman pointed to the other side of the bed. "You should try it too. See how it feels when he rolls over. This model doesn't bounce around as much as the less expensive ones."

Jemma opened her mouth to protest that she would *not* be sleeping next to the man already in the bed. Then she realized they probably did need to know how it worked for two people. Nathaniel seemed larger-than-life lying there. And— she hated to admit it—sexy as could be, even in his usual dress shirt and chinos. Gently lying down at the very edge of the bed, she said, "It is comfortable."

Nathaniel rolled over toward her, something she wasn't sure she wanted. Then she nervously giggled and snorted, which made Nathaniel grin at her and the saleswoman cover her mouth as she almost hid a chuckle. Jemma knew she needed to get over her nervousness. They were in a bed showroom with a salesperson standing over them. To test the bed, Nathaniel had to move on it. He wasn't making a move on *her*.

He asked, "Did the bed move too much?"

"Um, I'm not sure. Let me try." She flopped onto her side in an exaggerated way, staying where she was at the edge of the bed.

Nathaniel grabbed onto the nightstand beside the bed. "Even with that nasty jolt you gave the mattress, Jemma, it did well enough that I say we take it."

Still feeling awkward about the situation, Jemma agreed with him and they both got to their feet. Heading over to pay, he leaned close to her and whispered, "And I pity the man who has to spend time with you slamming the bed like that."

She nudged him with her elbow. "That was a flop test. I'm a sound sleeper. Except for snoring like a chainsaw."

Growing up, her sister had been able to sneak out when she was a teenager, and Jemma hadn't heard her even though her parents had accused Jemma of hiding the fact. Then one day Holly had spoken up and said her sister snored so loudly she couldn't have heard. For a second, Jemma considered mentioning that a future spouse would have to get used to her snoring, but decided against it. Nathaniel might make someone a good husband, but she didn't want him to think she'd be interested in him for that position.

Once Nathaniel had paid for his purchase, a couple of workers strapped a queen-sized mattress and box springs onto the roof rails on Nathaniel's SUV. When they pulled up at his house, Jemma breathed a sigh of relief, glad everything had remained strapped on for their slow drive home. Then she realized their work had only begun. Nathaniel put Chloe in the powder room so she couldn't run outside while they slowly maneuvered the mattress through the garage door and up the stairs.

As they turned the corner at the top of the stairs, for a second Jemma thought they'd lost control and the mattress was going over the balcony. Nathaniel blocked it with his body and pushed it toward the wall.

Jemma held her side. "This mattress is like a giant rubber worm."

"I know," Nathaniel agreed. They shoved it into the guest room and leaned it against the wall. "I'm not looking forward to the other half. I had time to have movers do this for my bed."

With the box spring halfway up the stairs, Jemma commented, "This is better. I think I could *almost* push it up the stairs myself." They rested it against the mattress.

Nathaniel ran back down for the metal frame to support it all, and apparently let Chloe out, because she raced into the room ahead of him and bounded around them as they assembled the frame, then topped it with the box spring and mattress.

They'd worked together well on this because he hadn't had to make many decisions, but she felt like he might be less than helpful today when it came to doing much of anything else. "Nathaniel, if you trust my taste, I can go buy the linens for the bed and some towels for the bathroom, unless you have enough towels from what you use."

"Go ahead and get whatever coordinates. I only need to do this once." With a glazed expression that seemed to reveal he was a man who could manage clients with many thousands of dollars but not decorate a room, he asked, "What about the other furniture?"

Jemma chewed her lip. "I have a solution. We're short on time, and I know a place nearby with furniture that would work. But I don't think you'll like it. You seem to enjoy clean and modern if your house is any example."

He waved away her words. "I don't have time to pick and choose. No one will deliver this late in the day. Where is this store?"

Jemma pointed across the street.

Puzzled, he wrinkled his forehead. Then the light dawned on him. "Great! Perfect. Do you have two nightstands and a dresser that will work?"

"Actually, I do. They don't all match, of course, not with what I do, but they will go together. If the bedding I buy fits with them and the wall color, I think you'll have a nice room. Cozy."

"Vintage Cozy?" He grinned.

She relaxed. Maybe he would be okay with this. "I'll do my best for you." She started to leave, then realized her words might be misread. "I'll do my best for you so *your parents* have a happy experience while they're here."

His expression turned edgy when she said "happy."

She added, "If you want me to, I can be here some, so it isn't so intense between you and your dad."

He sighed. "Thank you, Jemma. It means a lot to me to have you as my friend."

"If you're ready, come across the street with me. We can carry some, and you'll be pleased to learn I bought a hand truck yesterday so we can move the heavier pieces easily. One of the other vendors at Friday Fling was pulling out and selling their supplies for cheap, so I was in the right place at the right time."

"I can't say I'm not grateful. I already had a picture in my mind of dragging a dresser across the street."

When they stepped into her garage, she pointed at the one dresser she had finished. "Take out the drawers to make it lighter."

Giving the dresser an odd expression, he didn't say anything. Instead, he rolled it across the street on the hand truck, pushed it through the house, and the two of them clopped up the stairs with it.

They brought over the drawers and returned for the nightstands. Jemma gave him a choice. "I have three pieces of furniture that could work. Which two do you prefer?"

"Jemma, I have no idea. The whole situation with my father . . ." He shrugged. "I'm letting go here and giving you free rein on the room. Do your best and I'm sure they'll love it. At this moment that's all that matters to me."

Jemma chose the two she preferred, and they carried them over and set them in the room. Once they'd also brought over a bench they set in the corner of the room, Jemma felt like it would all come together nicely.

Nathaniel asked, "Should we get the headboard now?"

"No. I don't have any headboards."

With his brow furrowed, he asked, "I know I saw one over there not long ago."

Jemma nodded in understanding. "You did. It became a bench. That bench." She pointed to the corner of the room. "Don't worry. I'll add something to the wall over the bed to make it pretty."

She headed toward the door. "I'm going shopping now in Wasilla. I'm sure I'll find what I need, and I'll pay for everything. You can write me a check later."

"I have some cash." Nathaniel pulled out his wallet. "I'll be happy to write a check for anything over this."

Two stores later, Jemma had a long list of bedding and bathroom accessories purchased. Shopping with someone else's money was fun. Perhaps a backup career as a personal shopper should be explored.

She noticed a "Help Wanted" sign on the second store's door as she left. Maybe a job working in a department store would make the difference during the winter. At home, she'd work inside on things for next summer that didn't use smelly paint and stain, projects that involved sewing and crafts. With the job and working at home, she might make it through the winter in decent shape *and* be ready for next summer. But the plumbing bill meant she'd have to eat her own cooking to save money, and that wasn't a pleasant thought.

Her phone rang as she put the car in reverse. A glance at it told her she should probably put the car back in park and take the call.

"Hi, Mom."

"Any news about you and your neighbor?"

Jemma laughed. "Getting right to the point, huh? Nothing new." Surrounded by things she'd bought for his house, she wondered if that was completely true.

"I can dream, can't I? You aren't getting any younger."

Jemma rolled her eyes and sought a way to get her mother off the scent of this potential son-in-law when she did it on her own.

"Have you heard from your grandmother?"

Jemma pictured her sweet but feisty grandmother and wondered what situation she'd gotten herself into. "What's happened? Is Nana okay?"

"She's fine, Jemma. Don't worry."

Jemma let out a slow breath.

"At least I assume she's fine. She seems to be missing."

"Missing?"

"You know she calls every week like clockwork, says she doesn't need me to check in, but she always calls. After a week and a half, I called her. When I got no answer, I tried a few of the neighbors, and one had seen her leave with a suitcase. Another one said she's taking care of her houseplants while 'Mattie's away.'"

"Oh no." Jemma remembered the last time this had happened. Nana had spent a month at a mission in South America. Noble idea, but without thinking to tell her family, she had caused everyone to panic. "Do you think she went to Africa to see Bree?"

"That's the first thing I thought of, but Bree says she hasn't heard from her. And Mother knew Bree would be back in the US soon. I called you because she's said so many times that she'd like to spend time in Alaska."

"Well, I haven't seen or heard from her."

Her mother sighed. "I guess I'll just have to wait and see if she contacts us. She isn't really old at seventy, or feeble. Even so, I'd like to be sure she's safe."

When they ended the call, Jemma was concerned about her grandmother but relieved her mother had dropped the ball about Nathaniel.

Pulling into his garage twenty minutes later, she glanced over at her open garage workshop, and the many pieces of furniture in it seemed to be mocking her. As she climbed out of the SUV with a couple of bags, she muttered, "Don't give up yet, Jemma Harris. You can still beat the clock on your business."

Jemma knocked on the door from Nathaniel's garage to his

house first then opened it and stepped inside. He stood there, obviously waiting for her, holding Chloe in his arms.

Jemma set the bags down and ruffled Chloe's ear.

He said, "A fence company I called came while you were gone and gave me an estimate. It seemed reasonable, so I told them to go ahead, and they're starting tomorrow. I don't need something else going on"—he gave a sideways grin—"but I don't want her to run away again."

"Hold on to her. I'll be back with another load."

When she'd brought in four loads of bags, Nathaniel asked, "Should I be worried?" He pointed to the pile she'd deposited on the floor.

"Maybe. I admit to having fun with your money."

He laughed. Setting Chloe down, he hugged Jemma tightly. "Thank you for making me laugh today of all days."

When he let her go, Jemma wanted to pull him closer again. Maybe have another of those amazing kisses he'd given her. *Push the thought away, Jemma. He wants to be your friend.*

Upstairs, Jemma went to work putting the room together. She pulled the sheets out of their package and handed them to Nathaniel. "I think sheets feel nicer when they've been washed, so please put these in the washer."

When he came right back and hovered near her, she knew she had to give Nathaniel something else to do. He seemed more and more nervous as the minutes ticked by.

"Didn't you say you're taking time off while your parents are visiting?"

"I don't think I have a choice."

"I'm sure you must have something business-related that you need to do before they arrive. Maybe e-mails to send, phone calls to make?"

As he considered this, a slow grin spread over his face. "I'm acting like a child underfoot, aren't I?"

"Maybe just a little bit." She held her thumb and forefinger close together.

"I do have things I should do. I'll have to take some time every day to work, even when they're here, so maybe I should clear out everything I can. I'm leaving you to this. You obviously have a knack for it."

With the bedding lying on the bed just waiting for the sheets, she started on the bathroom, pulling out a glass jar she filled with cotton balls and a couple of decorative heart-shaped ceramic accessories she thought newlyweds might appreciate. Bottles of shampoo, conditioner, and shower gel in the shower, along with a bar of soap, finished that area. The room was almost ready for guests. She hoped the guests were ready for all this visit entailed.

Chapter Fifteen

At the airport Nathaniel stood at the gate with Jemma beside him. She'd offered to stay with his vehicle and pick them up outside, but if ever he needed a friend, this was the moment. Seeing her in dress pants and a blouse, both from this decade, he knew she'd dressed up to meet his parents.

Faces he didn't recognize came one after another. Then his mother appeared with a man at her side, a man who must be his father but had changed from a young dad into a dignified-looking fifty-something with gray temples and glasses.

Nathaniel stared at them when they stopped in front of him. Jemma nudged him with her elbow. He'd have to talk to her about doing that.

Stepping forward, he hugged his mother. "It's good to see you, Mom." Then he hesitated at his father. How did you greet a man you should be close to, should know better than anyone other than yourself, but that you hadn't seen or spoken to for more than half your lifetime?

His father extended his hand for a handshake. With tears in his eyes, he said, "Nathaniel, it's good to see you."

When he took his father's hand, he felt years slip away, but he wasn't transported to the bad years. He went instead to the earlier, good ones. He said, "It's good to see you too." And he meant it.

When standing there became awkward, Jemma took over. "Well, let's go find your luggage. Coming to Alaska even in the summer requires bulky clothes, so I'm guessing you didn't come with just a carry-on."

His mother blinked and for the first time seemed to notice the woman at his side, something that was rather amazing since his mother had been trying to get him married off or at least find him a serious girlfriend for the greater part of his existence.

She smiled at Jemma. "I'm Deborah Montgomery. Again." She gave one of those special newlywed smiles to her new husband, one that made Nathaniel cringe. "This is my husband, Charles. You are?"

"Jemma Harris."

His mother glanced over at him with raised eyebrows as if waiting for him to announce Jemma's role in his life. "Mom, she's my neighbor and my *friend*." He emphasized the last word so she wouldn't instinctively put the word *girl* in front of it.

"Oh, Mother told me the nice old lady who'd sold you the land passed away. You must be her—?"

"Great-niece. Yes, ma'am."

His father yawned. "Long day. Nathaniel, why don't you get your car and pick us up outside of the luggage return area."

When he started to protest being ordered around by a man who had no right to do that, he saw a tentative smile light his father's eyes, and the man yawned again. "Yes, sir."

Walking away, he realized his father had probably been under tremendous stress all day worrying about meeting him again. Nathaniel could choose at any time to reject his father, but his father had to wait for either rejection or acceptance from his son.

He heard Jemma say, "Let's go downstairs. It's a pleasure to meet both of you. Nathaniel has told me so many good things." Leave it to Jemma to shine a good light on the situation. He had said good things. He'd also said bad things, but those remained silent for now. He knew they'd have to come out eventually. He just hoped they could get through the next few days without any ugliness.

Jemma stood beside Nathaniel's parents, waiting for their luggage.

"There!" Mrs. Montgomery pointed at a pink leopard-print bag. Grinning, Jemma snagged it off the belt as it went around.

"Thank you, dear. I could have gotten it."

"I know, but I was afraid that man might take it." She gestured toward a senior citizen toting a solid black piece of luggage away, probably the last man on earth to mistake her luggage for his.

The older woman stared at him for a moment, then grinned. Laughing, she said, "I like you. Are you sure you aren't going to be my daughter-in-law?"

She grinned back. "We're friends, Mrs. Montgomery. We started out hating each other's guts, so it's an improvement."

"Then there's room for me to hope. Please call me Deborah and my husband Charlie."

Jemma wasn't sure she liked the extra layer of familiarity, but she had to use the names his mother suggested. Standing on the other side of Deborah, Charlie pointed out his luggage, a rugged piece in tan leather that must have cost quite a bit, making Jemma wonder what the man had done since he'd cleaned up his act. Come to think of it, she didn't know anything about his earlier career either. She directed them to Nathaniel's SUV, and he helped them load their luggage in the back. When Jemma started to get into the backseat, Deborah directed her to the front. "You sit next to Nathaniel. I'll probably doze." It was her turn to yawn. "You make such an attractive couple."

When Nathaniel gave a loud sigh as Jemma sat beside him, Jemma couldn't help smiling. His mom was working as hard as her mother. She was very glad her parents had returned to Tennessee, because she'd hate to experience having them all in the same room together doing the marriage push. Deborah did rest her head on her husband's shoulder and sleep. He jostled her awake when they pulled into Nathaniel's garage. When Jemma got out of his vehicle, she figured she could go home.

Nathaniel stepped next to her and whispered in her ear, "Help me get them settled for the night, Jemma." His eyes pleaded with her. He'd have to see his mother and father in the morning. The least she could do would be to see them to their room for the night.

When he reached for the doorknob, he paused. "I forgot to mention something. Remember Chloe Carleton from elementary school?"

Deborah answered. "Of course. She was a nice girl. With those big, brown, puppy-dog eyes, she was adorable."

Jemma grinned. He hadn't shared the reason for his puppy's unusual name, but now she knew.

"I've kept in touch with her mother over the years. Christmas cards exchanged every year, a wedding announcement"—Deborah gave him an expression that probably meant she wanted to send out wedding notifications for him—"that sort of thing."

"I remember her too," Charlie spoke up. "Didn't she have a crush on you?"

Nathaniel sighed. "It was embarrassing to have her follow me around the playground in the first grade."

Jemma heard a scratch at the door. "She's waiting for us."

Deborah's brow furrowed, much the same way she'd seen her son's. "But she's married. And I'm sure I remember children, multiple children." Her eyes widened. "Nathaniel! You haven't run away with a married woman, have you?"

When barking sounded through the door, Jemma opened it and Chloe shot out into her owner's arms. He held her close and stood. "Let's take you outside for a late night walk, *Chloe*." He grinned as he leashed her up.

"Shame on you for making me think that." Deborah shook her head. "Lead on, Jemma."

Jemma took the Montgomerys to their room. When they stepped inside, Deborah immediately stopped. Panic surged through Jemma. Had Nathaniel gotten his design style from his mother? Was clean and lean what she would have chosen? "But this is wonderful!"

"Thank you." Jemma sighed. "I'm happy with how it turned out."

Charlie turned to her. "Did you decorate it for him?"

Deborah's speculative glint returned.

Jemma felt heat rise in her cheeks. "I own a company that makes the furniture you see. Because of my design background, your son asked if I would put this together today."

"Today? You did all of this today? My mother had mentioned his lack of a guest room, but I assumed he'd taken care of it before now."

"No, ma'am. If you'll excuse me, I'll go home." She pointed across the street. "I know there's a hungry cat over there."

Nathaniel added blueberries he'd picked and frozen last fall to a coffee cake and slid it into the oven. Exhaustion had made everyone choose to go to bed early the night before. Even so, he had lain there for hours trying to sort out his emotions. The man staying down the hall was his father, a man he had loved and worshiped as only a child could. When things had turned ugly, he'd hated him with all the vengeance a teenage boy could conjure up.

Now a grown man who had made his share of mistakes, how did he see him? How did he reestablish a relationship with him? Did he even want to?

Somewhere around midnight or one o'clock, Nathaniel must have nodded off. And now he stood here making breakfast, waiting for his parents—plural—to come downstairs.

"Coffee. I smell coffee." His mother said from halfway down the stairs, his father beside her.

"Ha! You sound just like Jemma in the morning, only with her it's tea."

He knew he'd made a tactical error as soon as the words left his mouth.

His mother paused on the stairs, and she gave a meaningful glance to her husband. Suspicions that they'd spent time
talking about him and Jemma were confirmed when she said,
"Mornings with the neighbor, hmm? I told you, Charlie."

"Mom, I've taken her to events as her *marketing consultant.*" He left out the part about Lake Louise. That seemed
more personal. "She always wants tea first thing. Here." He
poured her a cup of coffee and added cream. Then he looked
at his father, but couldn't remember how he drank his coffee,
or even if he did.

"Black."

Nathaniel nodded. "I have a coffee cake in the oven and
will get some bacon and eggs on in a few minutes."

As soon as they'd finished eating, Nathaniel leashed up
Chloe, who had patiently waited for her walk, with the incentive of bites of food his father thought he sneaked to her.

"Why don't you drop off some coffee cake with that nice
Jemma? I'm sure she'd appreciate having breakfast brought to
her."

Uh-huh. Subtle his mother was not. "I'm sure she had
some toast or yogurt or something like that for breakfast."

"You know what she has for breakfast? I thought you just
covered the tea part for her?"

"Get those ideas, *all* of those ideas, out of your head. I
guessed she'd have something easy. She can't cook. Her sister
tells horror stories of cooking attempts gone wrong."

"Then how do you know *when* she eats?"

He pointed toward the front of the house. "Look out the
window and you'll see. She's usually at work in her garage
early." He silently added, *Sometimes too early to be using*

power tools. Now that he thought about it, she had gotten better about early morning noise lately. "But I think you're right. Jemma would like some coffee cake for a break, so Chloe and I will drop it off on our walk."

He ignored his mother's satisfied smile as he put some on a paper plate, added a plastic fork, and covered it.

His father said, "Nathaniel"—every time he said that, it sounded strange because the man had *never* called him by his full name when he was a kid—"thank you for inviting us to stay with you. That's a very nice room Jemma made."

"Yes, sir."

His mother got a strained expression on her face when he said those two words, but he wasn't sure why.

"Jemma's talented. I still have some reservations about her products—I won't lie about that—but they do seem to be well received."

His mom spoke. "I think your dad and I"—she emphasized the word *dad*—"would like to drive ourselves around this area. Could we borrow your vehicle?"

His father had an expression that said, "We do?" but he nodded agreement, which made Nathaniel like the man a little bit more.

Nathaniel handed the key to his father, saying, "If you have any questions about where to go, give me call." Once his parents had gathered their things and left, Nathaniel leashed up Chloe, headed for Jemma's garage with the coffee cake, and told her his mother thought she'd enjoy it. Though she did seem pleased to receive the treat, she cautiously said, "You know your mother's matchmaking."

"Gee, really?" He grinned. "She's gotten more assertive about it since I turned thirty a couple of years ago."

Chloe tugged on her leash.

"I wish I'd had that much time before *my* mother started her push. I think it was about twenty-seven, with no one serious on the horizon that did it. Now, with thirty looming this winter . . ."

"We'll resist them together."

The puppy tugged on the leash again.

"Just a minute, Chloe. Jemma, my parents are out driving around today. Anyway"—he scraped his foot in the gravel on her driveway, feeling like a sixteen-year-old asking a girl out for the first time, but it wasn't a date if they were friends—"I know you're going to Friday Fling soon, so you're busy today. I wondered if you'd like to come with us on Saturday. We're taking a picnic lunch to Eklutna Lake. It's a short drive and beautiful. Would you like to come? Then we're having dinner at my house. It will help to have someone on my side there." Having her nearby took his stress level about his father down about a million notches. Just thinking she might say yes about today had already dropped it.

Jemma chewed her lip and looked around her garage.

Following her vision, he realized she had work to do and a short time to do it in. "You're busy. Don't worry about it. Let's go, Chloe."

"No, wait. I want to come, and I think I can finish up most of my projects today. My hesitation is that I'm wondering if I should invite you to my house for dinner after the trip, you and your parents." Before he could issue the protest she saw him about to speak, she added, "I'll pick up food. Fear not." Jemma grinned. "I thought it might help to be in a different location. You will have been in close quarters for days." She picked up sandpaper and rubbed it on a painted picture frame, making it, to his eyes, look terrible, but he suspected she was creating a piece other people would like.

"I think Mom and my father would like that."

Stopping her sanding, Jemma gave him a look he didn't think boded well for the next few minutes of his life. "I've noticed you call your mother Mom, a term of endearment. You call your father just that, or sir. Neither sounds endearing."

This wasn't a conversation he wanted to have. "Jemma, the man did some things I've had trouble forgetting."

She threw the sandpaper to the side. "You're awesome!" she said with enthusiasm.

When he started to take her words as a compliment, he realized her narrowed eyes told a different story. "Why am I awesome?" He suspected she was about to say something he might not want to hear.

"You've never done anything someone has needed to forgive you for." She grabbed a small bottle of paint and started spreading it on the frame.

He hesitated. "I never said that."

Jemma pursed her lips. "No, I think you did. Your father, for whatever reason, went through a bad time starting, I'd guess, at about the age you are now. It must take sheer will, grit, and determination to overcome alcoholism and build a new life, yet he did it."

"You weren't there. You don't know what it was like."

"You're right. I don't. I only see a man who has worked hard to win your mother's love and who wants a relationship now with his adult son. What if something happened to him tomorrow? Or the plane went down Sunday? How would you feel then?"

"I want to like him. Inside there's a part of me who wants a relationship with his father, wants to love him and to be loved."

"Build from there." She picked up the plate he'd brought and sat down on a crate that, knowing her, she probably planned to transform into something else. "Now, about tomorrow, vintage or not?"

For a second he wasn't sure what she meant. Then he noticed she was back in her decades-old overalls and another bright top from another century. "Be yourself. Whatever makes you comfortable."

"I'm finishing up my special orders, those for the designer and the customer we met last weekend. The truck rental place isn't open Sunday, so I've rented a truck and will pick it up Saturday. Then I'll deliver everything early Monday." She stood and rolled her shoulders. "Would you have time to help me load things tomorrow before dinner? All of the paint will be dry by then."

The garage was stuffed with furniture. "All of this?" He waved his hand in front of himself. It would take hours to get everything she now had in her garage into a truck.

"No. Just these." She pointed to a corner of the garage that held about seven or eight things. "I went to an auction at a house where the owner had great taste." A worried expression crossed her face. "I spent a lot of money, more than I'd planned to spend on inventory this summer, but I didn't want to walk away from these treasures. That stunning table over there"—she pointed to the farthest corner—"is a genuine antique. I'm planning to find an antique store that does consignment. If it sells even close to what it should, the table alone will make up for spending the rest."

"Then I'd be happy to help. I would have helped anyway, but I wouldn't have been as happy about it."

"Great! And I'll be ready for our picnic tomorrow. Do you want me to make something?"

When he paused for second, wondering how to gently tell her no, he realized she had her cheeky grin. "Thank you for your kind offer Jemma, but no. It might be better if I take care of it."

"Tell me why I'm in a canoe." Jemma anxiously looked at the lake, the shore, the sky, trying to find what, he didn't know.

Nathaniel shook his head. "While I gathered everything from the garage that I thought we'd need for the day—ice chest, charcoal for the grill, etc.—Mom wandered around. When she saw the canoe hanging there, she asked if we could bring it. I said, 'Sure,' thinking that was easy to do, and if she wanted to go out in it, I'd be happy to take her. I brought the small outboard motor so she wouldn't have to paddle. You saw the rest."

"I saw you put the canoe in the water, your mom start to get in, then say I should see if I liked it. Now I'm scared spitless in the middle of a lake."

"I'm as confused as you are. It all happened so quickly. This has to be another one of her efforts with matchmaking in mind. Maybe she thought we should have fun together."

"Are we having fun yet?" Jemma shifted her weight to the right, and the canoe tilted that direction.

Nathaniel quickly pushed off the water on that side with his paddle, stabilizing the craft. "Jemma, have you ever been in a canoe?"

"Huh-uh." She shook her head vigorously from side to side and the canoe wobbled.

"Stay centered. I know that sounds very Zen, but I mean don't lean to one side or the other. Canoes aren't as easy to tip over as people think, but they will if you test them."

Jemma nodded, slowly this time. "Is the water deep?"

"Deeper than you are tall. After that, it probably doesn't matter."

"Cold?"

"A glacier melts and feeds the lake."

"Answers that question. You know what you're doing, right?"

"Yes. You're safe. And you're wearing a life jacket." He didn't mention that cold water made being in the water a challenge even if you were floating.

"I'm going to do my best to calm down and enjoy the ride."

He watched her roll her shoulders and scan the horizon. She *was* trying.

Nathaniel said, "I'm going to shift from paddling to the motor so we'll move a bit faster."

"Good idea."

He set aside his paddle and turned toward the motor, switching it on. As the canoe propelled down the long, narrow lake, movement on the mountain beside them caught his attention. "Don't move abruptly, but turn to your right and up, and you'll see mountain goats." As she saw the animals, a smile crossed her face and somehow went into his heart. She was a friend, and it felt good to have one again.

When they reached a halfway point, he twisted around and waved at his mother, whom he could barely see sitting at their picnic table. She could apparently see them because she waved back. Watching Jemma sitting stiff-backed, he decided to turn the canoe around. She'd had enough of a ride.

Just after he'd turned the craft, the water kicked up a bit with wind coming off the glacier. He'd been here once when the lake had gone from flat water to waves in minutes. He hoped it wouldn't do that again today. Jemma might never forgive him.

He edged the canoe to the right side of the lake. Jemma had apparently also noticed the growing waves because she sat even straighter, and when she turned her head to the side, he could see she wore the panicky expression again.

"Don't worry. There's a trail that runs the edge of the lake. I'll keep us near it, and we can land if we need to."

She gulped. Jemma Harris didn't back down easily, but she obviously did not love the water as much as he did. He reached down for a plastic container he always kept in the bottom of the canoe and dipped it into water that had splashed into the canoe. When he looked up and emptied the water over the side, he saw his mother now stood at the shore. She must have noticed the winds kicking up and become concerned about what she'd instigated.

Nathaniel decided his passenger needed a diversion. "This lake is always beautiful and pristine—it's actually a major source of water for Anchorage—but I've enjoyed coming here in the winter. Picture the lake frozen and still."

"I like that image. Have you been up here then?" Jemma turned to look at him and he paused, not letting her see the full container of water he held just below the gunwales, the top edge of the canoe.

"Several times. I've come here to cross-country ski." She

turned back, and he dumped the pail of water, quickly dipping for another as the water level in the canoe rose.

She waved at his mother. "You know, Nathaniel, I don't want to upset your mother, but I hope she doesn't keep trying to push us together."

"I hear you. I'll say something in a nice way. She means well."

"My parents too. Back on the more pleasant subject of a still and frozen lake, I'd like to come here then. I was reading about snowmobiles the other day."

"You can use them here, but I don't own one."

"I think I hear a "yet" in there. Is it on the list of toys you'd like to have?"

He laughed even as he bailed the canoe. "Definitely. There are several things I've become interested in while in Alaska."

"I know what you mean," Jemma said quietly, so quietly he could barely hear her over the wind and waves.

Minutes later he landed the canoe onshore. Hopping out, he helped Jemma step onto land, where she immediately folded up and sat down, hugging her knees. "I think I'll wait for my land legs to come back."

"It's all my fault." Nathaniel's mother crouched in front of her. "Are you okay, dear?"

"Yes, ma'am. And I'm certain I'd be better with some chocolate."

"A woman after my own heart. I happen to have a chocolate bar in my purse for emergencies. Dark chocolate okay?"

"Always." She glanced over at Nathaniel.

Nathaniel cleared his throat. "Mother, Jemma and I are grateful for the time we had on the lake, but maybe you shouldn't have tricked us into it. The beautiful nature—"

"Terrifying water-filled nightmare," Jemma muttered.

"But beautiful?" the older woman asked.

"Yes, ma'am. But if you don't mind, I'd like that chocolate and then to go home."

That night when Nathaniel and his parents arrived at her house right on time, as he always was, Jemma the party hostess was on duty and greeted them smiling. Things weren't all sunshine over at Nathaniel's house. She sensed tension between him and his parents, or at least between him and his father, and that didn't bode well for a happy evening. If she couldn't lighten the mood, she'd have to pass out antacids with the dessert.

"Thank you for inviting us, Jemma." Deborah sniffed the air. "Um, Nathaniel tells us you've bought food from a restaurant. It does smell delicious."

Jemma grinned. She liked this woman. "Yes. I did, and they do make delicious food." She named a local restaurant, and Nathaniel seconded her opinion. "I have appetizers, so let's sit down for a few minutes and enjoy them."

Nathaniel glanced in his dad's direction and took a seat across the room. His father's hurt expression told more of the story. Nathaniel obviously hadn't listened to her advice. If anything, the situation had escalated just since their picnic today.

"Deborah, could you help me in the kitchen?"

As soon as they were out of the men's hearing, Jemma asked, "I don't want to intrude, but I would like to know what happened?"

Deborah shook her head. "I don't know. I've gone over and over it in my mind."

Jemma stared out the window over her sink, watching Chloe run around, chasing a squirrel. "I believe they would both like to make things better before you leave tonight. I have a plan. But things might get worse before they get better. Are you interested?"

The older woman nodded once. "Let's heal this rift. I want my men to talk to each other. Love can come later." She seemed close to tears. "At least I hope it will."

Jemma unwrapped the rest of the meal, a roast turkey-and-dressing meal, and handed two platters to the older woman. "I ordered a menu reminiscent of Thanksgiving for a reason. Knowing this occasion, I'd already planned to start with a few words about being thankful. I'll build from there."

Deborah's determined expression told Jemma she also planned to get this resolved tonight, or heads might roll.

As they entered the dining room, Jemma leaned over and whispered in Nathaniel's ear, "Please be nice."

He glared at her in a not-too-pleasant way and said, "It's easy to see solutions for someone else's life, isn't it?"

She knew when she was being baited. "Yes, it is! Thank you for noticing."

His dumbfounded expression told her she'd hit the mark, and maybe he'd calm down a little.

When they were seated, Jemma spoke. "As I mentioned the evening that Nathaniel had dinner here with my family"— she glanced over at his mother—"in an underhanded match-making event, I use this large table as my desk and craft work center, so I've had to go to some effort to clear everything off for this dinner. I hope everyone enjoys their meal. Since the combination of turkey, dressing, and cranberry sauce always reminds me of Thanksgiving, I thought everyone should take a moment to say two things we're grateful for. I'll go first. Family and friends. Deborah?"

"Two things, huh? I'll break it down further: Charles and Nathaniel. Son?" She turned toward Nathaniel.

Jemma watched him turn to his dad with his face filled with all of the sorrow from his childhood. Had she pushed him too far? He looked from her to his mother and father. "I won't say this has been easy, but after the last couple of days, and seeing how happy my mother is, I know I'm grateful for my mother and father."

Nathaniel stood and held out his hand to his father in the ages-old sign of male bonding. His father stood, taking his hand and holding it for a minute. "Dad, every time you say, 'Nathaniel,' it feels strange. Wrong, even. Please call me Nate." Then he reached out and awkwardly hugged his father, who Jemma could see had tears in his eyes.

"Thank you, son. Nate."

At the exact same moment, the barrier she'd held in front of her heart slipped away, and Jemma felt her heart sink. She'd done the impossible, fallen in love with Nathaniel Montgomery, a man who probably could never love her back. His mother watched her with a satisfied expression as Jemma struggled to put a blank look on her face. Could the woman read minds?

The two men stared at each other with equally vulnerable, raw expressions. Then Nathaniel turned toward Jemma, pleading. If she guessed his expression correctly, it was time to move on. What did one say at a moment like this, a pivotal turning point in a family? She pushed aside the emotions she did not want to explore and focused on the present, opting for humor instead of seriousness. "I've had occasional issues with microwaves and overcooked food, so you may want to eat this now before it gets cold."

Laughing, the men sat down, and everyone started piling food on their plates.

At the end of the evening, Jemma bid Nathaniel's parents good-bye, with his mother hugging her and saying, "Until we see you again."

Jemma liked this woman, but she shouldn't expect more than her son could give. "You do understand that Nathaniel and I are neighbors and friends, nothing more, right?"

His mother simply smiled and said, "Yes, dear."

Watching them cross the street to Nathaniel's house, Chloe in tow, Jemma wanted to take back her emotions, take back what she felt for her sometimes impossible, sometimes sweet and charming neighbor. Panic surged through her. What did you do when you fell in love with someone who would never love you back? He'd helped her fall in love with Alaska, but no one could be clearer on his views about human love and permanence than Nathaniel Montgomery. Then again, she'd thought this evening could go badly, but he'd done the right thing and taken a big step to healing the rift between him and his father.

Chapter Sixteen

Jemma checked the time when she got home. Nine o'clock. She could reassemble her work area in the dining room and finish up sewing some simple projects for Friday Fling.

Humming to the pop music she had on, she stitched another seam for the bench cover she was working on. Pounding on her door made her leap to her feet. She heard, "Jemma! Jemma!" before she pulled the door open.

"Is something wrong?" Nathaniel had just driven his parents to the airport in Anchorage. She reached out and touched his arm. "Is it your parents? Are they okay?"

He pointed, and her hand went to her chest. Smoke poured out of the eaves of her garage's roof.

"I called 9-1-1 as soon as I saw the smoke. I hope they come quickly."

She took a step toward the garage, then reeled around. "Key. I've got to get the key to unlock the door. Get the hose." She pointed to the coiled hose connected to the spigot on the front of her house. Reaching inside the door, she grabbed the key and surged off the porch toward the garage. "Everything's in there. My future is in there."

Nathaniel picked up the hose and streamed water onto the garage. As she grabbed the padlock, he threw the hose to the ground and raced over to her, shouting, "No, Jemma! Don't open the door."

"I have to. My whole life is in this garage." She shoved his hand to the side when he tried to pull the key out of her hand and stuck the key into the lock.

Nathaniel swung her into his arms as she started to turn the key and carried her away from the building.

She pushed at his chest. "No, Nathaniel. Put me down! I've got to get in there!"

He set her down but held her tightly so she couldn't move. "Jemma, look closely. There are flames coming out of the eaves. It isn't only smoke anymore. If you open the doors, you'll feed the fire. Right now, we'd better move the truck so the firefighters can pull in here—and so the truck doesn't catch fire too."

Staring longingly at the garage door, she knew he was right. She'd seen that in any number of movies and TV shows, the fire exploding through the open door or window.

"Jemma, we need to hurry. Where are the keys?"

She pointed her thumb at her house. "On the table by the door."

When he moved that direction at the same moment the flame flickered higher, she came back to reality. "I can do it."

"Put in it my driveway so it'll be out of the way and safe."

With her brain feeling as hazy as the smoke-filled air around her, Jemma got the key and moved the truck. When she threw the door closed behind herself, she saw that the flames had risen higher and sparks now flickered into the sky, like the aptly named fireflies they'd had in Georgia, blowing around in the slight Alaskan breeze.

From Nathaniel's driveway she saw the fire engine pull up, blocking her view of the garage. Men jumped to the ground and fire hoses were uncoiled and hooked to the fire hydrant at the end of her property, something she'd barely paid attention to before this moment.

She hurried to the front of her house and noticed the breeze blowing sparks toward it. The firefighters saw that too, because one turned a hose on her house as others moved toward her garage.

A ladder thrown against the side of the building soon had a man with a chainsaw on it. Part of her wanted to call out over the chaos and stop him from damaging her roof. A slightly hysterical laugh coming from her mouth caught her off guard. She stepped away from the smoke and sat on her front lawn, watching the men work. As the ladderman cut a hole in the roof, the flames licked out of it.

One of the men came over to her. "Miss, I'm the fire chief. What do you have in the garage? A vehicle?"

"No. My car isn't here right now. I moved a rental truck." She pointed toward Nathaniel's house, and the man's gaze followed her direction.

"Good. Gasoline is, as you'd imagine, quite combustible."

He watched his crew for a minute, shouting commands.

"The garage is my workshop."

The fire chief focused on Jemma with a serious expression. "What do you work on?"

"I refinish furniture."

"Latex or oil-based products?"

"Both. Mostly latex, but there are a few cans of oil-based stain and some oils I used on wood."

"Spray paint?"

"I like to use that sometimes. Maybe six cans of it."

"Back!" the chief called to his team. "Pull back from the building. There are combustibles inside!"

The men immediately did as they were told. Flames surged through the hole on the roof so some of the oil must have caught fire. Larger pieces of roofing flew off the garage and blew toward the house. Jemma watched with her heart in her throat as the firefighters turned the second hose toward the house for a minute, then, when they apparently thought it was under control, back to the garage fire, which seemed totally out of control. The men kept the hose pointed at the building with flames shooting out of the roof.

She had a feeling she'd lost it all. The furniture. The tools. The dream.

Nathaniel sat beside Jemma on her front lawn, watching the firemen wrap the hoses on their truck. Tears streamed down her sooty cheeks. The back wall of the garage stood, the side he could see caved inward, and the front had burned all the way through. When he went over to thank the men, Jemma sat without moving, simply staring straight ahead.

Returning, he tried to find words that would make her feel better. "Everything will be okay."

"You don't have to soft-pedal the facts. Summer is short. This finishes me for the season." Turning toward her house, she sighed. "I've grown to like it here. With your help I seem to have fallen . . ." She paused, causing his heart to make a little leap as he wondered if she would say "for you." Then she continued, "For Alaska."

The fire truck drove off, and she rose and moved to stand in front of the garage. Nathaniel followed her there. A vulnerable feeling surrounded her like the cloud of smoke that had enveloped the garage, something very unlike her usual air of strength.

A sooty, soggy mess now lay where just a few hours earlier a building had been filled with furniture. And promise. The hope of the dreams Jemma had for every piece of furniture. Charred wood littered the cement floor. It didn't take a fire marshal to know that nothing inside her garage would be salvageable.

"Did you ever upgrade your insurance?"

She shook her head. "It totally fell off my radar. I stopped by the office a month ago, but they were so busy I said I'd come back or call."

"And you never did."

"Nope."

"It's going to be okay somehow, Jemma."

"I see burnt remains of a workshop." She pointed. "There. See? Nothing left."

Without considering the consequences, Nathaniel wrapped his arms around her and pulled her snugly against his chest. She leaned close, her tears turning to sobbing as she clung to him, her body racked with emotion. When she quieted down, he tried to step back, but she held on. He gently kissed her cheek, then rested his head next to hers. Jemma turned her head and kissed his cheek, the touch of her lips even there igniting something new inside him. He wanted to move his lips to hers, but now wasn't the time.

Then her lips found his mouth. He held himself still, not responding, knowing how shaky and vulnerable she felt right now. Jemma deepened the kiss, seeming to pour all of her emotion into it and he snapped, tugging her against him and giving her back kiss for kiss.

When she pushed away, he said again, "Jemma, it's going to be okay." Struggling for humor, he added, "At least I won't complain about the noise."

Jemma stepped back, her eyes big, and put her hand over her mouth. "I promise it will be quiet here from now on." Then, without another word, she ran to her house.

"Jemma, wait! I didn't mean that the way it sounded. Please talk to me!"

She turned on the porch and shook her head vigorously. "No, I . . . can't."

The last thing he heard was the slamming of her front door.

Chapter Seventeen

The next afternoon Jemma held a mug of tea in her hands and stared out her front window. The previous twenty-four hours had taken on a surreal feeling.

Last night she'd stood under the shower for a long time, washing off the soot, the smell of smoke, and the burnt embers of her dreams. In her pajamas she'd lain down on the bed and stared at the ceiling, certain she'd never fall asleep.

When she next opened her eyes, flickering morning light on her wall told her she had slept. Starting to get up, she'd fallen back onto the bed, and it had taken her another half hour to talk herself into actually getting up. Her business had vanished last night. "Poof! Gone," she said to the cat who sat and watched her, seeming to know something wasn't right.

The first thing that morning she'd stepped onto her front porch to see if it had all been a bad dream or the living nightmare she remembered; she found the latter. And a truck parked in Nathaniel's driveway that they'd filled with furniture she needed to deliver.

A few hours later the goods were delivered and received with praise that brought her partway home on a high. Then a fire truck passed her and reality hit again.

Now she stood in her living room with a full mug of tea and an empty future.

Turning around in the room, she could see through the door to the dining room, where a half-completed project sat next to her sewing machine. The cover for a bench seat would be pretty when done, but the bench it should go onto had gone up in flames. The picture that fit a refinished frame leaned against the wall, but the frame itself no longer existed.

Out the window Nathaniel stood in his driveway with Chloe on her leash, staring at her house. She watched him cross the road, walk up her steps onto her porch, and pass by her window. A minute or two passed before she heard his knock on the door, so he must have hesitated.

Jemma stood with the screen door between them. "It's all gone."

"I know, Jemma. Listen, I'm sorry about what I said last night. I would take the words back if I could." He touched the screen.

Backing away from the door as though he'd touched her, she said, "I need space." *Lots of space*, she thought, as she closed the door on her neighbor.

She called her sister.

"Holly, if you have time, could you"—she gulped back a sob—"come over this afternoon?"

"Are you okay, Jemma?"

"I'm not at all okay. Please come over."

"I'm on my way. I just saw my neighbor outside, and I know she'll watch the girls for me."

Jemma hung up the phone. She didn't want anything to eat, but refilled her mug, adding an extra squeeze of honey. Stitches meowed repeatedly from the floor in front of her, then jumped up beside her on the couch and bumped her arm. It finally sank in that the cat needed to be fed even if she didn't.

Holly didn't take long. She let herself in the door, reached down to hug her sister, and sat across from her in the living room. "Jemma, what happened to the garage? Are you okay?"

Jemma immediately burst into tears. "It's gone. It's all gone. I have to walk away from the business. And Alaska. And him." She pointed across the street.

"Oh, Jemma. Did you fall for Mr. Gorgeous?"

The range of emotions she'd felt with Nathaniel rushed though her, from anger to love. "I tried not to, but he's so nice."

"Really?"

"Oh, yes. He's been sweet to me, and you should have seen him with his parents. He's a good man."

The phone rang, interrupting her litany of Nathaniel's attributes. When she picked up the phone, the woman on the other end asked for Jemma Harris.

"Yes, this is Jemma Harris." When Holly raised an eyebrow in curiosity, Jemma put the phone on speaker so her sister could hear. She doubted this call held any secrets.

"I'm the bookkeeper at Design with Style. I want you to know your check is in the mail. Marina asked me to pass on her compliments. She loves your furniture and would like to purchase more in the future. And from the notes I see here, you appear to know a Nathaniel Montgomery?"

"Yes, I do."

"Then please let him know Marina is so pleased with your work that she says she won't accept the money Mr. Montgomery offered for trying your products."

"I will. Thank you for your call."

As she hung up, the woman's words sank in. Turning to her sister, she said, "Did she just tell me Nathaniel offered a bribe to get this woman to try my products?"

Holly bit her lip. "I think *bribe* might be too strong a word."

"You're a writer. At least you dabble in it. What word would you choose?"

Holly smiled weakly. "I guess bribe does sum things up well. Let's ignore this, and figure out what to do about your situation."

Jemma sighed. "Right, my situation. Finite money. Long winter. Burned-down garage. My choices are few."

"You couldn't stay for the winter, do some work for the company that just called, and try again in the spring? I want you to stay, Jemma."

"I do too. After the plumbing repairs, what she's offering won't be enough. I'd need more than one Marina. Even a job at a local business wouldn't really be enough. I'm having to start over, and without a workshop. He"—she gestured across the street, with an angry fling of her arm—"said he was helping me fall for Alaska. And he did. I love it here, even the wild, crazy canoe trip he took me on Saturday." She described what in retrospect seemed more adventurous than dangerous. "I don't want to move."

When Holly got up to leave, she repeated those words back to Jemma. Unfortunately, the plan taking shape in her mind meant she couldn't stay.

Nathaniel brought her a dinner that night that smelled delicious even as she opened the door, but at the same time he smelled like a rat. "I made something I think you'll like. And"—he held up a covered pitcher—"sweet tea."

Her heart broke a little more when she took in his kind gesture. Then she remembered the call she'd gotten earlier in the day. "Nathaniel, you paid someone to buy my furniture. How do think that makes me feel?"

"You found out, huh?" He smiled sheepishly. "Maybe that wasn't my best move."

"Not even close. I felt . . . humiliated that someone had to be paid to want my furniture."

"The owner sent me an e-mail saying she liked it. Isn't that what you were told?"

"No. Well, yes, the woman who called did say they liked it. And she said they would pay me the full amount of money and give you back your bribe."

"*Bribe's* a harsh word."

"No. It's not. It's the right word."

"But you found people who like your furniture. Did she say anything about buying additional pieces in the future?"

"Yes, but she was just being polite."

He seemed to fight a laugh. "No, Marina's never just polite. If she said she wanted to buy more, she meant it."

"It isn't enough." She started to push the door shut. "Thank you for dinner." Jemma closed the door and turned the lock. She took the meal she didn't have any appetite for through to her kitchen and put it in the fridge.

Back in her living room, she found her phone where she'd left it after what she'd always remember as the "bribe call" and, using some of the miles she'd earned in her corporate job, booked a seat on the next plane out of Anchorage. Even if she loved Alaska, it wasn't loving her back. She needed space from this sham of a business, her neighbor, and even this beautiful state.

Ignoring the little voice that told her running away from Alaska and Nathaniel wouldn't help, she phoned Holly, asking her to drive her to the airport and hurried upstairs to pack, shoving clothes and toiletries into a small bag. Stitches loved the girls, so he'd be fine living with Holly until Bree came for him next month.

A week later, Jemma sat on her parents' back deck in Tennessee, sipping a glass of sweet tea with what she knew must be a sour expression on her face. Sleeping in her childhood bed felt ridiculous. It never bothered her during the holidays, but it sure didn't feel right now. *Maybe,* a small voice inside her said, *that's because you're running away.* She carried her glass into the kitchen, then left for a walk through the neighborhood she'd lived in during her teen years. Coming here had seemed like a good idea, but it hadn't fixed anything. She had Holly managing the one solution she had for the problem, and her sister should be calling soon with more information.

An hour later, her phone rang and Holly's face appeared on the screen. "Hey, I was just thinking of you," Jemma said. "Everything okay?"

"Your signatures came through, so everything's on track. I checked your mailbox today and found an envelope from a local lawyer."

"What now? Go ahead and open it." She heard tearing sounds, then silence, she presumed while her sister read whatever was inside.

"Uh-oh. I can't believe he did this."

"Who? What?"

"On behalf of Nathaniel, his lawyer is asking if you could conduct your business in a quieter manner."

Jemma sputtered, but no words came out. Nathaniel had called a lawyer?

Holly's voice dropped. "I'm sorry, Jemma. I know you'd started to fall for him."

Started to? She'd fallen all the way in love with a man who obviously couldn't love her back.

"I guess this means you won't be coming back to Alaska. Ever."

Jemma felt her depression clear, to be replaced with anger. "I might find a way. It would serve him right to have his chaotic neighbor living across the street again."

As she walked, though, she decided that instead of even considering returning to Alaska, she should sever those ties and go back to Atlanta. Nathaniel didn't want her, she didn't have the money to make it through the winter, and her business had by default failed, so why would she go back?

Chapter Eighteen

Nathaniel heard gravel crunching and hurried to his office window. Was Jemma home?

Her sister's car stopped in the driveway, and a professionally dressed woman stepped out. When she turned to face him, he realized it was Holly, but she'd exchanged her usual jeans for business clothes. He'd seen her come and go during the last eleven days—yes, he knew the exact number—but she never stayed long. He hadn't seen Jemma since the day after the fire, so he'd come to the conclusion that she wasn't living there anymore. Holly must be watering the plants.

He turned back to his desk and finished up a project, hoping the quality was what it should be. He hadn't gotten much work done since the fire. Not seeing his friend nearby had left him having trouble concentrating.

A noise startled him. "What on earth is that?" He leaned back in his chair to see out the window, then shot to his feet. Holly was hammering a real estate sign into Jemma's front lawn.

He raced out the door, catching her just as she opened her car door. "Wait! What's going on?"

She seemed sad too. "Jemma isn't coming back."

His jaw dropped. "No? What's she going to do?"

Holly swallowed hard. "I don't know. She loves this house and Alaska and . . ." Her voice trailed off. "I'm getting my real estate license, so I'm helping her with this. Anyway, you'll have a new neighbor soon."

He stood with his mouth hanging open as Holly got in her car and left. Jemma wasn't coming back to him. When he turned toward his house, his front door stood wide open so it was a good thing the crew had finished the fence a few days ago. Chloe happily ran outside right now.

Back in his office, he paced, stopping at the window every few minutes to stare at the sign in the yard across the street. He didn't want to lose Jemma. Grabbing the phone, he dialed the one person he could think of for help.

"Mom!"

"Nathaniel, are you okay? Are you bleeding?" She'd asked the question she'd taught him as a child to show he had a true emergency.

"Inside, Mom. Only inside. Jemma's moving."

"Ah, I see. And this bothers you because . . . ?

"Jemma's my friend."

"Wouldn't you like to know she's happy somewhere else?"

"No! Yes. I mean, I don't want her to be anywhere else. I want her to be here."

"Because?"

"I told you. Jemma's my friend."

"And?"

"I love her!"

Nathaniel froze. Had his mother used the *l* word, or had he? *He'd* done it.

"I'm so glad, dear. I love her too."

"What do I do, Mom?"

"Do what you're good at. Sell yourself to her," his mother said in a matter-of-fact tone.

"I'm panicking and you're speaking in riddles."

"Nathaniel, pay attention."

He hated it when she said that. He felt like a five-year-old. He took a deep, calming breath, then said, "I am paying attention. What are you trying to tell me?"

"Do what you're good at. Sell yourself to her. If you were a product and Jemma the customer, what would you do to market yourself to her?"

He paced the length of the room, turned, and stopped at the window. The For Sale sign seemed to be blinking neon and amping up his panic level. How *would* he market himself?

Then it came to him.

"I'd show her I want her and everything she stands for in my life. I'm going to buy a very unusual gift for her. Yes, I know she'll at least stop and look. If she ever comes back, I'm going to be ready."

He heard his mother ask, "What?" as he set down the phone and went down the stairs.

Jemma stepped off the plane in Anchorage, still dazzled by the awesome way things had gone in her life in the last few days. Holly and the girls waved as she walked through the gate. After she'd hugged each of them, Holly carried her bag so she could hold hands with the girls as the group went down the escalators and toward the parking garage.

"Don't get me wrong. I'm glad to see you, but why are you here?" her sister asked. "Your last words were you'd lost everything—business, man, house—and you were never coming back. Exclamation point!"

Jemma chewed on her lip. "I may have been a trifle dramatic. It feels good to be back in Alaska."

Holly raised one eyebrow but didn't say anything.

"I found a way to make it through the winter. Or it found me. I'm still not sure."

Holly gestured for her to continue.

"I called my old boss to check on his offer of my job and didn't tell him I was just a few hours' drive away. Things had moved more quickly than expected, and they'd found someone they thought would be perfect. I figured, 'Here's another dead end.' Then he said they missed my efforts, which he now realizes went far beyond forty or even sixty hours a week. He offered me a part-time consulting position doing some of my old job—from Alaska, because he thought that was where I was.

At that moment I went back in time and pictured myself working in a job I hadn't liked. But then I saw the future. I can easily make it here. And I can work in my pajamas if I want to."

"Whoa. That's wonderful! The job . . . And the part about working in your PJs." Holly grinned. Then she added, "This lets you live in the house, but it doesn't do anything about your business or your man."

They stepped out of the tunnel from the terminal and into the garage.

"I know. I need a workshop. I thought I wanted a retail storefront, but I've started to wonder if that's what I really need for my business, when my actual dream is to make and sell my products."

Her sister didn't comment about "the man" again, but she excitedly said, "I have a workshop for you!"

Jemma stopped in the middle of the walkway. "What?"

"Come on." Holly kept moving. "Let's get the girls settled, and I'll tell you in the car."

It only took a few minutes for them to get going. Jemma could hardly wait to hear what Holly had to say. As they pulled out of the garage, Jemma said, "Give. Tell me about this workshop."

"My boss at the real estate company moved into a new house about a year ago. The previous owner worked on old cars, but his wife didn't want the building near the house, so he built a shop where she couldn't see it on their large acreage. My boss was complaining that he has to check it out a couple of times each week to make sure no animals or humans have gotten into it. I asked why he didn't rent it out. He said he didn't know anyone who would want just a workshop, and one that wasn't at their home. I told him I knew someone who did."

Jemma sighed. "I'm sitting much better financially now, but I want my business to make sense. What does he want per month?"

"Enough to cover utilities. He added that his wife likes him, so he doesn't need to be so far away." Holly grinned as she drove down the road.

"Maybe I shouldn't have run away."

"Did it help to take a break from your life here?"

Even though she'd left, images of her and her neighbor exploring Alaska together had followed her. She knew she'd have to struggle to block those out as she worked to build a new life here. "Leaving helped. Not being here made me realize how much I want my life here to succeed."

Holly checked the rearview mirror. "The girls were so excited you were coming home that they were bouncing off the walls and wore themselves out. They've already fallen asleep. So I'll ask again: what about the man?"

Jemma felt her eyes fill. "I don't know," she whispered. Sitting straighter, she fought for control. "I'm going to be living across the street from him again. Avoiding him will be difficult."

"Do you want to avoid him? Do you think he wants a relationship with you?"

"He has tried to call me about a dozen times. Texted. Left voice messages." Jemma pulled her phone out of her purse and considered calling him. Then she put it back. She felt too vulnerable right now to even try.

"So what did he say?"

"I don't know. I didn't answer the phone, and I deleted all of the messages." She'd spent most of the flight back wondering if she'd made a mistake in doing that.

"You what? I never thought of you as stupid before, but Jemma—"

"I hurt, okay?" she said loudly, then glanced in the backseat, where the girls were still sleeping. In a lower voice she said, "I hadn't wanted to talk to him anyway. I know I should have at least listened. I'll see him tomorrow. Of that I'm sure."

Nathaniel opened his eyes. Chloe snugged next to him in bed, sound asleep. What had woken him in the middle of the night? Tires crunching on gravel shot him to his feet and into his office, where he could see across the street. Jemma waved from her front porch as her sister drove off.

Jemma was back. He dropped to the floor, his face in his hands. She'd come home to him. He wanted to run over there tonight, but she'd be tired and might be happier to see him in the morning. He wanted her to be happy to see him more than anything he'd ever wanted in his life. He'd haul the things out of his garage and over there tomorrow morning, and hoped she'd respond well to his marketing attempt.

The next morning he watched out his office window for signs of life across the street, feeling a little like a stalker. She couldn't work in her garage anymore, but she'd probably go out to get groceries. Amend that: this was Jemma he was thinking about. She'd probably go out to get a meal.

About noon he heard a car and saw her backing down the driveway.

Opening the second bay of his garage, he stood over the pile of junk that filled the area. He picked up a nightstand, took it over to Jemma's front yard, and returned for another load. This time he chose a dresser, carrying the drawers separately from the dresser itself. Then it was a headboard, a couple of picture frames, and some chairs.

If she didn't say yes, *he'd* have to hold a yard sale. At least he understood the dynamics of one better after shopping for this lot.

Almost an hour had passed before he'd finished his task. He sat on his front step with Chloe, waiting for Jemma to return, and he didn't have long to wait.

She must have seen the pile when she pulled around the curve, because she hit the brakes. Driving slowly, she pulled forward and into her driveway. When she stopped, she stepped out of her car, looking confused, and seemed to notice him for the first time.

This was the moment he'd been waiting for. "Do you like your gift, Jemma?"

"You did this? Why would you of all people leave used furniture on my lawn? You're insane."

He stood and tried for a casual walk over to her, no easy task considering the way his whole body shook. "No. It may appear I'm insane, but I can assure you I'm not."

"What is all this?" She swirled her hand over the pile of junk.

"I've learned it could be seen two ways: one, raw material to transform into products to sell, or two, junk." He gave her a lopsided grin.

"I can guess who you're thinking of with both answers."

"You might be surprised." Nathaniel stepped over to her and gave her a hug, and she held on tight for a minute before releasing him.

"I'm glad to be back, but I'm not too happy with you right now, Nathaniel."

He felt his grand plans going up in flames every bit as hot as those that had destroyed her garage. "Because?"

"You had your lawyer send me a letter asking me to be quiet."

"I talked to him the day I met you. I'd forgotten about it by now. I'm sorry."

"And what about Marina, the woman you bribed so she would buy my goods?"

He gulped. "I thought we'd talked about this. I wanted to help."

Something about his pleading expression must have touched her because she gave a slight smile. "When it comes to my business, let's make a deal, friend, for you to talk to me first before doing anything."

Whew. Looking heavenward, he thought about his plans. If Jemma saw him as just a friend, should he open his heart to her? Yes, but he'd start small.

Wanting to appear sincere, he looked into her eyes and promptly lost his train of thought. Then for a few seconds, he went over things in his mind, and got back on track. "I believe I have a solution to your business problems. First, remember the design firm will buy more of your goods. You had one special order from an individual. You also sold a fair amount at the women's event, so you could do things like that, and they're year-round. I bet you'd do very well at a craft fair in December."

She nodded slowly. "I can see all of that."

"Come sit down on this chair." He pulled one from the pile that seemed like it might still hold the weight of an adult. When she'd seated herself, he said, "We'll find you a new workshop. And maybe the bank can loan you money to get through the winter. I know the president of the bank."

She stared up at him with eyes that shimmered with happiness. "That's so sweet of you! But it turns out I have a workshop *and* a way to get through the winter." She outlined everything for him.

"So you don't need me. I thought I could help. With your house for sale, I thought you could live here." He pointed to his house.

Her eyes opened wide and she stood. "With you? You're asking me to move in with you? Like roommates?"

"No." What was so hard about this? "We'd share the same room, of course."

"Nathaniel Montgomery, have I given any indication I want to live with you like that?"

He slowly shook his head. *Not much*, he thought. Had he misjudged what he thought were subtle signs she liked him, or even more than liked him? She'd certainly kissed him with enthusiasm after the fire. But she wasn't herself at the time. Then again, she'd also seemed to enjoy their kiss when Chloe had returned. He cleared his throat and started over. "I always think married couples should combine their money into one account."

"I do too, but what does that have to do with—" She clutched her heart and sat down hard on the chair, closing her eyes. "Did you just ask me to marry you?"

"No."

A single tear trailed down her check. He'd completely blown this.

He knelt in front of her on one knee. "*Now* I'm asking you to marry me," he said, his voice trembling. "Jemma Harris, would you do me the honor of becoming my wife?"

He reached into his pocket and pulled out a ring box, popping it open and holding it where she could see inside.

Jemma stared at the ring nestled in the royal blue velvet box. Estate jewelry, probably from the 1920s, if she wasn't mistaken, the ring had a center diamond with open filigree work all around it and down the sides, with small diamonds nestled among it. He'd managed to find a vintage ring that was understated, elegant, and stunning all at the same time, in her preferred white metal, not yellow gold. "White gold?"

"Platinum."

If only she could be sure he really wanted to marry her, and that he didn't somehow pity her and just want to help. She refused to be a rescue, like Chloe. She couldn't accept a pity proposal. But when she looked into his eyes, they held a hopefulness that made her heart leap. Was it possible? "Nathaniel, why are you asking me to marry you?"

"Not you too!"

"You asked someone else to marry you?"

"No, I tried to explain the situation to my mother, and she pressed me relentlessly until I said something that startled me."

His eyes held both fear and joy. Nathaniel cleared his throat nervously, making Jemma wonder if he could possibly care for her. Maybe she wasn't just another rescue.

He shifted to his other knee. "I love you, Jemma."

Giddy laughter bubbled up and exploded from her.

"You shouldn't laugh when someone proposes and says he loves you."

"This"—she gasped for air—"must be *the worst* proposal ever." She chuckled as she tried to stop the laughter that had obviously upset her would-be suitor. When his words struck her, she stopped laughing. "Hold it. Did you just say you love me?"

He looked sick but nodded. "I did, but I'm sorry to have burdened you with my feelings. I thought—no, I hoped—you shared my feelings. I knew we were friends, but I hoped we had more between us." He awkwardly came to his feet, seeming confused about what he should do next.

When he turned to walk away, she said, "Wait! I do love you. And if you're still asking, I will marry you."

He stood, staring at her. "Not out of pity?"

"Are you kidding? I've been hoping and praying you'd come to your senses and want me in your life."

He spun around and pulled her into his arms, kissing her soundly on the lips. "You scared me. Promise me you'll love me always."

"Promise." Then she leaned forward and kissed him before adding, "As you helped me fall in love with Alaska, you made me fall in love with you."

"I got scared when that sign went into your lawn."

Jemma whirled around. "Holly will have to make sure the house is taken off the market. But I don't know what we're going to do with two houses. Yours is better for entertaining, and you need to entertain for business. But I really don't want to sell Great-aunt Grace's house."

"It might make a good B&B. I think visitors would like to stay in an early Palmer home."

She turned to him, excited. "We could do that in the summer." She frowned as the concept sunk in. "With me it might have to just be a B for bed, with no breakfast."

"I could make muffins and other things ahead and freeze them. You could prepare them in the morning and set them out for our guests. You're good at that."

"Perfect. I think we'll work well together, Nathaniel Montgomery. I'm so glad everything came together so I could come home to Alaska. This is the place I'm supposed to be."

He put his arm around her. "I know we haven't had anything even close to a normal courtship, for lack of a better word. Are you certain you want to marry me?"

"Bit by bit, you made me fall in love with you. I won't say it was from the first moment we met."

He grinned. "I might not have been as pleasant as I could have been."

"'Might' nothing. You were downright rude."

"Jemma, I'll love you and your junk—well"—he picked up a battered picture frame—"most of it—forever."

Grinning, Jemma threw her arms around his neck, pushing him off balance and backward onto a dining room chair. As she heard wood breaking, she felt them falling, him backward onto his back, her dropping to her knees. Leaning over him, she pulled one of the chair's arms off his chest and said, "I need to teach you how to choose higher-quality furniture."

Nathaniel gently put his hand to her cheek and rubbed it with his thumb. "Jemma, I know how to choose the best." He pulled her down to him and kissed her slowly and sweetly, Jemma kissing him back with all the love in her heart. She *did* belong here in his arms.

And in Alaska.

Dear Readers,

Thank you for reading *Falling for Alaska*. Without you I wouldn't be able to do this work I love. I appreciate you so very much! If you enjoyed *Falling for Alaska*, I'd like to ask you to give a review on your favorite bookseller's site or on Goodreads. Reviews are *very* important to writers.

At www.shannonlbrown.com, you will be able to read more about Alaska and keep up with what's happening in the series. You won't miss a thing if you also sign up for the newsletter.

I was born and raised in Alaska, so I had many adventures. Three of those are in *Falling for Alaska*. I've hiked Gull Rock Trail, boated up to Tyone Lake, and canoed Eklutna Lake.

On Tyone Lake, we boated a little farther than Jemma and Nathaniel did in this story; we went until the lake started to turn into a river, and we could feel the current. Not knowing what lay ahead, we turned around. We didn't see a bear, but a caribou swam across the water behind our boat. That day is one of my best memories of Alaska.

The scene on Eklutna Lake played out much as the one in the book. The lake suddenly turned rough, and my husband bailed the canoe when I wasn't watching, only telling me what had happened once we were back on land.

Bree and Holly will both have their own stories with Bree's first. She'll quickly find herself in a gold mining area far from cities.

Thank you again for spending time with Jemma and Nathaniel!

About Shannon

Writing books that are fun and touch your heart

Even though Shannon L. Brown always loved to read, she didn't plan to be a writer. She earned two degrees from the University of Alaska, one in journalism/public communications, but didn't become a journalist.

Years passed. Shannon felt pulled into a writing life, testing her wings with a novel and moving on to articles. Shannon is now an award-winning journalist who has sold hundreds articles to local, national, and regional publications.

The Feather Chase was her first published book and begins the Crime-Solving Cousins Mystery series. The eight-to-twelve-year-olds in your life will enjoy this contemporary twist on a Nancy Drew–type mystery.

Shannon, like Jemma, enjoys hiking. But unlike Jemma, Shannon unwinds by baking, and people are happy to eat the things *she* makes.

Shannon lives in Nashville, Tennessee, with her professor husband and adorable calico cat.

Reading Groups

*Please contact me through my website,
www.shannonlbrown.com, to let me know if your book club
chooses to read* Falling for Alaska. *I have a special gift I'd
like to give your group.*

Book Discussion Questions

1. What's the first thing that comes to mind when you hear the word *Alaska*?

2. Do you think you would find living in Alaska as easy as Nathaniel did or, like Jemma, would you have to learn to love Alaska?

3. Jemma and Nathaniel have several adventures. Which one was your favorite?

4. Which location in *Falling for Alaska* would you most like to go to yourself?

5. Jemma's passion is taking old furniture and fabric, and turning them into beautiful new things. Do you have any furniture or fabric that Jemma would love to get her hands on?

6. Nathaniel had a difficult childhood that he overcame. Is there anything in his life struggles and successes that you see in your own life?

7. Do you think Nathaniel would have been happy if he'd had to move away from Alaska to follow Jemma to a different place?

8. Jemma and Nathaniel fell in love slowly, first becoming friends. Do you think that's the best way to find your spouse, or do you believe in falling in love quickly or "love at first sight"?

CPSIA information can be obtained at www.ICGtesting.com
Printed in the USA
LVOW08s0825290316

481221LV00001B/1/P